"Martin's story charges headlong into the sentimental territory and best-seller terrain of *The Notebook*, which doubtless will mean major studio screen treatment."

—*KIRKUS* (STARRED REVIEW) ON *UNWRITTEN*

"Charles Martin understands the power of story and he uses it to alter the souls and lives of both his characters and his readers."

—PATTI CALLAHAN HENRY, *NEW YORK TIMES* BESTSELLING AUTHOR

"Martin is the new king of the romantic novel . . . *A Life Intercepted* is a book that will swallow you up and keep you spellbound."

—JACKIE K. COOPER, BOOK CRITIC, *THE HUFFINGTON POST*

"Martin's strength is in his memorable characters . . ."

—*PUBLISHERS WEEKLY* ON *CHASING FIREFLIES*

"Charles Martin is changing the face of inspirational fiction one book at a time. *Wrapped in Rain* is a sentimental tale that is not to be missed."

—MICHAEL MORRIS, AUTHOR OF *LIVE LIKE YOU WERE DYING* AND *A PLACE CALLED WIREGRASS*

"Martin spins an engaging story about healing and the triumph of love . . . Filled with delightful local color."

—*PUBLISHERS WEEKLY*, FOR *WRAPPED IN RAIN*

"Charles Martin writes with the passion and delicacy of a Louisiana sunrise–shades of shepherd's warning and a promise of thunderbolts before noon."

—JOHN DYSON, *READER'S DIGEST*, FOR *WRAPPED IN RAIN*

"[*The Dead Don't Dance* is] an absorbing read for fans of faithbased fiction . . . [with] delightfully quirky characters . . . [who] are ingeniously imaginative creations."

—*PUBLISHERS WEEKLY*

# Praise for Charles Martin

"Another stellar novel from Martin. His fabulous gift for characterization is evident on each page. Layers of the story are peeled back to show the spiritual truth underneath the gripping plot. This is a reimagining of the prodigal son story from the Bible, and the reader's faith can't help but be enriched and encouraged after completing the book. Cooper is an intricate character with an amazing story to tell, and the supporting cast is just as important to provide additional depth and understanding. This novel should be on everyone's must-purchase list."

—*RT Book Reviews*, 4½ stars, TOP PICK! for *Long Way Gone*

"Martin crafts a playful, enticing tale of a modern prodigal son."

—*Publishers Weekly* for *Long Way Gone*

"Cooper and Daley's story will make you believe that even broken instruments have songs to offer when they're in the right hands. Charles Martin never fails to ask and answer the questions that linger deep within all of us. In this beautifully told story of a prodigal coming home, readers will find the broken and mended pieces of their own hearts."

—Lisa Wingate, national bestselling author of
*Before We Were Yours* on *Long Way Gone*

"*Long Way Gone* takes us to even greater reaches of the heart, as Martin explores the complicated relationship between father and son. He weaves all the pieces of this story together with a beautiful musical thread, and as the final pieces fall into place, we close this story feeling as if we have witnessed something surreal, a multisensory narrative for anyone who enjoys a redemptive story."

—Julie Cantrell, *New York Times* and *USA TODAY*
bestselling author of *Perennials*

"A beautiful story of redemption and love once lost but found again, *Lo Way Gone* proves two things: music washes us from the inside out Charles Martin's words do the same."

—Billy Coffey, author of *Steal Aw*

# SEND

# DOWN

# THE RAIN

# OTHER NOVELS BY CHARLES MARTIN

# SEND

# DOWN

# THE RAIN

## CHARLES MARTIN

THOMAS NELSON
*Since 1798*

Published in Nashville, Tennessee, by Thomas Nelson. Thomas Nelson is a registered trademark of HarperCollins Christian Publishing, Inc.

Thomas Nelson titles may be purchased in bulk for educational, business, fund-raising, or sales promotional use. For information, please e-mail SpecialMarkets@ ThomasNelson.com.

Unless otherwise noted, Scripture quotations are taken from the New King James Version®. © 1982 by Thomas Nelson. Used by permission. All rights reserved.

Publisher's Note: This novel is a work of fiction. Names, characters, places, and incidents are either products of the author's imagination or used fictitiously. All characters are fictional, and any similarity to people living or dead is purely coincidental.

### Library of Congress Cataloging-in-Publication Data

Names: Martin, Charles, 1969- author.
Title: Send down the rain / Charles Martin.
Description: Nashville, Tennessee : Thomas Nelson, [2018]
Identifiers: LCCN 2017044610 | ISBN 9780718084745 (hardback)
Subjects: | GSAFD: Love stories.
Classification: LCC PS3613.A7778 S46 2018 | DDC 813/.6--dc23 LC record available at https://lccn.loc.gov/2017044610

*Printed in the United States of America*

18 19 20 21 22 LSC 5 4 3 2 1

*For Lonnie*

# — PROLOGUE —

*Blessed is the man whose strength is in You,*
*whose heart is set on pilgrimage.*

—PSALM 84:5

NOVEMBER 1964

The breeze tugged at my hair and cooled my skin. The waves rolled up and rinsed my heels and calves. Seashells crunched beneath my bathing suit. The air tasted salty. Shirtless and tanned, I lay on my back, propped on my elbows, a pencil in one hand, a small piece of paper in the other. The paper was thick. Almost card stock. I'd torn it out of the back of a book. An amber sun was setting between my big toe and my second toe, turning from flame orange to blood red and slowly sliding down behind the ball of my foot and the edge of the Gulf of Mexico. I busied the pencil to capture the image, my hands giving my mind the space it needed.

1

I heard someone coming, and then Bobby sat down beside me. Cross-legged. He wiped his forearm across his nose, smearing snot across a tearstained face. In his arms he cradled a jug of milk and a package of Oreos. Our favorite comfort food. He set them gingerly between us.

I was nine. Bobby was two years older.

We could hear Momma crying in the house behind us. The sun disappeared, and the breeze turned cooler.

Bobby's lip was trembling. "Daddy . . . He . . . he left."

"Where'd he go?"

Bobby dug his hand into the package, shoved a cookie into his mouth, and shook his head.

The sound of a plate shattering echoed out of the kitchen.

"When's he coming back?"

Another cookie. Another crash from the kitchen. Another shake of the head.

"What's Momma doing?"

He squinted one eye and stared over his shoulder. "Sounds like the dishes."

When they got married, Daddy gave Momma a set of china. MADE IN BAVARIA was stamped on the back of each piece. She displayed them in the cabinet. Locked behind the glass. We weren't allowed to touch them. Ever. Evidently she was smashing them piece by piece against the kitchen sink.

"Did Daddy say anything?"

Bobby dug his hand back into the package and began skimming Oreos out across the waves. They flew through the air like tiny Frisbees. A final shake of the head. He unscrewed the milk jug top and held it to his mouth. Two more plates hit the sink.

Bobby was trembling. His voice cracked. "He packed a bunch of stuff. Most everything."

Waves rolled up and over our feet. "What about that . . . other woman?"

He passed me the carton. His words were hard in coming and separated by pain. "Brother, I don't . . ."

I took a drink, and the milk dripped off my chin. He flicked another Frisbee. I sank my hand in the package, stuck a cookie in my mouth, and then threw several like Bobby. The little chocolate discs intersected each other like hummingbirds.

Behind us Momma wailed. Another plate hit the kitchen sink. Followed by another. Then another. The change in sound suggested she'd made her way through all the plates and moved on to the cups and saucers. The cacophony echoing from the kitchen kept rhythm with the irregular drumbeat of our own shattering fragility. I glanced over my shoulder but could find no safe purchase.

Tears puddled in the corners of Bobby's eyes. His lip was quivering. When Momma screamed and had a tough time catching her breath, the tears broke loose.

I tucked the pencil behind my ear and held my sunset sketch at eye level, where the wind caught it like a kite. Imprisoned between my fingers, the paper flapped. When I unlocked the prison door, the crude drawing butterfly-danced down the beach and landed in the waves. I glanced behind me. "We better go check on her."

Bobby pushed his forearm across his lips and nose, smearing his face and arm. His hair had fallen down over his eyes. Like mine, it was bleached blond from saltwater and sunlight. I stood and offered him my hand. He accepted it and I pulled him up. The sun had nearly disappeared now, and cast long shadows on the house. Where our world lay in pieces around us like the ten billion shells at our feet.

Bobby stared at the road down which Dad had disappeared. A thin trail of whitish-blue exhaust was all that remained of his wake. "He said some . . ." He sucked in, shuddered, and tried to shake off the sob he'd been holding back. "Real hard things."

I put my arm around his shoulder, and his sob broke loose. We stood on the beach, alone. Fatherless. Empty and angry.

I made a fist, crushing a cookie. Grinding it to powder. When the pieces spilled out between my fingers onto the beach, a physical and very real pain pierced my chest.

Fifty-three years later, it would stop.

# — 1 —

Witnesses say the phone call occurred around seven p.m. and the exchange was heated. While the man seated at the truck stop diner was calm and his voice low, the woman's voice on the other end was not. Though unseen, she was screaming loudly, and stuff could be heard breaking in the background. Seven of the nine people in the diner, including the waitress, say Jake Gibson made several attempts to reason with her, but she cut him off at every turn. He would listen, nod, adjust his oiled ball cap, and try to get a word in edgewise.

"Allie . . . Baby, I know, but . . . If you'll just let me . . . I'm sorry, but . . . I've been driving for forty-two hours . . . I'm . . ." He rubbed his face and eyes. "Dead on my feet." A minute or two passed while he hunkered over the phone, trying to muffle the sound of her incoherent babbling. "I know it's a big deal and you've put a lot of work into . . ." Another pause. More nodding. Another rub of his eyes. "Invitations . . . decorations . . . lights. Yes, I remember how much you paid for the band. But . . ." At this point, he took off his hat and rubbed his bald head. "I got rerouted at Flagstaff and it just plain took the starch out of me." He closed his eyes. "Baby, I just can't get there. Not tonight. I'll cook you some eggs in the morn—"

It was more of the same. Nothing had changed.

Allie Gibson wasn't listening anyway. She was screaming. At the top of her lungs. With their marriage on the rocks, they'd taken a "break." Six months. He moved out, living in the cab of his truck. Crisscrossing the country. But the time and distance had been good for them. She'd softened. Lost weight. Pilates. Bought new lingerie. To remind him. This was to be both his birthday and welcome home party. Along with a little let's-start-over thrown in.

The diner was small, and Jake grew more embarrassed. He held the phone away from his ear, waiting for her to finish. Allie was his first marriage. Ten years in and counting. He was her second. Her neighbors had tried to warn him. They spoke in hushed tones. "The other guy left for a reason." The inflection of their voice emphasized the word *reason*.

Jake didn't get to tell her good-bye. She spewed one last volley of venom and slammed the phone into the cradle. When the phone fell quiet, he sat awkwardly waiting. Wondering if she would pick back up. She did not. The waitress appeared with a pot of coffee and a hungry eye. He wasn't bad looking. Not really a tall drink of water, but she'd seen worse. Far worse. The kindness in his face was inviting, and judging by the appearance of his boots and hands, he didn't mind hard work. She'd take Allie's place in a heartbeat.

"More coffee, baby?" She said coffee like *caw-fee*. Before he could speak, the obnoxious beeping sounded from the phone's earpiece, telling him Allie had hung up a while ago. Furthering his embarrassment. He whispered to anyone who would listen, "I'm sorry," then stood, reached over the counter, hung up the phone, and quietly thanked the waitress.

Leaving his steak uneaten, he refilled his coffee thermos, left a twenty on the table to pay his seven-dollar bill, and slipped out quietly, tipping his hat to an older couple who'd just walked in. He walked out accompanied by the signature tap of his walking cane on concrete—a shrapnel wound that had never healed.

He gassed up his truck and paid for his diesel at the register, along with four packs of NoDoz, then went into the restroom and splashed cold water on his face. The police, watching the diner video surveillance some forty-eight hours later, would watch in silence as Jake did twenty jumping jacks and just as many push-ups before he climbed up into his cab. In the last two and a half days, he had driven from Arizona to Texas and finally to Mississippi, where he'd picked up a tanker of fuel en route to Miami. He had tried to make it home for his sixtieth birthday party, but his body just gave out. Each eyelid weighed a thousand pounds. With little more than a hundred miles to go, he'd called to tell Allie that he'd already fallen asleep twice and he was sorry he couldn't push through.

She had not taken the news well.

He eyed the motel but her echo was still ringing. He knew his absence would sting her.

So amiable Jake Gibson climbed up and put the hammer down. It would be his last time.

Jake made his way south to Highway 98. Hugged the coastline, eventually passing through Mexico Beach en route to Apalachicola.

At Highway 30E he turned west. Seven miles to the cradle of Allie's arms. He wound up the eighteen-wheeler and shifted through each of the ten gears. Though he'd driven the road hundreds of times, no one really knows why he was going so fast or why he ignored the flashing yellow lights and seven sets of speed ripples across the narrow road. Anyone with his experience knew that a rig going that fast with that much mass and inertia could never make the turn. State highway patrol estimated the tanker was traveling in excess of a hundred and ten when 30E made its hard right heading north. It is here, at the narrowest point of the peninsula, where the road comes closest to the ocean. To separate the two, highway crews had amassed mounds of Volkswagen-sized granite rocks just to the left of the highway. Hundreds of boulders, each weighing several tons, stacked at jagged angles, one on top of another, stood thirty feet wide and some twenty feet high. An impenetrable wall to prevent the Gulf from encroaching on the road and those on the road from venturing into the ocean. "The rocks" was a favorite locale for lovers sipping wine. Hand in hand they'd scale the boulders and perch with the pelicans while the sun dropped off the side of the earth and bled crimson into the Gulf.

The Great Wall of Cape San Blas had survived many a hurricane and hundreds of thousands of tourists walking its beach.

No one really knows when Jake Gibson fell asleep. Only that he did. Just before ten p.m. the Peterbilt T-boned the wall, pile-driving the nose of the rig into the rocks with all the steam and energy of the *Titanic*. When the rocks ripped open the tanker just a few feet behind Jake, the explosion was heard and felt thirty miles away in Apalachicola, and the flash was seen as far away as Tallahassee—a hundred miles distant. Alarms sounded and fire crews and law enforcement personnel were dispatched, but given the heat they were relegated to shutting down the highway from eight football fields away. No one in or out. All they could do was watch it burn.

Allie was sitting on the floor of a bathroom stall hunkered over a fifth of Jack. Tearstained and tear-strained. From three miles away she saw the flash off the white subway tile wall. When she saw the fireball, she knew.

The several-thousand-degree heat was so intense that Allie—along with all the partygoers—were forced to stand outside the half-mile barrier and helplessly inhale the smell of burning rubber. They did this throughout the night. By early morning the fire had spent its fury, allowing the water trucks to move in. By then not much was left. A few steel beams. One wheel had been blown off and rolled a quarter mile into the marsh. The back end of the tank looked like a soda can ripped in two. At the blast site, the only thing that remained was a scorched spot on the highway.

Closed-circuit television cameras positioned on the flashing light poles a mile before the curve recorded Jake at the wheel. Facial recognition software, as well as Allie's own viewing of the recording, proved that faithful Jake Gibson with his characteristic oiled ball cap was driving the truck and shifting gears as it ventured north on 30E.

No part of Jake Gibson was ever found.

Not a belt buckle. Not a heel of his boot. Not his titanium watch. Not his platinum wedding ring. Not his teeth. Not the bronzed head of his walking cane. Like much of the truck, Jake had been vaporized. The horrific nature of his death led to a lot of speculating. Theories abounded. The most commonly believed was that Jake fell asleep long before the turn, slumping forward, thereby pressing his bad leg and portly weight forward. This is their only justification for the unjustifiable speed. Second is the suggestion that four days of caffeine overdosing exploded Jake's heart and he was dead long before the turn—also causing him to slump forward. The least whispered but still quite possible was the notion that Jake had an aneurysm, thereby producing the same result. No one really knows. All they knew with certainty was that he went out with a bang so violent that it registered on military satellites, bringing in the Department of Defense and Homeland Security, who both raised eyebrows at the enormity of the blast area. "Shame."

With the site surrounded in yellow tape and flashing lights, it was still too hot to approach. Firemen said it'd take a week to cool off the core and allow anyone near the blast site. Onlookers shook their heads, thought of Allie, and muttered in their best backstabbing whisper, "That woman is cursed. Everything she touches dies."

Rescue and coast guard crews searched the ocean and the shoreline throughout the night. They thought maybe if Jake had been thrown through the windshield at that speed, his body would have shot out across the rocks and into the ocean on the other side, where there's a known rip tide. If so, he'd have been sucked out to sea.

Like everything else, the search turned up nothing. And like everything else, each failed search reinforced the excruciating notion that Jake died a horrible, painful death.

The weight of this on Allie was crushing. Jake, the affable husband who simply worked hard enough to put food on the table and laughter in his wife's heart, was not coming back. Ever. The last year or two or even three had not been easy. He had worked more than he'd been at home, staying gone weeks at a time, months even. Allie knew what people thought . . . that she was just tough to live with.

She was left to plan the funeral and decide what to put in the box. But every time she tried to tell his memory that she was sorry, she was met with the haunting and deafening echo that the final three words she spoke to Jake were not "I love you." Instead, her last words to him had been spoken in a spit-filled tirade of anger.

And for those words, there was no remedy.

## — 2 —

Five hundred sixty-five miles northeast of Cape San Blas on the shoulders of Mount Mitchell in North Carolina, Juan Pedro Perez lit a cigarette. His knuckles were scarred, as was his forehead, and beneath his shirt were twenty more. He had long prized his ability with a knife, but his education came at a cost. Born in Juarez, he'd first walked across the border when he was six, and most of that distance he'd carried his sister. Now thirty, he'd lost count of his crossings. Raised in the fields, and tired of endless hours in the sun and countless unmet expectations, he'd robbed a border farmer, taken his gun, and learned to use it. Soon, he was hiring it out. A drug runner with a guerrilla fighter's pedigree. Such talent and disregard got him noticed. Those atop the food chain took him under their wing, making him well connected. While hunted, he was also protected. Pretty soon he brokered his own power.

He sat in the front seat of an old flatbed Ford, left hand loosely cupped over his mouth, cheeks drawn, eyes dark and cold. Cigarette smoke exited his nose and trailed up and out the car window. He spun the brass Zippo lighter on his right thigh. With every spin he'd flip it open, flick it lit, then slam it shut. Spin it again, repeat. The woman next to him in the front seat didn't watch the lighter so much as the hand that held it.

Catalina was twenty-eight—or so she thought. The two had met, oddly enough, at church. She was attending her husband's funeral while Juan Pedro was running a load and using the church as both a cover and a safe haven. She had no idea. Diego, her husband of five years, had been a good man and she had loved him. They married when she was eighteen and he twenty-eight. He was a dentist, and given his honesty, underinflated prices, and twenty-four-hour house calls, he had a lot of patients but little money.

Juan Pedro stared at her long dress and beautiful black eyes, then at the simple wooden box that held her husband. He pointed north, toward the border. "America?"

She looked at her two children, who were looking blankly at the box. Then she looked at the hell spread around her and figured it couldn't get any worse.

She had been way bad wrong.

Five years later, she had America, an oil-leaking, mufflerless truck for a home, and Juan Pedro's pistol for a pillow. His process was consistent—he would drive her and the kids to a community ripe for harvest, drop them at a shack, and disappear for weeks or months while a couple of his lieutenants kept an eye on them until he reappeared without warning, flush with cash and half a bottle of tequila. Thus far she'd lived in Texas, New Mexico, Alabama, Louisiana, Georgia, South and North Carolina. She'd seen him in two dozen angry and bloody knife fights. He liked to stand over the other men as they quivered and bled out. A sly smile. His blade dripping. His weapon of choice was a Dexter-Russell six-inch skinning knife. A butcher's knife. He'd first learned to use it at the meat-packing houses. Curved blade. Wooden handle. Carbon steel. Razor sharp. If his pistol was close, that blade was closer.

The first two times she'd tried to escape had not gone well. It took her nearly a month to be able to take a deep breath. The third time he almost killed her while the two children watched. Had it been just her, she'd have closed her eyes and let Diego welcome her home, but the terror in her children's eyes proved too much. So she pulled herself off the floor and yielded. Even now her left eye was still blurry from the impact.

Juan Pedro didn't like her children. He didn't like any children. As long as they weren't much trouble or expense he would let her keep them around, but Catalina knew time was running short. In his world, evil people bought children, and she suspected that Juan Pedro had already collected the deposit.

Diego was ten. Cropped jet-black hair. Black-rimmed glasses with lenses on the thick side. Square jaw. The gentleness in his eyes favored his father. He sat cross-legged in the back seat, a coverless Louis L'Amour paperback in his hand, silently biting his bottom lip, about to pee in his pants. In public he called Juan Pedro *Papa*. In private, he didn't call him at all.

Gabriela was seven. Long black hair hanging in matted knots below her shoulders. Her skin was dirty; it'd been three weeks since she'd had a bath, and she had a rash she didn't want to talk about. She sat on her heels, silently biting her top lip and about to scratch her skin off.

In addition to the shiny pistol just below his belly button, Juan Pedro kept a revolver at the base of his back. A third handgun was taped below the front seat, a fourth wedged up behind the dash. Two shotguns lay across the floorboard of the back seat, and three automatic weapons were stashed beneath the kids' seat. Behind them, the bed of the truck had been built with a false floor containing several thousand rounds of ammunition and cash. While Juan Pedro was hated and wanted by many, he was not stupid, and if he was going out, it would be in a blaze of glory.

The temperature hovered in the thirties. Catalina stared out the window as the freezing rain stuck to the windshield. They had driven through the night. And the night before. There would be no harvest in this weather, but she dared not state the obvious. Juan Pedro had been sent either to pick up or drop off. Their life had become a series of aimless destinations.

She placed her hand gently on his forearm and whispered, "Juan, the kids no have clothes for this." He looked at her out of the corner of his eye, then at the back seat, where Gabriela had started to shiver. He cranked the engine, flicked his cigarette butt out the window, and dropped the stick into drive. Catalina whispered again. "Diego has to go."

Juan Pedro glanced in the rearview in disapproval. He believed the boy to be soft, so he was toughening him up a bit.

He eased into Spruce Pine and pulled over at the Blue Ridge Thrift Store. He slid a roll of hundreds from his front pocket and thumbed through the wad until he found a twenty. He handed it to Catalina and nodded toward the door. When she motioned for the kids to follow, he extended his arm and shook his head once. The kids didn't move.

Catalina quickly found two matching used men's down jackets and two pairs of ladies' fleece sweat pants. They were too big and too long, but the kids could roll them up. She laid the bundle quietly on the counter, and the clerk, whose name tag identified her as Myrtle, rang up the order.

"Twenty-nine dollars and ninety-six cents."

With her back turned to the truck, and with motions that could not be seen from the sidewalk, Catalina slid seven dollars from just inside the waistline of her underwear, unfolded it, and without a word offered Myrtle twenty-seven dollars. Myrtle looked over the rim of her reading glasses and eyed Catalina for the first time. She did not look impressed. She tapped her teeth with a pencil, then glanced at the idling truck where the red glow of the single cigarette pulsated just above the steering wheel. Then she noticed the kids. She raised an eyebrow, scratched her scalp hidden beneath a beehive, then busily mashed several buttons.

"Sorry, darling, been a long day. Numbers are running together." She counted the twenty-seven dollars, reached inside the cash drawer, and gently slid a crisp ten-dollar bill back across the counter. While she took her time folding and bagging the clothes, Catalina rolled the ten into the size of a toothpick and slid it back into the waistband of her frayed underwear. When she had finished, Myrtle handed her the bag and said, "Sweet thing, you need anything else, you holler now."

When Catalina returned to the car, she found Diego trembling, a tear cascading down his cheek. She pleaded, "Juan . . . please?"

Juan Pedro snatched the bag of clothes, filtered through it, then tossed it into the back seat, where the kids did not touch it. He motioned to Catalina, who sat down and quietly closed the door. Juan Pedro waited for a car to pass and then pulled slowly out onto the highway. He was cautious. No need to spin the tires and speed off. Those inside the truck knew he was a bad hombre. There was nothing to be gained by reconvincing them. Those outside the truck didn't need to know it. Least not yet. One of the reasons he had survived as long as he had on this side was his cunning. His ability to not think rashly. He was a master at looking the part of the tired, poor migrant worker.

Juan Pedro had four cell phones, one of which contained the map that held his attention. He drove west on 19E out of Micaville and turned south on Highway 80 in front of the post office heading toward Busick. The small two-lane mountain road wound out of town, past the elementary school and the mattress spring plant. Juan Pedro saw the police officer sitting in his car alongside the road, but paid him no visible attention. He smiled slightly to himself as they drove by, his right hand sliding to his waistband. His left rear taillight was burned out, but he had a pretty good idea that the police officer liked being dry and warm. He tapped the fake ivory grips of his automatic. If the cop wanted to make it an issue, he'd get all the discussion he could handle. And then some.

The freezing rain did little to improve conditions. The roads were mushy and muddy. And the windshield wiper blades had quit working about ten years ago. Juan Pedro drove slowly, wiping the back side of the windshield with a dirty white T-shirt.

In the back seat, Diego trembled.

Juan Pedro followed the map through Bowditch, then Celo, and when the road made a hard right turn at the South Toe River, he let off the gas and began looking for signs. He turned right at Gibson Cemetery and downshifted into first as the big truck rattled onto the dirt road. Diego winced. Juan Pedro hesitated just slightly at the No Outlet sign. He didn't like being penned in.

They wound up the slowly increasing grade, passing the occasional house or cabin. It was growing dark. Passing a run-down geodesic dome where wood smoke puffed from a chimney, Juan Pedro rolled down the window, letting in the cold and rain, and stared off into the trees. A light flashed twice, then again once. Juan Pedro whistled and turned left onto the muddy road, where rhododendron limbs smacked the windshield.

He parked, left the truck idling, and carried a black bag through the dark toward a guy holding a flashlight in front of a metal barnlike building. Incoherent screaming rock music could be heard from within. As soon as Juan Pedro was out of sight, Catalina handed Diego an empty water bottle. Diego knelt on the back seat and furiously unbuckled his pants. Over the next minute and fifty-six seconds, Diego filled the twenty-ounce bottle, trying not to spill it. Screwing the cap back on, Catalina took the bottle and wedged it beneath her seat. Diego took a deep breath and all three watched the warehouse, hoping, praying Juan Pedro would not return.

A minute later, an expressionless Juan Pedro exited the warehouse with a different black bag, hopped into the truck, dropped the stick into reverse, and circled backward and slowly out the drive. When he glanced in the rearview and noticed Diego was no longer sweating, he slammed on the brakes. The sudden movement jolted everyone forward. The pee bottle as well. Juan Pedro eyed it and, as if loosed from a spring, backhanded Catalina, rocketing her head against the headrest. As blood trickled out the side of her split lip, he lit a cigarette, looked into the rearview, and growled out of the corner of his mouth, "That's your fault." He lit a cigarette. "Apologize."

Diego whimpered, "I'm sorry, Mama."

Catalina wiped the blood away and shook her head slightly.

Taking a deep draw on his cigarette, Juan Pedro continued down the dirt road. As he made the wide bend toward the asphalt, the headlights of the old flatbed Ford were met head-on by a waiting police officer parked perpendicular to the No Outlet sign.

The officer stood in his rain slicker, water dripping off his hat, a flashlight in his hand. He shined the high-powered LED light in Juan Pedro's eyes and held out his left hand like a stop sign.

Juan Pedro smiled, waved, and never even hesitated. He slammed the accelerator to the floor, roaring the big block V-8 to life, and, turning the wheel slightly to the left, slammed into the police officer, who spun out through the night air like a helicopter blade.

When Juan Pedro cleared the bright white dot from his pupils, he noticed that the police officer had been smart and not come alone. A second officer knelt alongside his car, pointing a rifle at the Ford's windshield. His door-mounted Q-Beam lit the entire front and back seating areas, which explained why he had not emptied the entire thirty-round magazine into the truck. The officer maintained his aim while wildly yelling into his shoulder-mounted radio mic. Juan Pedro drew the automatic from his waistline and, knowing the officer would not return fire, emptied his seventeen-round magazine through the officer's car door. When the smoke cleared, the officer lay on his back in the mud. One leg crossed oddly beneath the other.

While little surprised Juan Pedro, the third officer did when he moved around behind the first officer's car, trying to get a clear shot without endangering those inside the car. Using the truck as his backstop, Juan Pedro drew the revolver at the base of his back, exited the truck, and walked toward the officer, pulling the trigger six times. When he'd emptied the revolver, he returned to his truck and methodically dropped the stick into drive.

When he let off the clutch, he was met by his first unsolvable problem. All four tires were flat.

He eyed the police cars, but he knew they were equipped with highly sensitive GPS units that would allow someone sitting at a dry desk to track his every turn. His options were few.

Grabbing the bag, a backpack packed for just such an eventuality, and several weapons, he shoved Catalina and the children out of the truck and force-marched them back toward the metal shack.

Drenched and freezing in only a T-shirt, Catalina worked hurriedly to get the stumbling kids into their jackets. The fleece pants would have to wait.

Juan Pedro ushered them through the darkness, prodding them with the muzzle of his rifle. Reaching the side of the building, he slipped through the darkness like a shadow. Ten head-banging, wannabe rockers stood cooking dope inside. The four who sat guard outside were passing something back and forth and stoned out of their minds. Juan Pedro forced Catalina and the kids around the cookshack and up the small hill behind, then sat them next to a giant boulder and, with a clear view of everything below him, waited.

Ninety seconds later, Catalina watched him smile as the sound of sirens reached their ears. Thirty seconds later the night sky was filled with flashing red and blue lights as the entire Burnsville and Spruce Pine police departments descended on the cookshack. Stoking the fire, Juan Pedro fired four shots through the windshield of the first car and seven through the windshield of the second. Doing so brought all twelve vehicles to a rapid stop, whereby a hail of bullets passed between the cookshack, now in utter chaos, and the twelve officers who believed three of their fellow deputies were dead.

Juan Pedro knew it would be tomorrow or the next day or maybe even the next before they figured out that the driver of the truck was not in the building. He turned, slung his rifle over his shoulder, and motioned for Catalina to move up the hill. She didn't argue. Didn't hesitate. She simply picked up Gabriela and followed Diego, who had begun trudging up the steep, snowy trail. The trail marker read Woody Ridge Trail. She'd never been here, but based on the way Juan Pedro kept prodding, she had a feeling he had. With the echo of muffled gunfire below, they climbed for a mile, their feet slipping more with every step. Soon the grade grew so steep they were pulling on tree limbs and bushes to help their ascent. Freezing rain blew sideways.

An explosion rang out from below. Fire raged where the building had stood. Juan Pedro smiled again. Now it would be a week or two or maybe never before they figured out that he wasn't inside it. He lit a cigarette, spun the brass lighter in his hand, and laughed quietly.

Diego stumbled and Catalina caught him as Juan Pedro smacked the back of the boy's head. Catalina pleaded for rest through chattering teeth, but Juan Pedro pointed farther upward. He directed them around a small outcropping of rock and then back into the trees, where they came upon a natural break in the granite. Beneath an enormous rock outcropping was a cavelike space large enough to park two or three pickups. Someone had piled firewood and dried evergreen branches in the corner. Juan Pedro quickly lit a fire.

Catalina and the kids hovered near the flames, their shivering growing more intense as they warmed. Catalina helped the kids strip out of their wet clothes and settled them between the fire and the granite wall. She used long branches to hang their wet clothes against the rock wall, added larger logs to the fire, and circled the growing base of coals with rocks that would hold and reflect the heat. Staring at her two terrorized and exhausted children, shadows from the flames flickering on their faces, Catalina made up her mind: a bad death would be better than this living hell.

Because sleep could get him killed, Juan Pedro had trained

himself to go without. When he did sleep, he did so in one of two dozen shipping containers strategically placed throughout the Southwest. He could lock them from the inside out, and something about locking himself in convinced his subconscious that he'd be safe. But if he'd been awake several days and couldn't get to one of his trailers, he'd take something, a powerful narcotic, to knock him out for a few hours. Something that would medically override his system and force his instincts to shut down.

Catalina's problem was that she never knew when he would do this. Like everything else in his life, when and what he took was secret. Juan Pedro was a master at controlling information. It was what made him valuable. Given that, she never really knew when he was asleep or just pretending. She couldn't even trust his snoring. The only signal she'd ever been able to trust was the sight of his eyeballs moving back and forth beneath his eyelids. But he would usually cover his eyes with a hat.

Juan Pedro had been keeping himself awake for almost five days. Catalina knew he couldn't keep this up much longer. He had to get some sleep. And in all the hurry, he'd left his hat in the truck. Catalina made the fire as warm and inviting as she could. Juan Pedro yawned, walked outside the cave, and studied the worsening conditions. When he came back, he laid his backpack flat across the entrance to the cave, lay his head on the pack, cradled his rifle in his arms, and closed his eyes.

## — 3 —

I sat with my legs dangling. Roll of white paper spread beneath
me. Shirt off. Young doctor listening through his stethoscope.
Degrees and diplomas covered the wall.

"Breathe."

I did.

"And again."

Another breath.

"One more."

He placed his hand on my chest and tapped it with his other
hand. Same on my back.

"You've been short of breath lately?"

"A little."

"A little or yes?"

"I live at thirty-five hundred feet."

"Did you feel this way when you moved there?"

"No."

"How long have you lived there?"

"Ten years or more."

"How long you been feeling this way?"

"Couple."

He pointed at the antacids on the table. "How long you been taking those?"

"Long time."

He frowned. "And you're just now coming to see me?"

"Didn't seem important."

He crossed his arms. "At one time you were strong as an ox, weren't you?"

I weighed my head side to side. "I can pull my own weight."

"Except lately."

I didn't respond.

He hung his stethoscope around his neck. "What you're feeling is not indigestion."

"What is it?"

"You probably need a few stents. But I won't know until I look."

"Any hurry?"

He seemed surprised by my question. "That depends."

"On?"

"If you want to live."

I nodded.

He baited me. "You seem like an educated man."

I sucked through my teeth. "Never finished high school."

He crossed his arms and gazed at me skeptically.

I studied his various diplomas. "I attended school . . . just not in a traditional classroom."

He looked again at the clipboard in his hand. "You're sixty—"

I finished for him. "Two."

He nodded. "You've got some hardening. Probably some blockage. The diabetes can contribute to it. I won't know what I'm dealing with until I get in there and take a look."

"What's this going to cost?"

He did not look impressed. "Does it really matter?"

I shrugged.

He glanced at my chart. "You could get it done for free at the VA, but you probably already knew that."

"I wouldn't let them operate on my dead body."

"Can't say I blame you." He put his hand on my shoulder. "Why don't you let me schedule you for next week. It's painless, and you'll feel a lot better."

"And if I don't?"

"Well . . . one of two things will happen. You'll be dead before you hit the floor, or if you don't die, we'll split you up the middle and then crack most of your ribs trying to sew the pieces of your heart back together."

I mumbled, "Not sure medicine can do that."

He leaned in. "What's that?"

I pulled on my shirt. "Next week will be fine."

He glanced at my shirt pocket. Eyeing the pack of Camels. "You'll have to quit those."

"I don't smoke them."

He laughed. "And I bet you don't inhale either."

I stood and tucked in my shirt. He was an inch or two shorter than me. I looked down. "Doc . . . your bedside manner leaves a bit to be desired."

He bristled. "How so?"

"Before you accuse a man, you should know his story."

He was half my age. Young enough to be my son. Maybe it was my tone that convinced him. He changed his tune. "Why do you carry them then?"

"To remember."

"Remember what?"

"That this hard heart you keep poking at was once tender and knew how to laugh and love and feel deeply. No amount of stents will bring that back."

# — 4 —

The percolator gurgled behind me, and the aroma of coffee hung in the air. I filled two mugs, placed one opposite me across the table. Then I lit a Camel unfiltered cigarette and set it next to the second cup, where both steam and smoke trailed up. I closed the worn brass Zippo lighter, flipped it over, and ran my fingertip along the engraving. Remembering. I pricked my finger, checked my fasting blood sugar, which measured 177, then drew out three units of insulin and injected it into the fatty tissue just above my belt line. I swallowed four antacids, mumbled something to myself about uppity doctors, and followed them with a glass of milk and a few Oreos.

Outside the wind howled. Downward sleet had turned to sideways snow. On the table sat a Mason jar half full of sharks' teeth. I spilled a few on the table and picked through them. In one hand, the teeth. In the other, the lighter. Each a memory.

A familiar whining rose up from outside the front door. Rosco had returned. I slid my mug along the table, letting him know I was inside, and the whining grew louder. A moment later a paw scratched the front door. I shuffled my chair and he whined again. Rosco was working me and I knew it, but he'd always done that.

Up here, people pride themselves on their bear dogs. It is not uncommon for a prized bear dog to sell for upwards of twenty thousand dollars. Easy. Rosco was some shade of Rhodesian ridgeback mixed with a little North Carolina mountain mutt for good measure. He was a big dog. Came to mid-thigh, long lanky legs, big paws, big head, could run all day and night and then some, and he had powerful shoulders and jaws. Ridgebacks were bred to fight lions in Africa. But Rosco was a long way from Africa, and he was currently standing out in the snow and he was hungry.

I didn't own Rosco. He used me for food, a warm bed, to pull the ticks off him come springtime and rub him between the ears at night. Truth be told, he liked to wander for days on end, chasing every female dog twenty miles in either direction, but when he grew tired or hungry or lonely, he was a pathetic pansy with a pitiful moan.

I slid my mug again and smiled. He'd laid his muzzle flat against the threshold and was blowing snot beneath the crack of the door. The whining had transformed to a muffled bark. I pulled open the cabinet, which squeaked, and the tempo of the breathing doubled. I popped the lid off a can, and a rhythmic thumping told me Rosco was spinning in circles, his tail thumping the door at every turn. I dropped the contents of the can into his bowl, cracked two raw eggs on top, covered that with a layer of dry dog food, and then soaked the whole thing in heavy cream. When I finished, I looked out the side window. Rosco was standing in front of the house, facing the door, howling.

I turned the handle, and the howling immediately stopped. I stood in the doorway and raised my eyebrows. Rosco sat spine-straight. Ears trained on me. I folded my arms and he lay flat on his tummy, paws forward, head up. He'd been gone four days—he had to be hungry. A tiny whimper escaped his throat. I stepped to the side and nodded. Rosco stood, walked inside, and sat, his head pivoting on a swivel and his tail wiping the varnish off the wood floors. Staring at me, then at the bowl. Then at me, then at the bowl. I sat, crossed my legs, and nodded.

Rosco devoured his food. When finished, he licked his muzzle and stretched out on "his" bear rug in front of my fire. The wind had picked up, pushing the wind chill lower. In front of me, Rosco snored happily.

My cabin is well insulated, so I crack the window whenever the fire is lit. I telescoped the radio antennae and adjusted the dial. The radio signal strengthened, and her voice sounded through the air. As she welcomed listeners, I finished my coffee. Then I poured out the cold cup across from me and stamped out the cigarette, which had burnt itself down to a butt. I refilled both cups, lit a second cigarette, and snapped the brass Zippo closed on my thigh.

Putting on my reading glasses, I dialed the ten-digit number. Three thousand miles away, she recognized my caller ID and answered. The most widely listened to nighttime radio call-in show in the country. Live on the air. "Jo-Jo!" Her voice dripped. "How are you, baby?"

Every caller was her baby. I chuckled. "Alive."

"Still surprising to you?"

"Suzy, every day is a mystery, darling."

"I love it when you call me that."

I, along with a couple hundred thousand guys like me, could hear her smile.

"How're things in the mountains of North Carolina?"

"White and . . ." A glance out the window. "Getting worse."

"You still pouring two cups of coffee?"

A glance at my table. "Yes, ma'am."

"How many years you been calling in to my show?"

"A lot."

"And in all those years, and all the times I've asked about that coffee, you've never explained why."

"I know."

"One of these days you've got to let me in on that secret."

"I try to keep my promises."

"That would make you different from many in uniform." Her voice had fallen to a low whisper. Like lovers speaking between pillows. Suzy knew her place. While she was an advocate for the silent, which meant she got to stoke the anti-government vibe from time to time, she was also careful not to push it too far, knowing that the same people she was criticizing on the air were the back-channel people she called when the show ended.

I didn't respond.

She let the dead air filter out across the airwaves. After about ten seconds, she said, "Least you went."

"I try to keep my promises."

She laughed. The sound just millimeters from the microphone. Layered behind her voice, her squeaking chair sounded through the radio. "What brings you to my ears this moonlit night?"

"Sharks' teeth."

"You're such a romantic. Still dreaming about that beach, eh?"

"I've been called a lot of things. Romantic has never been one of them."

"Why sharks' teeth?"

I paused. Looking back. "I knew a girl once."

"Oh, do tell."

"Growing up, me and this girl used to walk the beach."

"Hmmmm . . ." She savored this, and in so doing allowed her listeners to do likewise.

I continued. "I'd lead her by the hand and we'd comb the beach looking for whatever washed up."

"Any walk in particular?"

The snow was falling heavy now, but the moon had risen so it hung behind the clouds like a flashlight shining behind a sheet. "It was October. Harvest moon. So bright you could see your shadow. When the tide washed over the shells, leaving them wet, the shells would reflect like black diamonds. We filled up a backpack."

"Was that before you shipped out?"

"A few months."

"Sounds like a good memory."

"It was innocence."

At some point in Suzy's back-and-forth, she usually dropped an emotional bomb that sent the listener reeling. Like having a

Band-Aid ripped off your heart. For me, that bomb was here. But I knew it was coming.

"Did you love her?"

"I'm not sure I remember that emotion, but I do remember feeling something I haven't felt in a long time."

In her conversations with guys like me, Suzy liked to walk her listeners up to the wire, stare beyond it, allowing our memories to take over, then retreat to safety. It was her way of forcing us to deal with what most of us didn't want to deal with. But she was careful. She knew not to push too far. Each of us had a place from which we could not easily come back.

Suzy had mercy. She offered me an out. "It was a long time ago."

I considered this. "I can still smell the salt air mixed with the smell of her shampoo."

Suzy sidestepped. "You two have a favorite song?"

"We had a thing for Creedence."

"Any song in particular?"

"I've always felt fortunate."

Suzy laughed. But didn't quite let me go. "One more question." I knew it before she asked. "Whatever happened to the girl?"

The memory returned. I cleared my throat. "She married another."

"I'm sorry."

"Probably for the best. I was in pretty bad shape."

"Did you know the guy?"

"Yes." The snow was blowing sideways. "He was my brother."

Rarely does a caller leave Suzy speechless, but I'd just succeeded.

———

She tried to recover. Her chair squeaked, suggesting she'd sat up to look at her producer for some help. Like an actor on Broadway, she stayed in character no matter what a caller said. It was how she protected herself from the pain she served on her radio waves. Having undressed me, Suzy peeled off her mask and spoke to me. Just to me. "Jo-Jo, I'm sorry. I knew I shouldn't have asked that one."

I let her off easy. "Long time ago. Besides . . . the boy she walked the beach with was not the man who came home."

Empowered, Suzy strapped her mask back on. "Sergeant?"

"Yes, ma'am."

She spoke to all of us. It's why we listened. She spoke the words we'd never heard. "Thank you."

I studied my hand, making and remaking a fist. "If you knew my story, you'd have trouble saying that."

She chuckled. "I'm not talking about who you were and what you did when we sent you halfway around the world."

I matched her chuckle. "I'm not either."

Suzy's voice reached through the phone and kissed the ears of every man listening: "Stay dry, Sergeant."

She switched back into her radio voice. "This is for every sergeant who ever fell in love, but signed up anyway."

I hung up as CCR burst into my anthem. The sound took me back to the beach and the stars and the feel of that tender and trusting hand inside mine.

It'd been a long time since I'd felt fortunate.

# — 5 —

I snoozed until after midnight, when Rosco appeared next to my bed, his ears trained toward the window. I'd heard it too. I lay in the dark listening. A noise well beyond the cabin echoed faintly. Rosco's ears were pointed toward the open window. There it was again. This time the hair stood on his back.

I tied on my boots, pulled on my coat, and grabbed my backpack. Live in the mountains long enough and you never walk out the door without a pack. It contained the just-in-case stuff I might need if something went wrong: a hundred meters of rope, compass, emergency blanket, flares, matches, butane lighter, paracord, knife, a second knife, warm hat, first-aid kit, and a dozen other things I might need.

For a minute we stood outside, snow stinging my face, listening. Rosco pressed against my side. Up here the acoustics can lie to you. Between the wind and the granite, voices carry. Out of the darkness, we heard something that sounded like a muffled scream. More like the second half of an echo. There it was again. Louder. And longer.

Rosco stood motionless, staring northeast toward the ridgeline above us, his muscles taut as a wound spring. I tapped him on top of the head, and he tore up the hillside and into the tree line, his paws flinging snow as he ran. I followed, slipping with each step. Four minutes later he was back. He stood thirty yards in front of me and spun in a circle. Then a second time. When I stepped toward him, he disappeared again into the trees. I fast-jogged up an old logging road toward a saddle between two six-thousand-foot peaks where two backpacking trails intersected at a waterfall, a popular summer hiking destination. No one really swam up here. At least not for more than a few seconds at a time. Even in summer, the water temperature never rose above thirty-six degrees. Right now it hovered in the upper twenties. The sound was growing closer. Someone was frantically calling a name.

I sprinted onto the saddle and let my eyes adjust to the snow and poor light. The attraction to this area of the trail was Big Tom's Fall. Big Tom was the unlucky fellow who happened upon the dead body of Elisha Mitchell, after whom the mountain is named, back in the 1800s. Big Tom's Fall is a sixty-meter cascading section of rock, steep enough and slippery enough to ride down on your butt before it empties into a small pool of water. The Fall drops off at about a seventy-degree angle. Too steep to walk unaided but doable with the right length of rope and sure footing.

I reached the top of Big Tom's to find two people, one larger than the other, leaning over the precipice, screaming down into the water. If they leaned any farther they'd join whoever was down there. Coming out of the bottom were the muffled cries of what sounded like a young girl. To the wide-eyed amazement of the two at the top, Rosco and I ran up alongside them and stared down. It took me about half a second to realize that as this woman and her two children had been walking the knife's edge between Big Tom Mountain and Craig Mountain, the little girl slipped. Their problem was threefold: snow, ice, and no rope. The little girl below wasn't moving, and her head was barely sticking above water. Either she couldn't swim or the cold wouldn't let her.

I clicked the carabiner tied to the end of my rope to the steel anchor sunk into the rock by the forestry department. I tossed the rope down, peeled off my coat, and began rappelling back-ward. Sure purchase was nonexistent, so I slid my way down. At the bottom, unable to slow my descent, I splashed into the waist-deep water. The shock took my breath away, momentarily paralyzing me. Rosco appeared out of a side trail that's longer and only accessible by a cougar or a cocky dog. He jumped into the water and swam toward the girl. I forced my body to start moving and walked sideways across the flow of the water. I grabbed the girl, who clutched my back with a whimper, and we made our way back to the rope while Rosco climbed out, shook, and disap-peared the way he'd come.

I pulled the girl around in front of me, draped her arms around my neck so she was hugging me, and said, "Hold tight." She was nearly limp as a Raggedy Ann doll and crying, which I took as a good sign. Trying to ignore the growing loss of gross motor movement in my hands, I began pulling us up, fist over fist. Step by slippery step. I used my elbows and forearms to hold the girl close to me. Above me I could hear Rosco barking and the woman screaming. Twice my hands slipped, causing my feet to fly out from beneath me, slamming me against the rock, where my forearms took the brunt of the blow while I tried to protect the child.

At the top I was met by the woman. Her lips were blue and terror covered her face, but she was laser-beam focused on the little girl.

The wind was howling, so I had to raise my voice. "You got anyplace you can get warm?"

She shook her head.

I held the girl in my arms and nodded. "My coat!" She snatched it off the ground, and I wrapped it around the girl and pointed. "My cabin. I got a fire." She nodded and I led the way.

The woman followed step for step, along with the boy and Rosco. We descended the trail as quickly as we could, almost a half mile, where it spit us out onto the logging road. A quarter mile later we could smell the smoke of my fire. Every part of my body was screaming with lactic acid buildup.

The woman opened the door, and all three of us converged on the fire. I set the girl down on top of Rosco's bear rug, and the woman immediately began stripping the clothes off the kids. I fetched two sleeping bags, added several logs to the fire, and helped the woman slide the kids into the bags. They were shaking uncontrollably, and the little girl was whimpering.

"You'd better get in there with her," I said. "I'll get you some dry clothes and put on some water to boil."

The woman peeled off her wet clothes, I handed her some sweats, and she wrapped the bag tight around the two of them. As they began to thaw and warm, the shaking became more violent, proving that they had been cold for quite some time. Seeing that the boy needed some extra warmth, I scooted Rosco up alongside him. The boy unzipped his bag, wrapped his arm around Rosco's tummy, and pulled the dog in closer.

Rosco stared at us like we'd all lost our minds. The boy snuggled up next to Rosco, and the four of them started the long—and painful—process of warming up. Getting cold is one thing. Getting warm again is another entirely. The only sounds in the room were the crackle of the fire, the chattering of their teeth, the little girl's cries, and the sound of Rosco's tail happily pounding the floor in rhythm as the boy scratched his tummy.

I stripped out of my wet clothes and laid an extra wool blanket over each of them. The young girl was the worst. I don't know how long she'd been in that water, but she was irritable and having a tough time sounding coherent. I made some hot cocoa and topped it with spray whipped cream. The can was probably a year old, but when I turned it upside down and pushed the nozzle, it made that *shhhhh* sound and produced a mound of white. I handed the mug to the woman and she held it while the girl sipped, poking the end of her nose and cheeks into the whipped cream.

Seeing an opportunity, Rosco exited his sleeping bag and began licking the girl's lips and cheeks and nose. At first she was irritated by it, which further encouraged the dog, but then she began to giggle. I made a second mug and handed it to the boy. He looked as if he wanted to smile but was waiting for permission. Finally I made one for the woman—who watched me carefully. She held the mug between both hands and hovered over the steam. The fear had not left her face.

She shot a glance at the door and spoke with a thick accent. "A man is following us." Her eyes darted. "A bad man." She lowered her voice. "If he finds you . . ."

The children's faces confirmed her words. "How far?" I asked.

"Close."

I pulled on my dry pair of boots and a black jacket and beanie. She climbed out of the bag. Her hand was trembling when she touched my shoulder. "He will kill you." Another pause. "Without thinking."

While she talked, I rubbed my hand along the soot on the outside of the fireplace and began wiping it on my face. "Where's he from?"

"Juarez."

"Drugs?"

She nodded.

"He killed men?"

Her eyes were cold. She never hesitated. "Many."

"How old is he?"

"Thirty."

I didn't know squat about Mexican drug lords, but if he came from Juarez, the mere fact that he'd lived this long told me he was good at his job. I pulled a double-barreled shotgun from behind the door, broke it open, loaded it, and handed it to her. "You know how to use this?"

The way she held it told me she did.

I handed her my Jeep keys. "If I'm not back by the time this storm lets up, you drive out of here and flag down the first police officer or fireman or ambulance driver you can find. Understand?"

Her face told me she was not going to do that.

"You don't want to do that?"

"They'll send us back . . ." She glanced at the window. "He has friends."

I handed her a box of shells. "Then hunker down and shoot straight."

I looked at Rosco, who, having watched me dress, now stood at the door with his nose pressed against the crack. "Stay." He backed up, but the muscles in his shoulders were taut. I pointed to the boy but spoke to the dog. "Lie down." Rosco lay down next to the boy. His whimper told me he didn't like me leaving without him. I zipped up my coat and pulled the door behind me. I needed to get away from the house—without creating more footprints. That meant I had to backtrack.

Tricky.

Mount Mitchell is the tallest mountain east of the Rockies: 6,684 feet. Running north from the summit is a twelve-mile hikers' trail called the Black Mountain Crest. It follows the ridgeline along eleven other peaks, each greater than six thousand feet, ending at a place called Celo Knob. This vast and steep wilderness is encompassed by what is called the Pisgah National Forest. It's a rugged landscape. More vertical than horizontal. Most people live down below in the valleys, but I am not most people. My cabin sat at five thousand feet, with the closest neighbor more than two miles away.

I stood along the tree line, listening, staring back at the cabin. I couldn't remember the last time I had visitors. If ever. The snowfall had tapered off, leaving our footprints half full. Bread crumbs. Whoever he was would have seen my larger footprints as well as theirs. That meant he knew about me. I closed my eyes and listened for the quiet crunch of snow beneath careful feet.

It didn't take long.

# — 6 —

An hour after daylight I washed my hands in the snow and knocked gently, standing off to one side. Out of the line of fire. The blast wouldn't penetrate the cabin wall but it'd blow right through the door. I slid open the door and was met by a growling Rosco, baring his teeth and standing between me and them. Beyond him I saw the barrel end of my shotgun. I knew my blackened face would scare everyone, so I showed them my hands and said, "It's just me."

The woman sat, exhausted. Evidently she'd not slept. The gun rested across a chair in front of her where she'd kept the muzzle pointed at the door. Five shells were laid out in front of her. She leaned back, separating her shoulder from the stock of the shotgun. She had only one question.

The boy sat up, the girl lay sleeping. I washed my face and hands, trimmed the lantern wicks, and then sat on the hearth. I reached into my back pocket, pulled out a worn beef butcher's knife in a sheath, and set it on the ground in front of the boy. He stared at it, afraid to touch it. As if it might wield itself. Slowly he reached for it and took hold, then laid it flat across his palm and stared at it. The woman's mouth cracked open just slightly and her eyes turned slowly to me. The boy just sat there. Holding the knife like a bomb. The woman stared from it to me, back to it and back to me.

She pulled the boy to her chest, and tears streaked down her face. Tears without sadness. She wrapped her arms around the children and began shaking.

The boy spoke with his face pressed against her bosom. "Mama?"

"Yes."

The little girl was awake now, and sitting up. "Is Juan Pedro going to find us?" she asked.

Her mother looked at me. "I don't think so, baby."

"Looks like you three had quite the hike." I tried to smile at the children. "You are two of the toughest kids I've ever met. Most folks can't do what you did in summertime with a pack full of food and water. You hungry?"

Their blank faces told me they hadn't thought about it.

"Let me get cleaned up. I can scramble a mean egg. Just ask Rosco."

My cabin doesn't have running water, so I take bucket showers with room temp water. Given that my cabin was one room, and that I lived alone, I'd never made concessions for privacy. With six curious eyes watching my every move, I hung a wool blanket in the corner, creating a divider, and then stripped and stepped into the tub. Pretty quickly the water started turning red. My fingers found the source, I dressed the wound, and then I started stitching up the cut in the fat just below my left rib cage. The absence of a mirror and the location of the cut made it difficult to work on, so I pulled on my pants and poked my head around the blanket.

"Could I trouble you?"

The woman rose, almost obediently, and stood at the blanket. Head bowed. I pulled back slightly on the blanket, allowing her to see what I didn't want the kids to see. She quickly stepped behind the curtain, knelt next to the tub, and began carefully bathing the skin in peroxide and then stitching the skin together. Her precision told me that she'd had either some medical training or some prior experience.

When she finished, she stood, waiting for me to dismiss her. But there was a second emotion. There was shame. Along with a growing posture of servitude. Since I'd mastered her master.

I pointed toward the kitchen side of the room. "There's food. Whatever you like. The matches are sitting on a shelf above the stovetop."

She shot a quick glance at my stitches.

"It's nothing. Rosco scratches me worse when we wrestle." A forced chuckle. She looked at me briefly, then turned and exited through the side of the blanket. When I walked out, dressed and having put on deodorant for the first time in years, she had fried bacon, scrambled eggs, cooked some grits, browned some toast, and brewed a fresh pot of coffee.

The kids were sitting at my table watching their food get cold. I gestured. "Please. Eat." Having been released from their cages, they pounced. They inhaled their food more than chewed it, putting down a dozen eggs, six pieces of toast, half a jar of jelly, nearly a pound of bacon, and the entire pot of grits.

While the kids ate, the woman and I sat near the fire. "Did he bring you across the border?"

"Yes."

"How long ago?"

She shrugged. "Maybe five years."

"You got any family in the States?"

"A brother in Florida. Maybe more."

"You want to see them?"

I don't think she had thought past the next five minutes, because planning requires freedom. "I don't know exactly where they are or how we'd get there. I have . . . nothing."

"I can put you on a bus."

She paused, afraid to make eye contact. "I can't pay you."

There were two conversations going on here. The one we were having on the surface, about my having money. And the one we were having beneath the surface—about her being a vulnerable woman, with a woman's body, who needed money. I studied her expression, wondering if something about me made her feel this way or if she was so accustomed to having life taken from her that she was unable to think otherwise. It was as if her soul had been tattooed and she'd not asked for the ink.

I stood and let the fire warm my back. "There's a bus station in Spruce Pine. I can put you on the late afternoon to Asheville. From there you can get a ticket most anywhere."

She nodded. Again without looking.

I spoke softly. "You don't have to pay me. Not with money or anything else." I don't know whether she believed me or not, but the look in her eyes told me she was struggling with the idea.

# — 7 —

By the time we got down the mountain, through Busick and the Carolina Hemlocks, through Micaville and into Spruce Pine, it was almost two o'clock. I checked the schedule and saw that the bus to Asheville didn't leave until five. I bought three tickets and only then realized that the aroma of the burger joint next door had caught the kids' attention.

The girl backed up when I spoke to her. "You hungry?"

She didn't answer.

I pointed at the neon marquee. "Cheeseburger?"

She looked up at her mom, who nodded, and the little girl nodded, though still not smiling.

"You like French fries?"

Another glance at her mom, followed by a nod.

"Single or double?"

She looked confused.

I held out my hand, barely separating my thumb and index finger. "One patty, or . . ." I widened the gap between the fingers. "Two."

She held up one hand and two and a half fingers. Seeing the one finger stuck in the half position, she reached up with her other hand and folded it back down, extending a perfect peace sign.

The restaurant was a grease pit, but the food was hot and the kids needed calories. We ordered, and because making small talk had never been my strength, we waited in silence. Given a few minutes, I checked my blood sugar, calculated, and injected two units of insulin into the fat of my stomach. The three of them watched me with curiosity but said nothing.

A television hung above the counter. The local news was just starting. The underlying soundtrack suggested a breaking news story. The news anchor behind the desk started his monologue.

"An explosion at what authorities are calling a methamphetamine cookshack rocked the small town of Celo last night, mixed with several minutes of automatic gunfire." The anchor turned his attention to a second reporter standing in front of the Burnsville Emergency Room. "Frank Porter reports. Frank, tell us about it."

"That's right, John. It began with a routine traffic stop and turned into what authorities are calling a gang-related drug war. Last night around six p.m. a Yancey County deputy attempted a routine traffic stop. The driver, attempting to escape, ran over one deputy and the spike strip the police had stretched across the road. Unable to drive on four flat tires, he exited the vehicle and opened fire on the other two deputies. He then returned to the metal cookshack disguised as a utility barn where he was joined by at least ten men armed with automatic weapons. When more than a dozen officers responded to the 'Shots fired—officer down' call for help, they were met with a barrage of bullets. No one really knows what caused the explosion, but eight men inside were killed, and four sustained critical injuries from burns to gunshot wounds. And in what authorities are calling the most bizarre aspect of the entire night, deputies stumbled upon the mangled body of a man named Juan Pedro Santana Perez—a known Mexican drug runner with over thirty arrests and just as many deportations. Mr. Perez was declared dead at the scene. Medics who attended him say he died of blunt force trauma with multiple broken bones in his extremities and skull."

John interrupted. "Frank, can they put any of these pieces together?"

Frank shook his head. "They won't comment officially, but they believe Mr. Perez was not injured in the explosion. He was found unresponsive, zip-tied, and lying in the back of a patrol vehicle with several weapons and a backpack full of both drugs and cash. He was wanted in several states but"—Frank thumbed over his shoulder—"not anymore."

While my ears had been trained on the TV, my eyes had been watching the three of them. When the show broke for commercial, the little girl spoke first. "What's your name?"

"Joseph. But most folks call me Jo-Jo."

The woman had not looked at me. She was staring at the three tickets, with a narrowed space between her eyes where a wrinkle had creased the skin. Her statement in the cabin, *He has friends,* came to mind. I doubted a guy like that had a single friend in this whole world, but he might have some loyal lieutenants bucking for promotion by honoring his memory. And if they were so inclined, they'd check the buses. This didn't set well with me.

"What's your name?" I asked.

The woman placed her hand on the girl's shoulder. "Gabriela." Then the boy. "Diego." Finally she touched herself in the chest. "Catalina."

I pointed at Gabriela. "And how old are you?"

Gabriela held up both hands and a total of six fingers. "Seven."

I reached across the table and gently raised one more finger. She smiled.

I looked to Diego. "And you?"

He held up both hands, and all his fingers, and smiled.

When our burgers arrived, Diego pulled the six-inch butcher's knife out of its sheath, which now hung on a loop on his belt, and used it to cut his sister's burger in half. Then his mother's. Then his. Once finished, he carefully cleaned the knife and returned it to its sheath.

Catalina watched him and finally looked at me, but didn't speak.

Our waitress reappeared. A short, somewhat pudgy redheaded girl. Maybe a bit absentminded. She was quick with a refill followed by, "How 'bout a couple of milk shakes?"

Diego's eyes widened and his head jerked toward his momma. She was trying to shake him off when I asked him, "Chocolate or vanilla?"

"Chocolate."

Gabriela quickly said, "Banilla."

The waitress disappeared. While she did not wear a wedding ring, the indentation in her finger suggested that she had. Even recently. As she walked away, her faded jeans, which had fit her two or three sizes ago, showed the outline of something in her back pocket. Something that would fit in the palm of your hand. When she stopped at another table and bent over to pick up a fork that had fallen, the thing in her pocket wiggled itself loose and hung just slightly over the edge.

A baby's pacifier with a blue handle.

She stuffed it back into its hiding place and then grabbed the waistband of her jeans and tried to wiggle them above her tummy. She could not.

While we ate, Diego kept looking at me. Specifically, my hands. I held out my right hand. He looked at Catalina, who said, "Go ahead." He reached out and placed his hand flat across mine. He then slowly turned my hand over and studied the scars—including two recent cuts.

Catalina spoke for him. "Your hands tell a story."

I nodded. "And if they could talk, we'd be here awhile."

Leaning forward, she chose her words carefully. "To Diego, no one was stronger than Juan Pedro. Ever. That knife is the emperor's sword."

Across the restaurant somebody clanked a knife on a plate. In the kitchen one of the dishwashers hurled obscenities at the short-order cook. The beleaguered waitress ping-ponged between the tables, trying to satisfy impatient customers.

Diego tapped his foot against the central leg of our table, and his eyes blinked several times. And across from me, Gabriela squirmed slightly like she had ants in her pants. I pulled an index card from my shirt pocket, flipped it over to the unlined side, and quickly sketched Diego's face. I'm no artist. Just caricatures really. I can pencil somebody's face in less than five minutes. It's a habit I picked up when I needed to find a way to occupy my mind and hands with something other than what I was doing with my mind and hands.

I handed him the picture of himself. "You like to read?" I asked.

He pushed his glasses up on his nose and studied the picture. "Yes."

I glanced at the time. "We've got a while. Maybe we could find you a couple books for the drive to Florida." Gabriela was having a tough time sitting still. "She okay?"

"She has a rash."

Gabriela was studying Diego's picture.

Our waitress appeared with two milk shakes. "Anything else, honey?"

"Check, please."

She set the check down, cleared a few plates, and left us quietly. Gabriela kept looking at my stomach and the insulin syringe.

Sometimes kids need permission. "You want to ask me something?"

With her top lip covered in milk shake, she asked, "Does that hurt?"

"It's a small needle."

"Are you sick?"

"I have a thing called diabetes." I tapped the syringe in my pocket. "This is my medicine."

She struggled with the word. "Dia-tee-tees?"

"Perfect."

"How'd you get it?"

"That's a good question. I'm not sure there's a good answer."

"How do you think you got it?"

"Long time ago, I didn't treat my body maybe the way I should have."

"What were you doing?"

"Stuff we shouldn't have been."

"Who were you with?"

"Bunch of young people as foolish as me."

"Where were you?"

"California."

"How long were you there?"

"Couple of years."

Her head tilted sideways. "Seems kind of silly."

I laughed. Truer words are seldom spoken. "*Silly* would be a good description of a lot back then." A pause. I sat back. "You ask a lot of questions for such a small girl."

"Papa say I ask too many."

"Papa?"

She glanced at the TV.

"Well . . ." I never took my eyes off her. "He's an idiot. Don't listen to him."

A spontaneous combustion of a giggle broke loose through her lips, and this time she could not conceal all her teeth. The giggle bounced in the air around us like a butterfly. Having satisfied her curiosity, she drank her milk shake. Evidently my encouragement served to break the dam. After a few gulps, she looked over her shoulder and then whispered, "Is he coming to get us?"

"No."

"Did you stop him?"

"Yes."

"Did you do all that man said?"

"Yes."

"Were you afraid?"

"No."

She finished her shake. "Mr. Jo-Jo?"

"It's just Jo-Jo."

She chewed on this. "Mr. Jo-Jo?"

I smiled. "Yes."

"I think you must be a good man."

I quickly sketched her milk shake–covered face, curious eyes, and matchless smile. While I sketched, she and Diego watched. When finished, I handed her the card.

She stared at it. "Can I keep it?"

I nodded.

"Where'd you learn to do that?"

"California."

"How many have you done?"

I considered this. "Hundreds." A shrug. "Thousands maybe."

"Do you ever keep any?"

"No."

"Why not? You're good."

"I don't do it for me."

"Then why?"

"It allows me to capture a moment and then turn it loose all at the same time."

She considered this. And me. She shot another glance at the TV. "Did you learn to do all that in California?"

Catalina put her hand over Gabriela's mouth and spoke rapidly in Spanish, momentarily hushing the child.

I considered this. "Yeah. I guess I learned that in California too."

She nodded confidently and then slurped the bottom of her milk shake. "California sounds like an interesting place." She looked at her mom. "We should go there sometime."

Gabriela's nonstop twitching suggested that she was about ready to peel her skin off. And she acted like her underwear was constantly crawling up her backside, causing an uncomfortable wedgie.

I paid our check, left the tip, and we walked out. As we piled into the Jeep, where Rosco was waiting to lick Gabriela's face, our waitress exited the restaurant. She was crying. As I shifted into neutral and let the engine idle, she walked up to the window and placed her hand on my arm. She clutched a wad of cash in her hand. I doubted she made that much in a week. Maybe two. She managed, "Thank you."

I handed her my handkerchief and she wiped the tears off her face, smearing her mascara and making her look a bit like a raccoon.

I wanted to say something to make her feel better. "Life isn't always this hard." She nodded but didn't let go of my arm. The pacifier dangled off her left pinky. "What's the baby's name?" I asked.

"James Robert. I call him J. R."

"I knew a fellow named J. R. one time. Good man. Good name, too."

She nodded, squeezed my arm, then squeezed it again and disappeared into the restaurant. Catalina's eyes followed her.

Gabriela was bouncing around. Nonstop motion. Looked like an addict suffering withdrawal.

"She okay?"

"She needs a doctor."

"What's wrong?"

Catalina's embarrassment was obvious. "She has worms."

# — 8 —

Diego and I sat in the waiting room while Catalina took Gabriela back with the nurse. Five minutes later, the nurse called Diego back, and he disappeared through the same sterile door. Twenty minutes later, when the three of them reappeared, Catalina was carrying two bottles of pills. Band-Aids on their arms suggested all three had been given a shot.

"Better?" I asked.

She nodded but with more embarrassment.

"Do you need the hospital?"

"No." She shook her head. "We all have them."

I bought Diego a few dime-store Louis L'Amour Westerns, along with a tattered copy of *Treasure Island* and a few word-search books. Gabriela picked out a couple of princess coloring books, a hardcover of *Winnie-the-Pooh*, and a giant box of crayons, because she said she wanted to sketch like me. Twenty minutes later we found ourselves standing awkwardly in the bus station. I turned to Catalina and handed her a folded wad of hundred-dollar bills. "To get you settled."

She thought about refusing it but knew she needed it, so she slid it into her jeans pocket and stared at the kids.

There was no easy way to do this. I leaned over. "You two take care of your momma. Okay?"

They nodded. Diego extended his hand and shook mine while Gabriela wrapped an arm around her mom's leg. Catalina said, "Thank you, Mr. Jo-Jo."

I smiled. "It's just Jo-Jo."

FIVE MINUTES OUTSIDE OF town I pulled over and stared through the windshield. The man of my youth would not have deliberated. But I'd tried to kill him with booze and fifteen other things, so his voice was muted. The man of my forties would not have left the station without them, but I'd tried to kill him too, with success and travel and women and money, so it was tough to make out his voice over the idle of the engine. That left me with just me in the Jeep. Diabetes. Arthritis. Antacids. Reading glasses. Scars. Memories tough to look at. Through the course of my life I'd spent so much time and energy trying to silence the voices that now when I needed to hear what was true, I was having trouble.

They were sitting on the bench waiting to board when I turned the corner. Catalina was slumped down on the bench, shoulders rolled off at both ends, staring at the tickets with that pained look on her face. The kids were oblivious, engulfed in their books. Both looked up at me with surprise when I sat next to their mother.

"I was thinking . . ."

Catalina said nothing.

"I could drive you . . . to Florida?"

"What?" The space between her eyes narrowed. "Why?"

I hadn't practiced conversation much in the last few years, so I was rusty. "Riding that bus is not a good idea." I opened my hand. Palm up.

This woman hadn't let her guard down in a long time. I'd been there. You can kill my body and you'd be doing me a favor, but kill my soul and there's no remedy for the pain. And when you're in that place, and the pain is real bad, and you've been leaning into the thing causing it so long that you don't know how to do anything other than lean, hope and hopelessness blur and you lose sight of who's trying to hurt you and who's trying to help. Sometimes you need somebody to stand between you and the sharp thing that hurts. To lean for you. I touched her hand. "It'll be okay."

Slowly she laid the tickets flat in my hand.

When we reached the Jeep, Rosco was spinning in circles in the back seat, whining excitedly. His tail was creating its own wind cycle. Catalina reached into her jeans and handed the money to me.

"Keep it."

Her hand was shaking. She was struggling. Hope has a funny way of cracking people down the middle. Cutting through the tough places. Half of her wanted to trust me. Half of her wanted to run. She offered it again.

Rosco sat in the middle, between the two seats. He fluctuated between trying to lick our faces and watching the world pass by through the windshield. I spoke as I shifted. "I will take that back, but I would be grateful if you would let me give it to you."

She held it out.

"I don't have kids. No wife. No mortgage. I've owned and sold several businesses, and at one time in my life I made some money. I'm not stupid rich, but . . . I don't need it."

I have seen dogs, beaten by the people who owned them, unable and unwilling to let anyone pet them. They approach, then stand at arm's length, never closing the gap. Their experience teaches that all hands are the same, and while some might scratch between the ears, in the end all bring pain. Catalina had known a lot of hands.

"Why are you doing this?"

An honest question. "If I don't, who will?"

"What do you want?"

"Nothing."

"Every man wants something."

When people become afraid on a soul level, when the terror of their lives has taken up residence in their belly, it becomes the wall behind which they sequester themselves. The only way through is to tunnel under. Meet them inside their perimeter. Problem is, the depth of their pain determines the thickness of the wall. "I don't want you to be afraid."

"That's all you want?"

"I think so."

"You've got to do better than 'I think so.'"

I wanted to. "I don't know how."

She glanced at the money, then at me, and raised one eyebrow. She whispered in a tone of voice the kids would not understand. "I can pay . . . just . . . not where they can see."

"Ma'am—"

She straightened. "Catalina."

"Catalina, save Rosco, I live alone. Have for a long time. I'm not around people very much, so I don't always understand what they mean when they say things. Maybe I wasn't in class the day God taught us how to read between the lines. I've known some hardship. Maybe a lot. There was a time in my life when you would not have wanted to know me. When every bad thing you could say would have been true. I don't know how to navigate all this. It's tough to get a compass reading. But—" I waved my hand back toward the bus station. "I've known some bad men. Know how they think. Maybe I even thought like them at one time. I'm not saying I'm proud of that. I don't blame you for not wanting to trust me. If I were you, I'm not sure I'd trust me either, but . . . I have this thing that happens with the hair on my neck, and I'd feel a lot better if you'd let me drive you."

Catalina pulled her knees into her chest, bit her bottom lip, and wrapped her arms around herself. Holding herself. As if she were afraid the pieces would fly out the window if she failed to hold them all together. As the station disappeared behind us, the tears that she'd been holding for a few years broke loose.

# — 9 —

When we reached Micaville, Catalina tapped me on the shoulder.

"Yes, ma'am."

"May I please spend some of your money?"

I'd been on my own a long time. Never had any kids and never had to think like a parent. "Sure."

We stopped at a Walmart, and the three of them ran in while Rosco and I waited in the truck. I figured maybe they needed some privacy. Twenty minutes later, they exited the store, each carrying a shopping bag and wearing new clothes. When they climbed in, a new-clothes smell plus the pleasant aroma of perfume filled the truck. Took me a minute to realize it was the smell of deodorant.

When I turned into the parking lot of a storage unit, they looked at me with curious eyes but said nothing. Evidence that Juan-idiot-Pedro had sunk his claws in deep. I rolled up the storage unit door to reveal a late-model Crew Cab Ford F-150. They eyed it as if it were the president's limousine.

I swapped out the vehicles, and while the kids stretched out across the back seat, fighting Rosco for sleeping room, Catalina sat with her arms wrapped around her. She looked cold. I pushed a button on the dash. Two minutes later she started fidgeting and finally unbuckled, sat up off the seat, and began brushing off her back and legs. "Something's wrong."

I pulled over. "What?"

"Ants are biting me."

"Where?"

"My backside."

I guess if you're not expecting a seat heater, it can throw you off. I pushed the button twice more, turning the seat heater to low. I tried to explain, "The seat has a heater in it. You can control it here."

She sat on her palms. For the next twenty minutes she touched the button and raised or lowered the seat temperature, finally settling on medium. After a quiet ten minutes, her face flushed red. She rubbed the back of her neck and a giggle broke loose. It was the first time I'd heard her laugh. It was beautiful. I also heard relief.

I DROVE SEVERAL HOURS through Marion, Union Mills, Rutherfordton, and finally exited the back roads at Tryon onto I-26. We drove south a short while to I-85 and turned southward yet again toward Atlanta.

The kids slept while Rosco stood guard.

As we put the mountains behind us, she opened up. Her parents had owned a small restaurant. Made tortillas from scratch. She'd waited tables. Graduated high school. College wasn't an option, so she married one of their customers. A man she loved. He'd given her two children. She'd helped him in his dental practice. Learned the trade of a hygienist. He'd taught her to suture. He was a good man. Often didn't charge for his services. That endeared him to many. To others, it made him a target. He was robbed and shot in the street in front of their home while she stood on the doorstep, the kids at her feet. They'd seen the whole thing.

At the funeral she'd met a man who pretended to be something he was not. Said he was a diplomat and businessman who traveled freely into the States. Had a home there. Offered to take her away from all that and bring her here. She decided out of a broken heart. A bad decision. They'd been paying for it ever since. They'd been in several states. Lived in multiple migrant communities. Cement block homes. Rats. Roaches. Scabies. They had gone hungry, cold, and been left alone a half dozen times. Juan Pedro had beaten her three times. The last was the worst.

She explained about the cookshack, the shootout, the climb up the mountain, and how she'd waited for his eyes to move side to side. She'd herded the kids into the snow and cold and darkness. She did so knowing that none of them would see the light of another day. When he woke and found them—and he would—she knew he'd kill the kids while she watched and then drag her back to Mexico and give her to his men. They'd kill her over the days that followed. She didn't have a plan, but she was pretty sure that was Juan Pedro's, and he was just a day or two from acting on it.

---

I pulled over at a Hilton Garden Inn and paid for two rooms. We ordered dinner and had it delivered to our rooms. Watching them smear tomato paste across their faces, I was again amazed at the amount of food those kids could put away. After five pieces of pizza, Gabriela whispered something to her mom. The only word I could make out was "cream." Catalina hushed her and said, "No." A few minutes later Gabriela whispered a second time. Catalina responded in much the same way, though this time with a stern top lip.

Admittedly I can be slow on the uptake. "She want some ice cream?"

Catalina waved me off and did that windshield wiper thing with her index finger. "No."

Minutes passed, but when Gabriela moved to the window and stood staring down at the red neon sign of the Wendy's next door, I put two and two together. "You sure?"

I RETURNED WITH FOUR large Frosties, and the sugar rush, mixed with the fat of the pizza, brought with it a pretty heavy crash. When I shut the connecting door to my room, the kids were sound asleep. Rosco lay on my second bed. He had sunk his muzzle into a Wendy's cup and was pushing it around the bed trying to lick the bottom. When he lifted his head, the cup covered his entire mouth. I stretched out on the bed and he curled up next to me, resting his head on his paws, licking the sides of his face. I spoke both to him and to me. "No, I have no idea what I'm doing."

A few minutes later, I heard a quiet knock.

I'd been afraid of that.

Catalina pushed open the door and sat across from me on the opposite bed. The kids were asleep. She was almost wearing a terry cloth robe she'd bought today. It was draped across her more than tied, so it wasn't tough to tell that she wore nothing underneath. The light of the bathroom showered her legs and body. Her dark, shiny wet hair hung down, covering half her face. Her eyes were staring more at the floor than me. Her silence, and posture, said what her mouth did not.

Trust me, I'm a man. She's beautiful. And I'd be lying to you if I told you that the thought had not crossed my mind. I may be old, but I'm not that old. Problem was, I'd seen the damage we people do to one another. I'd done some myself. Soul-wounds are scars on the inside, etched with permanent ink.

I sat up. "Catalina, you don't need to . . ."

She said nothing. The robe falling slightly more off one shoulder. The fact that she'd not moved told me that her experience with men had taught her more than my words. And what I'd hoped was getting through to her, was not. I patted her knees. She'd shaved. Her skin was soft. "Why don't you go get some sleep?"

She lifted her head, pulling her hair behind her, and then sat up straighter, causing the robe to fall completely off her shoulders. This was getting more difficult. She made no effort to cover herself. "You don't find me beautiful?"

"No, ma'am. Never said that." I rubbed my neck.

One end of her lip turned up. "Your face is red."

"I reckon so."

She probed. "And?"

"I've seen bad men do bad things. This would fall into that category." The flickering bathroom light danced on her skin.

She pointed at my chest. "You?"

I nodded.

She waited.

"I've known men like me to take advantage of women like you."

"What kind of woman am I?"

"The kind that needs a little help getting out of a bad situation."

"What'd these men do?"

"Took what they wanted. Disappeared when it was over. Leaving the girls worse off."

"I don't mind."

"You might not now, but one of these days you'll meet a guy, fall in love, and he'll fall in love with you and those two kids in there, and when you open up and try to give him your heart, you'll find a scar made by my knife. It's the nature of this."

"How do you know?"

I stared at the radio. "I just know."

She rested her hands on top of mine and studied me. Finally she kissed me on the cheek. Oddly, it wasn't sexual. It was gratitude. Something in the same shade as trust. She stood and held the robe at her hips. One last chance. I tried not to look but it was difficult. I laughed. "You're not making this easy."

She turned, "Good night, Mr. Jo-Jo." She closed the connecting door behind her.

I whispered, "It's just Jo-Jo."

# — 10 —

Catalina said her brother lived in a community of workers on the west coast of Florida, south of Tampa. She'd been there once before but it was daylight and Juan Pedro was driving, so trying to find it in the dark might be tough. To find him, we'd need to get there either early before they left for work, or closer to dark when they returned.

We pulled out of the hotel parking lot just after four a.m., drove about thirty minutes, and started looking for a migrant community without a formal name. Sunup came and went and we were still looking. We stopped at a diner for breakfast and then made sandwiches on the tailgate for lunch. My problem was not Catalina's internal GPS. Her compass was pretty good. Our problem was finding a community that by its very nature didn't want to be found. We drove close to three hundred miles in ever-expanding circles while not traveling more than fifty as a crow flies. Finally, after winding through some farmland, clear-cuts, and a couple of miles of dirt roads, we stumbled upon it.

Catalina pointed and spoke excitedly in Spanish. Rattling off a hundred words in six seconds. I wiped my forehead and rubbed my eyes. The edges of my vision grew fuzzy so I checked my blood sugar, but my numbers were normal. That meant something else so I forced myself to methodically count telephone poles.

The road led to a collection of trailers, campers, tents, and lean-tos in need of a match and some gasoline. Several trailers were half-charred from long-ago kitchen grease fires, split in two from the flames, long since abandoned. Trees had flattened a few, and then the trees were used as firewood. Only the trunks remained. Many were covered in blue or gray tarps, and based on the sight of buckets and basins strategically placed to catch rain, few had running water. Communal cook fires were enclosed in cement blocks and large jagged pieces of stainless steel and iron. Rusted, wheel-less cars sat on blocks. Unburnt trash was piled in mounds. Used refrigerators. Dishwashers. Baby strollers. The wheel of a tractor trailer, absent the tire, had been turned on its side and covered with a grate—serving as a charcoal grill. The ground was sandy white coquina mixed with sections of mud in areas of high traffic.

When I rolled the window down, the smell told me that the plastic-wrapped buildings in the rear were outhouses. The strong smell of human waste brought with it a wave of nausea. Between Catalina's rapid-fire speech and the putrid smell, I switched objects and started counting trailers rather than poles. It didn't help. My heart was already pounding in my ears.

The place was empty. Not a soul in sight. We drove around to a trailer with *Leasing Office* spray-painted on the side and sat there as the truck idled. I was a little hesitant to let Catalina walk in and ask around. If somebody came looking for her, I didn't want her to register her face, which would get noticed on anybody's radar. Catalina was beautiful in a place absent beauty, and because of that she stuck out like a sore thumb. But we both knew that whoever was inside would never talk to an older gringo with gray hair around his ears asking about a Mexican man who wasn't legally here in the first place.

Across the park an older, bowlegged lady walked out of her trailer and carefully walked down the steps that led to and from her trailer. Judging from the way she was using the stick in her hand, she couldn't see too well. I drove over, and Catalina stepped out and quietly spoke to the older woman. The woman nodded, finally smiling, exposing toothless gums and white, fogged-over, cataract-filled eyes. She patted Catalina on the arm and shoulder. Then she pointed toward the rear of the lot. Catalina stepped up into the front seat and we drove around back looking for a bright-blue front door and something about a few pink flamingos.

Catalina's brother's name was Manuel, followed by four other names. She said it so fast I couldn't follow her past Manuel. We found a trailer with a blue front door. The owner hadn't bothered to lock it, because the doorframe was rotten. And he, or some previous owner, must've had a thing for yard-art flamingos. Twelve perched atop the roof. Five lying down. Seven standing.

While we stood there snooping around, a forty-person yellow school bus swung wide in front of the trailer park and slowed to a stop, followed by a massive backfire. I felt the sweat trickle down my back and tried to focus on a single spot.

It was too late. My head was already spinning.

Seventy-odd people wiggled out of that bus. All shapes, sizes, and ages. Men. Women. Children. They scattered to some thirty different trailers. Most carried machetes. As the crowd thinned, a short, stocky man with an ear-to-ear smile ran toward us and then hugged Catalina, who was hugging him back. He looked to be in his early thirties. Dark, tanned skin. Hardened hands. When he shook my hand, the meat in his palm told me he had never been a stranger to hard work.

They laughed, hugged again, and talked excitedly. A thousand words a minute. Moments into their conversation, his face turned serious. The two began nodding and she spoke in hushed tones, talking as much with her hands and pointing at me. Finally, Diego showed Manuel the knife hanging on his belt. Manuel looked at me, then back at Catalina, and she nodded.

Manuel took off his straw cap and spoke in broken English. "*Gracias, mi amigo. For mi familia.*" He paused, trying to find the English. "Must you please stay for dinner."

Catalina said Manuel had been in and out of this trailer for several years. He rented it depending upon harvest. We were lucky to catch him, as the crops around here were about picked and he was a day or two from leaving with some of the other men for Texas and Louisiana.

I walked behind the truck and sat on the tailgate with Rosco. He wanted out of the bed of the truck, but given the umpteen dogs running around, I figured he was better with me. He thumped the edge of the truck bed with his tail and whined in my ear.

At one of the fire sites, several women started making tortillas. Off to one side, a man was carving strips of meat off a side of beef. The beef had been freshly butchered; it was still draining blood. The man's hands were red up to the elbows and the meat pink and crimson.

While Catalina talked with Manuel, Rosco and I watched from the stable safety of the tailgate. Diego and Gabby played with several other kids who, as best I could understand, were second or third cousins once or twice removed. At a second fire a few feet away, a woman poured half a five-gallon bucket of peanut oil into a large pot and set it on the side of the fire to warm.

The kids, now about a dozen in total, began kicking a soccer ball. Around the fire. A large man, bare-chested and muscular, stepped out of the trailer next to us and spoke in a harsh, rapid tone to the kids. Pointing his finger. While the kids moved their game off to the side, he walked to a woodpile between our two trailers and, swinging his machete, began chopping bigger limbs into smaller and placing them in a pile next to the fire. He worked at a fast and determined pace. At one point, a few of the chips flew over and into the bed of the truck. I stretched out, closed my eyes, and tried to imagine the taste of the fajitas.

Around me swirled rapid conversation in Spanish, the occasional waft of the outhouse when the wind swirled, the rhythmic echo of wood being chopped, and the sight of the butchered cow. I was dangerously close to needing to leave.

In truth, I was beyond that.

In a few short moments, the park had transformed from a silent and empty mud hole to a thriving, noisy community. Everybody had a job and knew what it was without being told. Behind me the chopping continued. Across from me the butcher was boning out the ribs off the beef. Blood covered his hands like gloves. I lay back, counted kids, adults, dogs, flamingos. I pulled the mint ChapStick from my pocket and covered my lips and the edges of my nostrils. Just across the fire sat the elderly blind woman. I slipped a card from my pocket and studied her features. Cataracts. Hunched shoulders. Crow's feet. Gnarled hands. Toothless gums. Bowlegs. Stained apron. She was a study in mileage.

A soccer ball rolled into the vicinity of the fire, bounced off the pot of peanut oil, sloshing it, and then rolled toward my truck. Gabby, who was faster than most and that included many of the boys, followed it. Barefooted. She bounced past the peanut oil, nudging the pot, and then hopped over one side of the fire en route to the back of my truck to retrieve the ball. The chopping behind me stopped but not the noise. The muscular man behind me turned toward Gabby, pointed at her, and began speaking loudly and with greater emphasis and irritation. Then he moved toward her with great speed. Gabby picked up the ball and froze, her eyes growing wide. She tried to dodge him but he hooked her with a massive arm and snatched her up, and she dropped the ball. He lifted her so fast, her hair whipped back and forth from the movement. He spoke with animation and irritation.

Then I heard Gabby cry.

A few moments later, I found myself lying on the ground

between the trailers with that big man between my arms. He was limp. A rag doll. A group of men had circled me, each wielding a machete pointed at me. But standing over me was a woman—holding a machete—and pointing it at all of them. Speaking loudly and in a language that was not mine.

Coming out of it is always tough. A few seconds of knowing nothing. The only thing I knew to do was keep my mouth shut and wait. Eventually the fog would clear. And in the meantime, don't let go of whatever I had hold of. I may not remember why I was holding it, but at one time I must have had a good reason. I shook my head, my eyes focused on both Gabby and Diego, who were standing behind the old woman, looking at me. The limp man in my arms was breathing, and blood trickled out of a busted lip. I sat up, looked around at all those people looking at me. Catalina had straddled me and was speaking fast and forcibly in Spanish, pointing that machete at all those men.

After I sat up, Manuel knelt at arm's length. "Señor—" He looked concerned. "Are you okay?"

I thought before I spoke. "Yes."

He offered his hand to help me stand.

The man in my arms began regaining consciousness. I sat him up next to me. Catalina shooed the group of spectators and they returned to their jobs. A few minutes passed while they let me dust myself off. Somebody brought the muscled man an orange soda, and he sipped it while leaning against the trailer. A pretty good bump was rising on his forehead. Catalina tended to him and whispered words I couldn't hear. He nodded and glanced at me around her body.

Manuel sat with me. Saying nothing. I needed to know. "What happened?"

Manuel reconstructed the last few moments with both his hands and broken English. "You jump on Javier. Like cat. You and him wrestle. Fight. Then he go to sleep."

I pointed at Catalina. "And her?"

"Javier good man. He grabbed Gabby just as she was about to step in the hot oil pan. Just trying to keep her safe. He was tickling her when you . . ."

"I thought I heard her crying."

Manuel shook his head. "She was laughing."

I put the pieces together. There was no good way to fix this.

Javier stood, steadied himself against the trailer, and then smiled and laughed at the men in a circle around him. He said something in Spanish, patted me on the shoulder, and Manuel laughed. "What'd he say?"

"He said he is going to call you El Gato."

"What's it mean?"

He smiled. "The cat."

Manuel helped me to my feet while Catalina and Gabby brushed me off. I tried to apologize, but so few of my listeners spoke English that I felt like I was making matters worse, so I quit. I sat on the tailgate, finished my sketch of the old woman. I thought about giving it to her, but when I realized she couldn't see it, I just set it on the table nearby, where the kids gazed at it and whispered. Quietly I ate my dinner, watching the good-natured Javier replay the events with a smile and good humor.

After three plates of what might have been the best Mexican

dinner I've ever eaten in my life, I sat back and loosened my belt. A stuffed tick had more room than me. That's when I noticed the women dropping something in the hot oil. The sound of something frying had my full attention, as did the smell. A few minutes later, they sifted golden brown handfuls of goodness out of the oil, drizzled them in honey, and served me six on a plate. "Sopapilla," a woman said softly.

Evidently, word of my participation in Catalina's departure from Juan Pedro had spread, and despite my near decapitation of Javier, a steady line of folks were smiling at me and patting me on the back. Most everyone in the park came through to shake my hand and say, "Gracias, mi amigo." Several chuckled, patted me on the arm, glanced at Javier, made a fist, and said, "El Gato!"

I felt bad for Javier. A golf ball–sized bump had risen on his head and his left eye had swollen. Almost shut.

Mexican doughnuts are not what a diabetic needs to eat, but not wanting to be rude, I ate twelve. The combination of fat and sugar hung on my eyelids, pulling them down.

As the moon rose, an older man brought out a nylon string guitar and sang in the most beautiful voice I'd heard in a long time. When he finished some forty-five minutes later, Gabby was asleep in my lap, Diego was asleep on Rosco's stomach, and both fires had been reduced to warm red coals. I stood and patted my pocket, looking for my truck keys, but Manuel waved his finger like a windshield wiper at me. "Señor, you stay here. My guest. Please."

The thought of not driving sounded good. I carried Gabby inside his trailer while he carried Diego, and we placed them on bunk beds. He then led me to his room, where Catalina had just changed the sheets. He pointed. "Please."

"Manuel, this is your room. I can't—"

Catalina spoke from behind him. "Mr. Jo-Jo, it would honor my brother if you'd say yes. He is very happy to have you and wants to thank you for what you've done. He doesn't have anything else to offer you."

Rosco stood looking up at me. The look on his face said *Old man, let's take the bed.*

I thanked Manuel, pulled off my shoes, lay down, put one hand on Rosco, and closed my eyes. Behind my eyelids I watched the replay of the video, now some forty years old—the man with the machete. I was nineteen at the time. I could still hear the words and how he spoke them so fast.

Sometime during the night, I woke drenched in sweat. The sheets I had been sleeping on lay in a pile on the floor. Catalina stood in the doorway, holding a lit candle and looking at me. Somebody had placed a cold, wet hand towel on my forehead. Rosco had laid his head near mine. His paws were tucked up under my arm.

AT DAYLIGHT THE PARK again came alive. Fires were lit. The smell of breakfast. Within twenty minutes everyone was bathed, fed, dressed, and lined up for the bus. I walked out of the trailer and noticed that somewhere between last night and this morning, someone had washed my truck and wiped something shiny on the tires.

Manuel appeared with a small backpack over his shoulder, machete and hat in hand. He thanked me again and then joined the mass of men heading off for the bus. I sat on the tailgate and listened to multiple cries of "El Gato!" as the men waved, laughed, and patted Javier on the back. Javier's eye was black and swollen, but it seemed to have little effect on his smile.

The men squeezed into the bus and within minutes only the exhaust remained, leaving me alone with Catalina and a few of the older women, who were cleaning up breakfast. Catalina had not spoken much to me this morning. I pointed to the trailer where the kids slept. "You going to be all right?"

Catalina nodded. "My brother is moving tomorrow. Texas or Louisiana. We will go with him. It's a larger community. There's a school. The homes are cement block."

I pulled the cash out of my pocket, several hundred dollars, and offered it to her. She waved her hand. "No."

I looked around. "You might need it."

She leaned forward and hugged me but would not take the money.

I grabbed a pen and the receipt from our Walmart shopping trip, flipped it over, and wrote my cell number on the back. "If you need anything . . . Rosco usually answers by the third ring."

Gabby and Diego appeared at the trailer door, rubbing the sleep out of their eyes. Catalina said, "Wait . . . please."

I didn't like good-byes. Would have preferred to slip out while they slept. Catalina lifted Gabby onto her hip, and the two stood staring at me.

Gabby reached around the side of my face. "How's your head?"

I didn't know my head hurt. "Okay, I guess."

She touched the side where the blood had dried and caked to my hair. I had no memory of that. The side of my head was puffy and tender.

"You fell out of your bed last night."

"I do that sometimes."

"Did it hurt?"

I didn't have the heart to tell her. "No."

"You could get a seat belt."

I laughed. "For my bed?"

"Yeah, and a helmet."

"You have good ideas."

She whispered. Just between us. "Juan Pedro told me I was stupid."

I pushed her hair out of her eyes. "He's an idiot."

Diego shook my hand, the knife on his belt speaking loudly against the backdrop of the silence of his mouth. Catalina approached me and didn't shake my hand so much as hang hers inside mine. For several seconds she just stood there. "Thank you, Mr. Jo-Jo."

Rosco whined behind me. I handed her the index card. I'd sketched her from the side with her hair falling down across gently sloped shoulders. She was looking away.

I climbed into the truck and cranked the engine, laughing. "It's just Jo-Jo."

# — 11 —

I dusted myself off, turned north, hit I-75, and soon felt the tug of my childhood pulling me eastward. It'd been awhile since I'd driven those coastal back roads. I had time. I hugged the coastline on Highway 19. A two-lane in need of some tax dollars. I was in no hurry. The highway ambled northwest and then west as it followed the coastline and 19 turned into 319 and finally 30A. Occasionally the Gulf of Mexico would appear on my left. Miles up the coastline, a black plume of smoke spiraled miles into the air. Evidence of a hot and still-burning fire. I'd seen large explosions do the same thing.

When 30A turned hard right, or north, I continued straight, or due west, onto Cape San Blas Road. Cape San Blas is a seventeen-mile spit of barrier sand that juts off the skin of the state of Florida into the Gulf of Mexico like a hangnail. Before me, a plume of black smoke rose like Jack's beanstalk and disappeared into the stratosphere. Two state troopers stood guard by a cordoned-off road. Staring at the smoke, I felt the old pain return. I stretched my left arm and popped a few antacids.

I rolled down the window and spoke to a trooper who was looking at me through dark chrome glasses and holding his hand up like a stop sign. "Looks like something not real good going on," I said.

"Just a bit."

"What happened?"

"Old boy drove a hundred-mile-an-hour tanker filled with fuel into the rocks at the turn. Been two days. Core of the fire still burning."

"Know who it was?"

"You live here?"

I shook my head. "Grew up here."

"Local news said his name was Jake Gibson."

I knew the name. "Road to the Cape closed?"

"No, but fire is still so hot you can't walk within a hundred yards. One-lane road going around through the marsh at the site." He eyed my truck. "Little soggy but you could probably make it."

"Thanks."

TALL PINE TREES LINED the road, along with power lines and signs advertising homes for rent. Homes on stilts appeared through the trees on either side, with large wraparound porches, docks, and waterfront views. I passed through the quiet military observation installation where they've been "observing" for years, but nobody really knows what they're looking at or why.

At its widest, Cape San Blas is only about a half mile across. Where it narrows, and the marsh of the bay on the right had crept within two hundred yards of the ocean on the left, a man-made wall of enormous rocks had been constructed by the highway department to protect the road from tide encroachment and washout. This road was the only way onto or off the island, so the state had determined long ago to try to protect it. Some of the rocks were as big as cars. Some bigger.

Unlike Jake Gibson, I made the turn successfully.

I followed the road, slowed, and turned right in a wide northerly arc. Another trooper routed me through the marsh. The middle of my turn gave me a good view of what remained of Jake's semi. It perched grotesquely mangled in its final resting place atop the charred multi-ton rocks. The cab and its enormous, exploded gas tank rested among the rocks like a beached whale, still spewing black smoke.

Seven fire trucks surrounded the site; three were sucking and pumping saltwater onto the core. I rolled up my window. The heat was still intense.

A few miles north I got a room at the local motel, stashed my stuff, and headed out to the Blue Tornado. It had been a long time, and I wasn't sure how she'd respond, but I knew I needed to check on Allie.

# — 12 —

The Blue Tornado was the product of an unlikely union between a Detroit-based, cold-calling vacuum salesman with an entrepreneurial bent and a homespun west Florida girl working the checkout counter at Tops Hardware. While Mr. Tops wasn't too interested in Billy Pine's Blue Tornado vacuum or his research-backed promises that it would suck the carpet off the floor, his daughter, Eleanor Dane Tops, found the new and updated Tornado II a fascinating modern marvel; she sat pleasantly through the forty-five-minute presentation and ordered seven for the main store and four for the annex two counties over. Billy, six weeks on the job without having actually sold a single vacuum cleaner, and having now made his quota for the next four and a half months, invited Eleanor Dane to dinner, which she gladly accepted. The two shared a burger and a milk shake and then took in the latest double feature. The first was a John Wayne movie entitled *Rio Grande*. The second was an animated Disney film, *Cinderella*. During the movie, Billy bought Eleanor Dane a popcorn and soda and acted the total gentleman. Following the movie and a quick ice cream, he returned her home three minutes before her ten p.m. curfew.

Three weeks later, when Billy delivered the eleven shiny new vacuum cleaners to Mr. Tops, he quickly learned that Eleanor Dane did not have the authority to order eleven vacuum cleaners. In fact, she couldn't order a stick of bubble gum without the old man's signature. Stuck with a trunk full of inventory he might never sell, Billy Pine sat in his borrowed car and stared from his gas gauge to a map. He didn't have the money to get out of Florida. His destination was clear. All roads led to unemployment.

A bit of an optimist, he straightened his tie, walked back into Mr. Tops's office, and said, "Sir, I'd like to apply for a job."

This bravado seemed to both surprise and impress Eleanor's father, though he tried not to let on. He raised an eyebrow. "Other than *not* sell vacuum cleaners, what can you do?"

Billy adjusted his tie. "Sir, if you teach me, I can do most anything."

Thus began Billy Pine's employment at Tops Hardware. In two months he was managing the annex. In four months he and Eleanor were engaged. With Mr. Tops's permission, he set up a Blue Tornado display at the front of the hardware store. By the time of their wedding, Billy had sold ten vacuum cleaners. The eleventh he gave to Eleanor as a wedding gift.

The couple were married in 1950 under a setting sun and honeymooned on Cape San Blas, where they walked the beach and promised each other they would return and purchase property. When Mr. Tops died just a few weeks after their wedding, leaving Eleanor a few thousand dollars in inheritance, the newlyweds did just that. They bought a home, a car, a dishwasher, and an oceanfront piece of property on a sliver of land most found worthless.

Ever the entrepreneur, Billy pointed to the sunset falling over the Gulf. "With that view, good food will bring people from most everywhere."

And he was right.

What started small grew into two stories, beachfront tables, seating for over a hundred, live music, romantic lights strung across the outdoor porches, a waiting list on weekends that eventually spread across the week, a venue for weddings, and even a few small bungalows or weekend cabin rentals. In honor of their first meeting, Billy and Eleanor named the restaurant the Blue Tornado. And because patrons loved knowing the history of what birthed so unique a restaurant, Billy retired the actual vacuum cleaner and installed it in a glass case just inside the front door. Above it, Eleanor posted a handwritten sign: *How my husband stole my heart.*

Love had come to Cape San Blas.

In 1955, five years into marital bliss, Eleanor gave Billy a blue-eyed, towheaded wonder they named Allie.

The Blue Tornado became a cash cow and put Cape San Blas on the map. The heyday lasted about five years; then Eden gave way to the secret Billy had kept hidden from his wife.

Billy loved a challenge. Sales. Eleanor. The hardware store.

Marriage. The Blue Tornado. But when those measured risks paid off and prosperity came, Billy learned he wasn't in love with money. He was in love with the challenge of getting it. The chase.

The lure of gambling was strong. Cards led to dice, and dice led Billy to the realization that he was a terrible gambler. Pretty soon the jewel of Cape San Blas, the resort he and Eleanor had built with their own two hands, only earned enough to service the interest on his debt.

None of which Eleanor knew about.

The combination of insurmountable debt and an unwillingness to share his secret with his wife led Billy to find comfort in the bottle. And while it did little to comfort, it did cause him to forget—temporarily.

Billy was both a terrible gambler and a belligerent drunk.

He managed to lay off the bottle Monday through Wednesday, but come Thursday he'd start tipping it back and by Friday morning he would erupt into a full-blown binger that would last through Monday morning, when he'd start the cycle over again. For Eleanor, the Blue Tornado became a safe haven away from the storm at home.


A FEW MILES AWAY, my father returned home to my mom in 1955 from service in the Korean War and promptly gave her me as a homecoming present. I only had a few years to get to know my dad, nine to be exact, but during those few short years he was a hard, silent man. What tenderness I knew, I learned from my mother.

In 1963, when I was eight, my dad gave my mom an ocean-view house for their anniversary. It wasn't waterfront, but you could see the water from their second-story bedroom window.

The home behind us belonged to a family that owned a restaurant called the Blue Tornado. Judging from the sound of the screaming that erupted from those windows, they were living with another one.

Given the remote location of the island and the cost of connecting to the main line, indoor plumbing had made it to the restaurants and businesses, but most homes still used outhouses. One night I got up to go to the bathroom around three a.m. and found the daughter, eight-year-old Allie, sitting on her back porch. Legs bouncing. Eyes and ears focused on the outhouse.

I whispered across the backyard, "You okay?"

A single shake of her head.

I walked closer. "Something bothering you?"

She pointed at the closed outhouse door.

"You scared?"

A nod.

"Of what?"

"Whatever's in there."

We hadn't been living there long, but we'd already overhead a couple of her father's outbursts. I looked over my shoulder. "Where's your dad?"

She thumbed behind her.

"He been drinking?"

No response.

I held out my hand, she took it, and I led her to the outhouse where I found the door unlocked and three curious raccoons rummaging around inside. I turned on the light, shooed them outside, and was walking to my house when I heard Allie's voice speak to me from behind the door. "Jo . . . um . . . Jo?"

"Joseph."

Her voice cracked. "Jo-Jo?"

I seldom tell people that the origin of my nickname rose up and out of an outhouse. "Yes."

"Will you walk me back?" A pause. "Please." The tremor told me she was scared of more than raccoons. I walked her to her house and waited until she waved at me from her bedroom window. We did that a lot.

As her father's drinking worsened, so did the destruction he caused. Many a night I stood in the backyard listening to what sounded like a bull wrecking a china shop. The sound would start on the first floor and then travel up the stairs. As the sound of the havoc grew closer to Allie's room, her window would slide open and Mrs. Eleanor would pass Allie down to me from the second story. Both would climb down the lattice attached to the side of the house, and me and Momma would sit with them at the kitchen table while Mr. Billy deconstructed their house and Allie shook like a leaf in the chair scooted up next to mine.

Given that the beach was our backyard, and the fact that she didn't like being home with her dad, we spent most of our daylight hours outside. And most of those we spent combing the beach. Shells, driftwood, pieces or parts of boats with foreign writing. Every new discovery excited us because it was proof of a world beyond ours. Our favorite was finding sharks' teeth after sundown. When the sun dropped below the horizon, the receding tide rinsed the shells, and the teeth shone like black diamonds. We found thousands. Allie's father favored a brand of bourbon sold in blue Mason jars, and we put the empties to good use. We lined a shelf in her bedroom with jars filled with various sorts and sizes of shells and teeth.

But not all of my life was Eden.

When I was nine, for reasons I never understood and my mom never talked about, my dad ran off with another woman. Deserted us. I couldn't explain it then. Can't now. To quote my brother, Bobby, "He just left." His absence left a hole in my chest the size of the Milky Way. The man who was supposed to pick me up when I fell, put his arm around me, tell me I had what it took, and say, "I'm proud of you," didn't. For me, the whisper of his departure said, "I'm not proud of you." For Bobby, his departure whispered, "You don't have what it takes." Both were lies. But in the absence of any voice to the contrary, they sounded true.

The silence of my father's absence sent some bad signals through a young boy's mind. My mom tried to raise us, but as much as we loved her, she couldn't fill that hole. Couldn't speak the words we needed to hear. That empty place, in both Bobby and me, began to fill with some ugly stuff. Maybe the best way to describe it is to say that I reacted outwardly, while Bobby reacted inwardly.

Bobby was two years older and didn't have a mean bone in his body. Whenever we played neighborhood sports, I was picked first and he last, if at all. Same mother, same father, different gifts. Bobby's gift was empathy. He picked ticks off stray dogs. Fed homeless cats. He was quick to listen and never in a hurry. His body posture, along with a thick set of glasses, told you that what you needed to say was important. Folks used to say that Bobby was "more sensitive." They said it like it was a weakness, but I never saw it that way. I felt like Bobby drank life through a fire hose; if I felt an emotion, he felt it ten times as strong. It was as if his emotions were hooked up to electricity. Magnified. As a result, I think our dad's absence may have been harder on him.

Given his willingness to listen, everybody talked to Bobby. I was a 98-mph freight train with no ears. I charged headlong, didn't really care what others had to say, listened when it suited me. Complicating matters, I had found a switch inside me. When I flipped it, I could get angry fast.

Bobby had anger, but no such switch. Or, if he had a switch, its effect was internal. Not external, like mine, where the world could applaud what it accomplished. Medals and wins. The defeat of others. Whereas my gifting tore down, his built up. The world around us perceived me as brave and dismissed him as not, but Bobby was no coward. He just reacted more slowly. More measured.

Without a man to toughen us up, Mom had worked out a deal with the local martial arts school. Two for the price of one. We worked our way up the belt system in tae kwon do. This required self-control, the perfecting of complicated patterns of forms and physical dexterity and strength. We both had that. In truth, Bobby was a better technician than me. His form was more exact, and he just looked more graceful. When we tested for black belt, Bobby actually scored higher. But there was also a competition and tournament aspect to tae kwon do. Involvement in tournaments was not required in order to advance up the belts, but I jumped in because it meant I got to kick people in the head. I thought maybe if I kicked them hard enough, my dad would hear about it and come home. Tell me he was proud of me. That I measured up. That I had what it took.

Bobby watched me compete with no interest. He appreciated my ability, but he thought the idea of two guys trying to knock the sense out of each other rather silly.

One year I was sick in bed with the flu when our team was competing at a national competition. My instructor, Master Steve, came by the house to pick me up in the team van, but I was half delirious with fever and Mom put her foot down. Seeing me lying in bed, Bobby stepped up. Not because he had any desire to fight anyone, but because I couldn't go. Because he was my brother. That's all. Master Steve had a real dissatisfied look on his face when Bobby appeared in the doorway with my gear bag, but he relented.

Sometimes I wonder how differently our lives would have turned out had Bobby not gone.

When they returned that evening, the van slowed just enough to let Bobby roll out. He had been knocked out in his first match. A spin hook kick he never saw coming. When he woke up, Master Steve immediately threw him into another match, where some kid threw a back kick followed by a round kick. Bobby was out for the better part of ten minutes. Our team lost.

Master Steve reinforced verbally and publicly what my father's absence had spoken silently. "You don't have what it takes." It became the lie that defined him. The ridicule and taunting from my team members were unrelenting. They nicknamed Bobby "Cockroach" for the way his hands had stiffened as he lay on his back, straight as a board, eyes rolled back in his head.

The following weekend, in a similar tournament, I flipped my switch and knocked out both kids, standing over them in angry triumph. My first of several national championships. I had wanted revenge for what they'd done to my brother. For what my father did to us. And I got it. Or so I told myself. What I didn't realize was that Bobby had watched with both pride for me and shame for himself. Once more, I had done what he could not. Word spread, and even parents in the neighborhood picked up on it. Bobby became known as the kid who could not. I became known as the kid who could. He retreated to his books and hung up his belt.

By the time I turned thirteen, I had one real love. Cars. The faster the better. Wanting to get my hands on everything chrome, I volunteered after school at the auto repair shop in town. This meant they let me sweep the floor and wipe down greasy tools and listen to stories about fast cars. Come weekends, me and both my underarm hairs thought I knew enough to rebuild engines and replace brakes.

Fifteen-year-old Bobby worked afternoons at the grocery store. Gifted with an affable demeanor and gentle humor, he was everybody's favorite bag boy. People looked at me with skepticism, wondering what trouble I was either in or about to get in, while people trusted Bobby and liked being around him. His tips proved it. We looked so similar, though, that people often con-fused us or thought we were twins.

I was lying under Mom's wood-paneled station wagon one Saturday, wrestling with the oil drain plug and spilling oil all over the garage, when the hollering started. Doors were slamming and Mr. Billy was screaming, "Allie!"

I guessed that she had blockaded herself in her room. I wasn't sure where her mom was, but from the sound of things Mr. Billy was about to break down her door.

I slid out from beneath the car and found Bobby coming out our front door. I looked at him, wondering what to do. His eyes were blinking real fast. He took one uncommitted step toward the Pines' house and said quietly, "We . . . we better do some-thing."

Wrapped in Allie's scream was a new sound. Fear. Bobby and I bolted through our yards and hit the Pines' back porch at a dead run. I climbed the lattice and lifted Allie's window. She was sitting on her bed, knees tucked up into her chest, staring at the splintering door and screaming, "No, Daddy!"

Bobby and I landed on Allie's bedroom floor just as Mr. Billy broke the door off its hinges. Mrs. Eleanor took the first blow, which splattered blood across the wall and sent her rolling back-wards like a bowling ball. She hit the base of Allie's bed with a thud, where she lay muted and motionless. Mr. Billy stood there laughing, holding the brass doorknob in one hand and a Mason jar in the other.

I looked at Bobby, who was looking at Mr. Billy. Bobby's pants were wet, and he stood frozen in a puddle of his own pee. He took a weak step toward Mr. Billy, who laughed at him and said, "Why don't you go bag some groceries."

I was sick and tired of people picking on Bobby, and I was sick and tired of Mr. Billy beating Allie and her mom. I jumped between Allie and her dad, straddling Mrs. Eleanor. He stood two feet taller than me. "Mr. Billy," I said, "you need to back up."

# — 13 —

When I woke up in the hospital, Allie was sitting next to me. Tears on her face. Lip trembling. Holding an ice pack on my cheek. Mrs. Eleanor, whose face was equally swollen, sat holding my mom's hand, their chairs scooted up next to the bed.

I was nauseous, my vision was blurry, and my head was splitting. The last thing I remembered was Allie's hand grabbing my arm as I stood between her and her dad. Mr. Billy had broken my jaw with the Mason jar, and surgery had wired my mouth shut. When I tried to speak, my words sounded all garbled, making Allie recoil and cry even more. I motioned for a pad and paper and, struggling to write with a split middle knuckle on my right hand, scrawled *Milk shake?*

Allie smiled, and the tears that had been hanging in the corners of her eyes cut loose and trailed down her cheeks. Two milk shakes later, she curled up in a ball next to me and slept.

Throughout all of this, Bobby had been sitting quietly in the corner of my hospital room. He never said a word. I would find out later that he pulled Mr. Billy off of me and bit off the top of his ear. Which explained both Bobby's puffy black eye and the odd shape of Mr. Billy's ear.

When I asked my mom about the split skin on my knuckle, Mrs. Eleanor said I'd made it up the lattice with a crescent wrench in one hand. When Mr. Billy came at me, I knocked out his front teeth with the wrench and threw one good punch before he turned out my lights.

Mr. Billy spent ninety days in jail, which sobered him up but did little to erase the debt no one knew about. With great contrition he returned home, but the damage had been done. If a little girl is born with a hole in her heart that only her father can fill, Allie's had been permanently closed. Mrs. Eleanor had had enough, so Mr. Billy moved into one of the honeymoon cottages on the property and helped his wife run the business from there. They remained married, but I doubt the two were ever affectionate after that.

These events, and the ripples that resulted, created a wedge between Bobby and me. We were quickly learning that the world we lived in valued knights who stormed the castle. Got the girl. Rescued the city. Bobby was a boy like the rest of us. He desperately wanted to be a knight. He just wasn't any good at it. And when he tried, everyone let him know how miserably he failed and how immensely I succeeded. I compared myself to everyone. He compared himself to no one. I was constantly trying to be "better than." Bobby was constantly trying to be "with."

In 1964, the stop-motion animated Christmas special *Rudolph the Red-Nosed Reindeer* debuted. It was a good picture of our life. I was ever the young buck off at reindeer practice, showing all the other bucks how well I could fly and fight. "Pick me, pick me, pick me . . ." Bobby, on the other hand, had been banished to the Island of Misfit Toys.

I used to lie awake at night and listen to Bobby cry in his sleep. While we could not have been more different, one thing was true for both of us—pain had rooted in the middle of our chests. I medicated mine with the drug of competition. Fast cars. Bravado. Bobby medicated his with the drug of offending no one.

As the distance between us increased, Bobby began hanging out with the island crowd. The unaccepted who accepted him.

I hung out with one girl.

# — 14 —

The Blue Tornado had been an icon on the west coast of Florida for over sixty years. The walls inside were covered in photos of Allie and her mom with famous A-list actors who'd flown in from California to Europe just to eat here and walk what was routinely voted Most Beautiful Beach in the US by most every travel magazine.

I pulled into the parking lot to the realization that a lot had changed since I'd last been there. The restaurant looked as though it hadn't been open in months. The boarded-up windows and doors, faded and chipped paint, and half dozen No Trespassing signs suggested Allie was no longer serving the best seafood anywhere and wouldn't be anytime soon. Rosco and I walked around, one of us looking and the other sniffing, but other than a few footprints of people crossing the property en route to the beach, there was no sign of life.

A pattern of rusted nails was the only remnant of the fifty or so picnic benches that once populated the porches. A couple of floorboards were missing, exposing the sand dune beneath. Deep grooves were all that remained from the sixty rocking chairs that previously lined the front porch to help alleviate the discomfort of the average two-hour wait. Rusted eye hooks screwed into the rafters above looked naked absent the swings that once hung there. The takeout window had been covered with a sheet of plywood on which someone had spray-painted *Trespassers will be shot* in blue paint. I peeked into a side window and was amazed to find the kitchen had been stripped bare. Either stolen or sold, not a single stainless piece of equipment was in sight. No fridge. No fryer. No sink. No grill. Only dangling and disconnected exhaust pipes, frayed wires, and cut water lines. On the other side of the building, somebody had cut a hole in the wall of the kitchen big enough to drive a truck through.

I went back to my oceanfront motel a mile down the road. My second-floor room offered a breeze and panoramic view of the beach for several miles in either direction. For dinner, Rosco and I split a can of Vienna sausage, a can of sardines, and a pack of saltines. At nine o'clock I pulled a chair out onto the walkway, leaned against the wall next to my air conditioner, propped my feet on the railing, and stared down on the waves rolling up on shore just below me. I adjusted the radio antenna, thinned out the static, and attempted to dial her in, but the signal was still too weak. A few more minutes and the AM signal would clear up. It was only six o'clock in California. I checked my sugar, gave myself a few units of insulin, and laid my head back against the concrete block.

As her show reached a certain level of success, Suzy began calling more of the shots. About ten years ago she'd built a studio in the barn of her California farm just north of Malibu. Hosting a nightly show while staring out across the Pacific. Not a bad gig. She played a healthy variety of most every kind of music known to man. People tuned in because they loved the sound of her soothing, raspy, understanding, empathetic, easily animated voice, and they called in their heartfelt questions because of her uncanny ability to listen and offer sage advice. Given her style and intimate, wrap-you-in-her-arms sound, a lot of callers asked her to marry them. Sight unseen. They'd propose on the air and she'd laugh and play along, and then dig deeper and try to figure out what hole they were trying to fill. She was brilliant.

If you listened long enough, you got to hear her story. You could also buy her *New York Times* number one bestselling autobiography. Suzy was the beautiful blue-eyed daughter of a Vietnamese model who'd fallen in love with a GI Joe. Given his death somewhere in southeast Asia, Suzy had never met her father—a Marine helicopter pilot. She had accidentally become the spokesperson for an entire generation when, nearly two decades ago, she began talking openly about the framed telegram and the folded flag her mother kept on her father's side of the bed— for years after his death.

Her quest started with a simple question: "Hi, my name is Suzy. Does anyone know what happened to my father?" No one knew. Not even the military. He was initially listed as MIA. Eventually that changed to KIA for reasons that were never explained to her.

In an effort to discover the truth, she took to the airwaves.

Her personal approach drew listeners. By the thousands. And what became one person's quest soon became the mantra for a generation. Hence, her audience grew, and grew loyal. As her platform expanded, so did her focus. From a missing father to missing children to getting women and children out of the sex trade to interventions for those lost to addiction. Suzy focused on reaching lost loved ones.

She would have made a great medic. She was not afraid to run back across the battlefield. But every November and every July, Suzy would faithfully honor the military crowd in the buildup to both Veterans and Independence Day. She invited men to call in and share their stories or make a request. Anything to get them talking. Most requested classic sixties and seventies rock with a rather strong emphasis on Lynyrd Skynyrd and Creedence Clearwater Revival, but some had an affection for Janis Joplin. Suzy was a regular honoree at Bike Week in Daytona and at the annual Ride to the Wall, where a couple hundred thousand black-leathered and tatted men rode eardrum-splitting bikes from all over the US to converge on Washington, DC. She was a regular on the news networks regarding anything having to do with veterans and had made a name for herself as the spokesperson for the silent generation—those who went, were lied to, lost, came home, were spit on, and never said a word.

Suzy True became known as the voice of the voiceless.

In an odd twist, she became a connector in a world where connections had been severed. Through letters or call-ins, Suzy was able to help more than one military wife or child come to know the true story of their father's death or disappearance in a country twelve thousand miles away. Oddly enough, in all her searching she had never been able to learn her own father's fate. But in a world characterized by stoic silence, Suzy had garnered such affection that more than one man had pledged undying fidelity and sworn he'd take a bullet for her. When critics challenged her methods or her subject or her steely unwillingness to "just let it go already," thousands came to her vocal defense. They also loved her for her uncanny ability: while some people possess the gift of never forgetting a face, Suzy never forgot a voice. Some guy would call in once to request a song or send out happy birthday wishes to a buddy he lost or tell a story about a dog he'd rescued from a village. A year later he'd call again and she'd pipe up, "Oh yeah, you're Bob from Topeka. Served with the 3rd Special Forces unit. Two tours. Seventy-one, or was it '72? Lost a leg to a bayonet in a tunnel, I think it was."

Many of the bikes that made the trip to DC were covered in *Suzy 4 Prez* bumper stickers.

Suzy had a way of crawling through the phone line and soliciting trust from any ear on the other end. Her popularity put her in the unique position of being able to solve puzzles that the government could not. Soldiers who had been shunned by the very country that sent them into harm's way and then spit on them when they returned tended not to trust the authorities who sent them. But Suzy was another story. Suzy was one of them. One of the abandoned and rejected. This trust had gained her valuable contacts inside both Langley and the Pentagon—all with top-level security clearance. These back-channel sources allowed her to gain and provide truth to those in need—and also provided her with an iron-clad method of exposing the liars who sought to profit off America's newfound sympathy for her soldiers.

In what might have been her greatest talent, she could spot a fake a mile—or three thousand miles—away. At the first whiff of something fishy, she'd solicit her back-channel contacts. Within a few hours or a day, that man's entire life would be laid open for all the world to see. On several occasions she'd surprised the man on the air and publicly undressed him before all the world. Given this, few attempted to fool her.

The idea of the "soldier of fraud" was nothing new. Men had done it for centuries. Cowards who skirted the war only to return with a flag draped around their shoulders. But given the post-Iraq culture and America's long-overdue empathy for the boys that she'd asked to become men before their time, more men began crawling out of the woodwork with never-before-told stories of both terror and heroism. And because many of America's dodgers who burned their notices on their way to throwing rotten fruit and spitting through the fence were now looking for a way to say "I'm really sorry" to an entire generation, fewer tellers of tales were questioned or asked to validate their claims. Especially those told by men who were sent to go and kill a yellow man. Not only was it insensitive to press for credentials, but given the decades of history that had passed, how could they? Vietnam was a long time ago and halfway around the world.

While Suzy's voice was sexy, seductive, and suggestive in a dozen different ways, Suzy herself was no taller than five-foot-four and weighed close to 280 pounds, proving that some people wear their pain on the outside.

She had searched for years for the answer to the mystery of what happened to her father. Various vets had called in with leads or well-meaning lies. None proved true. A network had picked up on the search, sent a team to Vietnam, produced an hour-long documentary. But in over two months of searching, they could not find what only the buzzards and maggots knew.

Her father's dog tag, watch, and the Bible her mother gave him were never found.

Over the last decade Suzy solidified her status as *the* voice of the forgotten generation. Between prime-time TV and drive-time radio, she became a household name, face, and voice. Everybody knew Suzy. A presence to be seen, a force to be reckoned with, a voice to be heard, and a message not to be denied. Further, she was a hugger. She hugged everybody. People stood in line to get a picture and a hug with a woman so large they could barely get their arms around her.

Comfortable in her calling and career, she put her show on the road. Once a month "On the Road with Suzy" broadcast from all over the country, from a park bench on Coney Island to a saddle in Wyoming to a fishing boat in Alaska to an RV in the Keys. Family members of veterans wanting to highlight their lives and stories would write or call her, tell of their loved ones' exploits or selfless actions, and Suzy's team would evaluate where to go next. At each location she'd spend a day or two or three and slowly draw out the story of one man's life that the rest of the country needed to hear. These men, stained with spit and rotten tomato puree, silent for decades, slowly unwrapped their stories.

Healing comes in both the telling and the hearing. Maybe that is Suzy's greatest contribution.

As I LISTENED FROM my perch on the motel balcony, Suzy joked with some callers, talked intimately with others, and finally closed out her show at midnight. I clicked off the radio and sat staring at the moon's reflection on the water. It was a calm night. Barely any waves. Gentle breeze. A tender welcome.

Southward a figure appeared, walking the beach. A serpentine path. Left, right, left again. As the figure closed the distance, it acted more like a squirrel. Darting left, picking something off the beach, throwing it down, darting right or scurrying forward only to dart left again.

I hadn't seen Allie in years, but even in the darkness it wasn't difficult to identify her. Some images never go away—no matter how you try to delete or drown them. She was scouring the beach, but she was stumbling. Frantic. And exhausted. Dead on her feet. At one point she fell and lay there several minutes only to rally and crawl to her knees, lacking the strength to rise to her feet. Several minutes later, having scarred the beach like a sea turtle, she collapsed again, this time closer to the water. Here the waves washed up and over her feet and thighs. When the waves gently rolled over her shoulders, she lifted her head, peeled herself off the beach, folded her arms around her like she was cold, and made it about three steps before she collapsed.

Rosco and I walked out onto the beach. I lifted her off the sand and began carrying her toward the motel. She was soaked head to foot, and her palms were raw from crawling. I got her to my room, stripped off her wet clothes, and laid her in my bed, tucking the covers around her. During all of this, she never woke. I wondered if she had walked all the way north from the crash site. As I sat staring at her, several thoughts raced through my mind. The first was that the woman before me was not the girl I'd known.

# — 15 —

When daylight came, I pulled Allie's clothes out of the coin-operated dryer, folded them, and set them on the bed next to her along with a note. *Went in search of coffee and a doughnut—Joseph*. I also left Rosco, who had curled up on the corner of her bed.

I drove south a few miles to fill up with gas and grab a bite to eat at a combination gas station and doughnut shop. While I lifted the lever to start the flow of gas and inserted the nozzle into the side of my truck, a guy walked out holding a cup of coffee in one hand and two doughnuts in the other. He was wearing flip-flops, his shirt was unbuttoned, his skin was deeply tanned, and his shorts were frayed at the edges. Total local.

I said, "Morning."

He glanced at my Carolina tag and spoke with glazing smeared across his top lip. "You're a long way gone." It was a statement posed as an invitation.

I palmed the sweat off my face. "Don't you folks have any sort of winter down here?"

He finished shoving a doughnut in his mouth and then spoke around it. "Not really. 'Round here it goes from just plain hot, to Africa hot, back to Mexico hot, then mildly Nicaraguan warm and back to Sahara hot again."

"Where's the best place to eat?"

Another bite. "Ain't one."

I waved my hand in a circle about my head. "What about all these signs?"

He pointed half a doughnut north. "Up thataway. Called the Blue Tornado. Used to be the best restaurant in Florida. Now that was some good food. Legendary."

"You eat there?"

He smiled. "Had my own booth."

"What happened?"

He pointed a quarter doughnut south. "You passed part of the reason when you drove in."

"How's that?"

"You see that tractor trailer jackknifed on the rocks?"

"Yep."

"Driver was the husband of the owner. Woman named Allie. Beautiful woman, too."

I waited while he sipped and swallowed.

"Bad marriage led to bad restaurant. Couldn't service the debt. Bank foreclosed."

"What happened to the woman?"

"Waiting tables in Apalachicola."

That stung me a bit.

I screwed the cap back on my gas tank and returned the nozzle to its slip. Without my prompting, he continued. "He weren't never here nohow."

I had a feeling my new friend enjoyed being the town spokesperson. Evidently retirement was not what he'd imagined.

"He only made money when that truck was rolling, so he stayed gone months at a time." He pulled a foot-long cigar from the saddlebag of his bike, cut both ends, and displayed considerable talent and practice lighting it. He offered it to me. "Smoke?"

A single shake of my head. "Never acquired the taste."

He admired his cigar. "Havana. Buddy smuggles them in for me." He drew on it and continued with his story. "But . . ." An exhale. "It's a shame."

"Shame?" I said, shaking my head.

"That woman had the same thing Colonel Sanders had."

I laughed. "Special recipe?"

"Her fried shrimp would make you slap your momma."

"That good, huh?"

A long inhale followed by a slow exhale. "No lie."

I climbed into the truck and rolled down the window. I knew the answer, but I wanted to see his reaction. I squinted one eye. "And the hush puppies?"

He straddled an enormous Harley and pulled his sunglasses over his eyes. He shook his head. "You had to go there, didn't you?" He rested his hands on the gas tank and stared down the road, saying nothing.

I waved and rolled north. Eating a doughnut.

I SAT NEXT TO the bed, sipping my coffee. The note I'd left was clutched in her hand. She stirred around eleven o'clock and looked at me. My face registered as did the motel room and the dog at her feet. I sat at the end of the bed, feet propped. An index card and pencil in my hand.

She whispered, "Hey."

I warmed her cup in the microwave and handed it to her. "Hey."

She sat there several minutes, sipping and staring at me.

I offered, "I got to town yesterday, saw you wandering the beach. You passed out—" I pointed. "Out there."

She glanced toward the water, then south. "Thank you."

I touched her foot. "Allie, I'm real sorry."

She nodded and a tear broke loose. She glanced at the clock. "Would you do me a favor?"

"Anything."

She wiped her face. "I need to go to the funeral home, make the arr—"

She couldn't finish. I patted her foot. "I'll drive you."

She was staring through the window, out across the water. "I have to pick out a coffin, but . . . I don't have any idea what I'm going to put in it."

I said nothing.

Another tear trickled down her face. She was shaking her head. "My last words to him were so hateful. So—"

I tried to stop her. "Hey. Don't—"

She blew her nose. "I told him I hated him and he could go to hell. And then I hung up." Her eyes searched mine. "Those were my last words to him."

Rosco scooted up next to her hip and laid his head on her thigh. I let her talk.

"Ours wasn't a good marriage, never was, but . . . he'd been driving for four days straight. Tried to make it home. His body gave out—" She sat there, hands trembling, shaking her head.

"Easy. One thing at a time." I stood and pointed at her clothes. "Rosco and I will wait outside." I laid the index card with her likeness on the bedside table. "My truck is parked downstairs."

WE DROVE TO THE funeral home, where we were met by a guy I'd known in grammar school and hadn't seen in at least forty years. Austin Walsh had inherited his family's funeral business and made a good life for himself and his family. He saw Allie step out of my truck and met us at the door. He was round at the middle, bald on top, and soft-spoken, with a demeanor that suggested he was really good at his job. He led us in, expressed how sorry he was, and we small-talked for a few minutes. Then he led us to the display room. Ten coffins of varying wood type and finish lined the room.

Allie walked between the rows, letting her fingers touch the wood and the satin padding. After fifteen minutes, she was no closer to a decision. She turned to me. "What do you think?"

Unfortunately, I had some experience with coffins. I pointed to a solid oak, no-frills option with stainless handles. As for price range, it was middle of the road.

Austin nodded. "Good choice," he said quietly. "One of my personal favorites."

She stood over it, staring down. "This would be great."

Austin said, "Allie, um . . . given the nature of what happened, there aren't really a lot of arrangements to be made. We can be ready whenever you like."

She understood what he meant. "Would tomorrow be too soon?"

He shook his head. "No. No problem at all. I'll handle everything."

She thanked him and we returned to my truck where we sat staring out the windshield at the spiral of black smoke still rising from the crash site. She turned toward me. The tremor in her lip was constant. "Can I ask one more—?"

"Of course."

Her eyes followed the path of the smoke. "Would you go with me? It's been too hot—"

# — 16 —

We parked on the beach side, along the rocks. The fire trucks and troopers were gone, having left only the yellow tape surrounding the mangled remains of the trailer. What was left of the truck sat oddly perched on the rocks. Teetering like a seesaw. Allie walked around to the cab where the door, seat, dash, almost everything attached to the frame, had been blown off. Everything remaining was burnt or melted, and the primary smell was that of burnt rubber. The frame itself was strangely curved where it should have been straight. The blast was long gone, but it was still rocking the world around us.

Allie covered her mouth and the tears fell in a solid line down her face.

I put my arm around her and led her to the rocks, where she sat staring. "I thought maybe I could find something, anything, to put in the coffin."

I sat listening. Rosco inspected the area around us, sniffing in the dunes between the road and the water. He poked his nose out of the palmettos a quarter mile south and I whistled, bringing him back. He returned with a long stick in his mouth. As he neared, I realized it was no stick.

The dog trotted up in front of us and Allie covered her mouth, trying to stifle her sobs. Rosco had found Jake Gibson's walking cane. I took the cane from his mouth and Allie gently accepted it. Held it like a newborn baby. Or a folded flag. She then clutched it to her chest and spoke incoherently. Finally she knelt in front of Rosco and managed, "Thank you."

We sat there for an hour, the sound of the waves washing over us. When she stood, she stared at the warped truck. "I just want to tell him I'm sorry."

I put my arm around her. "The dead have already forgiven the living."

She looked up at me. "How do you know?"

I stared about ten thousand miles behind me. "I've seen it in their faces."


ALLIE WAS LIVING IN one of the four honeymoon cottages that were once a part of her father's plan for "the Vacuum," as we affectionately called the Blue Tornado. To consolidate her debt, she had mortgaged it. Given her father's gambling, the cost of her first husband's drug, rehab and relapse issues, upkeep on a restaurant next to the ocean, and the cost of Jake's new Peterbilt—which cost nearly a quarter of a million dollars—not to mention a few other short term, higher interest, bridge-the-gap loans whereby she'd tried to hold it all together, her debt had been considerable. When her marriage to Jake soured and she was unable to make the payments, she folded her hands and finally let it go. While the bank had foreclosed on the restaurant, each of the cottages was separately deeded and not tied to the loan. She slept in one while the other three rotted. To make ends meet, she'd taken a job waiting tables at Billy Bob's Beer House and Oyster Shack in Apalachicola. She'd been at the bar when Jake called.

I got her home. Her face was drawn, eyes sunken. She looked like she could sleep for a week. I told her to rest and I'd be there when she woke. She did not need convincing. She curled up in bed with the cane and was asleep before I shut the door.

She woke the following morning to Rosco licking her hand and the knowledge that today she would bury her husband. Or at least his cane.

The cemetery lay on the northern end of the island. Allie's folks lay next to one another, and a fresh hole had been dug a few feet away. The funeral was small. Graveside only. The pastor, hired by Austin, said a few kind words, comforted Allie. He and Austin left us alone with the empty box. She laid the cane inside, I shut the lid, and we stood there staring. Behind us, two blacked-out Yukon Denalis pulled onto the coquina road. They stopped, and two black-suited bodyguards complete with earpieces and mirrored sunglasses exited the vehicle. One held the rear door open while the second surveyed the landscape.

A man stepped out, waved, and walked toward us. He had

aged. Looked smaller. Gray hair. He hugged Allie, kissed her cheek, and said, "Allie, I'm so sorry. Really."

He then turned to me and extended his hand. "Hey, Jo-Jo. It's good to see you."

SENATOR BOBBY BROOKS WAS a five-term icon in Washington, known to most everyone as simply B. B. He was beloved. Routinely won in landslides and had done more to strengthen the military than most of the rest of the senators combined. He was a regular advisor to the president, a regular contributor to the networks, and was constantly asked when he was going to run for president. He always declined, saying he had no interest. If there was a beloved war hawk on Capitol Hill, it was Senator Brooks.

"Bobby." When I shook his hand, his bodyguards stepped closer. He grasped my hand with both of his. It'd been a long time.

When I released, they studied me and, apparently considering me little threat, withdrew a few steps.

Bobby put his arm around Allie and said again, "I'm terribly sorry."

She nodded.

He turned toward her and took both of her hands in his. "I had them pull the satellite imagery." He paused. "He didn't suffer. It was too quick."

She choked back a cry and said, "Thank you."

"If you need anything. Anything at all. Really."

He meant it, and I knew that. Bobby had never lacked sincerity. It was one of the reasons so many loved him.

Allie hugged him, and then he turned to look at me again. He then glanced toward the corner of the cemetery at our parents' graves, slid on his sunglasses, returned to his car, and drove out of the cemetery.

Two boys appeared and lowered the coffin into the ground. Allie stood crying quietly. I fed my hand inside her arm, turned her gently, and led her away from the hole back to her house, where she once again climbed into bed and slept like Jake.

SOMETHING WAS BOTHERING ME. The location of Jake's cane. Nearly a quarter mile behind the crash site. Yes, the blast could have blown it that far. Farther, even. But it was unscathed. Not a scratch. And things that have been blown up usually show evidence of that. While Allie slept I returned to the crash site and nosed around. I was no expert on semis, but nowhere on any piece of metal or frame or door or anywhere did anything say Peterbilt. Which struck me as odd.

As I was studying the wreckage, two black Denalis pulled in behind me. My brother stepped out. No jacket. No tie. Sleeves rolled up. "Got a minute?"

I followed the Denalis back to the cemetery. Bobby got out and waited for me, and we walked together toward Mom's and Dad's graves. Rosco made the rounds of each headstone, peeing on several. Ending on Dad's. I chewed two antacids.

Bobby looked at me, then down at the grave and back at me. "Been awhile."

"Yep."

Mom died two decades ago. Dad followed some time later. He bought the plots when they married, which I always found rather morbid. It wasn't my decision to put him here. I hadn't seen him since we laid her to rest.

Bobby asked, "You make his funeral?"

"No."

"Me either." We watched as a yellow trail of Rosco's urine snaked across the sand. "When was the last time you saw him?"

"The day we buried Mom."

"Really?" He looked surprised.

My brother and I hadn't talked this much in a long, long time.

"On my way off the island, I stopped to fill up with gas. Evidently Dad had heard about the funeral and had come to either pay his last respects or dig through her personals for a few nickels. I bumped into him at the counter. He didn't recognize me. I was taller. Thicker. He shoulder-bumped me, mumbled something angry, and then stood pumping gas into a worn-out ragtop Mustang. I returned to the pump where he was still mumbling something derogatory about my being a 'punk with a ponytail.' I remember chuckling, and he asked me what was so funny. I said, 'You are, old man.'

"He got swol' up and cussed me. Said something about teaching me some respect. I realized he had no idea who I was. I broke his jaw, fractured his left eye socket, and left him lying unconscious on the concrete. Driving out, I pitched his keys in the retention pond."

Bobby laughed. "Did you feel better?"

"Not really."

He watched me chewing the last of the antacids. "You still drinking milk and eating Oreos?"

I smiled. "Yeah."

He slid off his sunglasses and turned them in his hand. "How you been?"

"Good days and bad. You?"

"Same." He could never lie in front of Mom. "You need anything?"

I chuckled. "You guys invented a time machine yet?"

He smiled and shook his head. "Not yet."

"Let me know when you do."

"You'll be the first."

"And you could tell those guys at the VA to stop hassling me over my insulin."

"I'll get right on it." He glanced at the fresh, upturned earth of Jake Gibson's grave. "Allie going to be okay?"

I shrugged. "She's sleeping now."

"How'd you hear?"

"It's a long story, but in short, I saw the smoke. And you?"

"She called."

I nodded. "Makes sense."

"It's not like that." He shook his head. "Truth is, she asked me if I knew how to find you. I told her I did not. I told her I thought you had a cabin somewhere in the mountains, but as for a phone . . . I had no idea."

I stared at Momma's headstone. "Sometimes it's just better if the world can't find me and . . ." I laughed. "I can't find the world."

Bobby nodded at the two graves. "They'd be proud."

"She would." I spat. "Not sure what would have made him proud."

He stared into Dad's name and back into our childhood. "Strange how something so little can determine so much of your life."

I nodded but said nothing.

He brushed the acorns off Mom's grave. "Well . . . she'd be proud."

"Of what?"

"You and me . . . standing here talking. With me still alive."

I looked at him. "Bobby, I never wanted you dead. Not even on the bad days." I paused long enough to raise his eyes to mine. "You still looking over your shoulder?"

He looked at me, glanced away, and then stared at me out of the corner of his eye. The real reason he'd brought me here. "Should I be?"

"One thing my senior trip taught me is that killing a man doesn't kill the pain."

He studied me a long minute. "You sure about that?"

I weighed my head side to side. "I'm pretty sure."

He smiled. "You remember when Allie's old man beat down the door and you hit him with a crescent wrench?"

"And you bit off half his ear?"

We laughed. The sound surprised us both, but rather than speak, we let the echo drift through the trees. When it disappeared, I said, "I ate through a straw for six weeks."

"That's my image of you. Standing over her mom. Shielding

Allie. Looking up at that crazy, drunk old man and telling him that he can't do what he wants to do. Not today."

I ate another antacid. "Standing up always costs something."

He laughed and waved his hand across the front of his pants. "Cost me a change of pants."

I laughed. Squinted one eye. "My image of you is a little different."

"Not sure I want to know this."

"You're standing next to Allie, in the church."

He knew the picture. "Not my best moment."

"Have to agree with you there." I paused. "That one hurt."

Moments passed. When he did speak, his tone was softer. "I used to look for you in crowds. Windows. Back alleys. Cars driving by. I was convinced you were waiting on me."

"That's because I was."

"Thought I was just being paranoid."

"Miami. Second reelection campaign. Had a suite next to yours at the Biltmore. Top floor. When you walked out on the patio at two a.m. to talk on the phone, I was standing three feet from you."

"That was a long way down."

"Six years later, you were acting as master of ceremonies at some Disney function. I drove your car in the parade. A shotgun inside my costume."

He raised both eyebrows.

"And later, you were speaking in Pensacola at the Air and Space Museum. I was in the stall next to you in the bathroom. A guitar string in my hand."

"Why a guitar string?"

I shrugged. "Just something I learned."

"Senior trip taught you that, too?"

I nodded.

"What stopped you?"

I shrugged. "Same thing that's been stopping me for four decades. Same thing stopping me now."

He eyed his two goons. "Which is . . ."

"It won't help. You, or me."

"You sure?"

"I've got some experience."

He nodded. "Jo-Jo?" He spoke softly, with his chin resting on his chest. "Don't underestimate the other man's pain."

I turned toward him. His bodyguards took a defensive step toward me. He waved them off. I said, "You sober?"

He looked away. "Yes."

I waited until he looked at me. "Really?"

He rubbed his palms together. "Yes."

I spoke what we both felt. "A tough stretch of years. We all lost a little something."

He agreed. "More so for you than anyone."

This was a realization he'd never voiced. "What makes you say that?"

"I saw your file."

"You mean I actually have one?"

He laughed. "Not officially. Wasn't until I got clearance. It's top secret."

"How'd you get ahold of it?"

"I'm chairman of the Senate Committee on Armed Services. I see what the president sees—" He smiled. "Often before he sees it."

"Ironic, don't you think?"

He nodded. "Yes."

We stood a long moment. "You should burn it."

He put his hand on my shoulder. An offering. The first time my brother had touched me in decades. "Good to see you, Joseph." There was no malice in it.

"Bobby?"

"Yes."

"Your secret's safe with me."

The hawk on Capitol Hill didn't seem so hawkish. "I wouldn't blame you if you decide otherwise."

"I don't want what you have. What good would it do me? Would it take us back in time?"

"Sometimes . . . No, most times, when I'm sitting at my desk, I don't ask myself what I think I should do. I ask myself what would you do?"

"No wonder you have so many critics."

He laughed.

I picked at a stone with the toe of my shoe. "Bobby, I can never reconcile our history, but I've never hated you."

"Never?"

I stared back through the years. "Hate is a powerful weapon. But it is powerless when it comes to cutting chains off the human heart."

When he looked at me, he slid his sunglasses back over his eyes. "What does?"

I stared up, then down at Mom's grave. "Many nights I used to envision holding your throat in my hands. Squeezing. Until your eyes popped out of your head. Until I felt your neck break."

"What stopped you?"

"The memory of one good day." I crossed my arms. "You were nine. I was seven. We were running up and down the beach. No shirt. No shoes. Tanned skin. Our hair streaked blond from the sun. You found three dollars, and we ran a mile down the beach to the store. Bought a—"

He interrupted me with a smile on his face. "Gallon of milk and some—"

"Oreos."

He spoke softly. "A *good* Oreos-and-milk day."

"We walked back out on the beach, swigging from that jug, licking off the cream-filled middle, flinging the cookies like Frisbees . . . and then we just sat on the sand as the tide rolled over our toes and the sun fell off the edge of the earth in front of us. The one day when all the world was good and right and nothing hurt us." I paused. "The thing that stopped me was the thought, or hope, that someday we'll get back to good."

He touched my shoulder and left me standing with Momma.

# — 17 —

Despite the inner turmoil at home, the Blue Tornado continued to prosper. Mr. Billy had been right. People drove from all around to sit on a bench, run their toes through the sand, sip something cold, and watch the sun go down over the Gulf. Business doubled, then doubled again, then doubled again. Six employees turned into two dozen, porches were expanded, more lights were strung. Bonfires maintained. More "honeymoon cottages" were built along the dunes, and stayed occupied most of the time. Weekends were filled with white dresses, live music, fresh shrimp boil, and good tips. Given the climate of the country, Cape San Blas became a vacation destination. Construction boomed. Allie's folks had hit a gold mine. And to his credit, Mr. Billy stayed away from the bottle. For us, the Blue Tornado was one of the happiest places on earth. We were insulated and isolated from everything save the mail and an occasional hurricane.

Following my attempt at heroism in Allie's bedroom, Mrs. Eleanor loved me and gave me free rein to do what I wanted at the Blue Tornado. I worked every time the doors were open. I bused tables, washed dishes, cut and nailed lumber to expand the decks, hung lights, ran speaker wire, waited tables, swapped out kegs, and backed the bar, which Bobby had begun tending. Given his easygoing style, his uncanny ability to hear the same story a thousand times, and the fact that he'd never met a stranger, he was a natural. While he stood behind the bar and made people feel better, I worked behind the scenes. If it needed doing, I did it. And I didn't wait for someone to tell me it needed doing either. As a result, I learned to do most everything and I made money hand over fist.

I bought my first car when I was just barely fourteen. An old Ford pickup. Inline six. Three on the column. Bought it out of a junkyard. My mom thought I was crazy, but it was my money. In a week I had it rolling. And in another week I had it running. By the third week my mom was driving it to get groceries. We were walking out of the grocery store when a man stopped us. He said to my mom, "You wouldn't want to sell that truck, would you?"

She looked at me. I said, "How much will you give me?"

After expenses, I quadrupled my money, and it didn't take me long to learn how to "flip" cars. Given a rough economy and the fact that the bank's prime interest rate was in the teens, folks were looking to stretch a dollar, and I was all too happy to help them. Take something dead and used up, find out what killed it, fix that—or replace it—and then move on to the next thing. I understood cars and could diagnose what was wrong with them.

Sure, I read manuals and even bought my own set of Chiltons, but something in my brain was hardwired to understand machines and what made them work, and not work.

Allie was never far. Often, it was us three. Me, Allie, and Bobby. Scouring the beach became our version of a treasure hunt. Given the entrepreneurial spirit she'd inherited from her father, Allie began making shell-covered mirrors; her mom hung them in the honeymoon cottages and sold them at the restaurant.

If there was one place on planet Earth where the three of us were happiest, it was the shoreline of Cape San Blas. Nothing angry or evil or sad found us out there. Not Mr. Billy. Not the TV news. Not my mom's tears. Not the pained looks on Mrs. Eleanor's face. Not my father's absence. Twice a day, the beach cleaned itself. Leaving no residue of yesterday. Maybe that's why we liked it.

In the summer of 1970, when I turned fifteen, I bought myself a wrecked 1967 ragtop Corvette. Over the course of a summer I rummaged junkyards and pieced it back together. New rear end, gears, brakes, interior bucket seats, canvas top, electrical wiring.

One of my other junkyard gems was a wrecked Monte Carlo. It'd been rolled and then wrapped around a telephone pole. Wasn't much left. Except the engine. It was perfect. To my great fortune, the guy running the junkyard didn't take the time to pry back the hood and take a look at it. Had he done that, he'd have never sold it. Beneath the hood was a Chevrolet 350-cubic-inch engine. The technical name was LT-1. That designation meant several things: higher compression, angle plug heads, four-bolt main, larger exhaust, larger intake, two carburetors, radical cam.

In English, that meant it produced a little over 500 horsepower with normal aspiration. Meaning, no supercharger. The guys at the auto repair shop were drooling.

Because I wanted to know what made it tick, I took it apart, then meticulously put it back together. But better. I then bolted that orange and chrome beauty into my Corvette, replaced the rear-end gears with .411 posi-traction, linked it to a Muncie four-speed rock-crusher transmission, and scared my mom half to death the first time I took her for a ride.

When I pulled back into the drive, she unlatched her white-knuckled death grip on the door handle, unbuckled, and shook her head. "Jo-Jo, you just made your mother pee herself."

In the first month, I had a dozen offers to sell.


By THE EARLY 1970s the nightly news was filled with images of American boys returning home in flag-laden boxes. Like the rest of the country, my mom watched Cronkite at six thirty with religious regularity, and when she tucked me in she'd kiss me with tearstained lips.

"Mom, why are you crying?"

Bobby was two years older. Thick glasses. Loved history. He raised chickens in our backyard and spent his egg money on books. One night, with the moon shining through our window, Mom glanced at my brother's bed. His sandy-blond hair was spread across the pillow. His eyes were darting back and forth beneath his lids. Churchill's *History of the English-Speaking Peoples* lay next to his head.

She wiped her nose on my sheet, kissed my forehead, and closed our door quietly behind her. After that I started paying attention to what Cronkite said, and one word he kept saying over and over. "Draft." I thought it had to do with a poorly built house, so I asked the boys down at the auto shop. They explained the numbers to me and what they meant. Didn't take me long to figure out why Mom was crying.

Bobby's number was getting closer.

It was just a matter of time. He was in junior college, working at the restaurant full time, constantly looking over his shoulder. I had started doing the same.

On the first day of our senior year, Allie sat down in the front seat of my Corvette. Mrs. Eleanor placed her hand on my forearm, both holding and squeezing it. "Joseph?" She rarely called me by my real name.

"Yes, ma'am."

"You see who's in this car with you?"

"Yes, ma'am."

"And she's my only child?"

"Yes, ma'am."

"And you understand she's my whole world?"

I could barely hear her over the hum and glorious lope of the engine. "Yes, ma'am."

"And you understand that she tells me everything, and I do mean everything."

I nodded.

"And you understand what those black numbers mean on those white signs alongside the road?"

I gave her a confident, knowing look. "They tell you what highway you're on."

She squeezed my arm tighter. "Those are not the numbers I'm talking about."

I knew that. I smiled. I revved the engine to about 5,000 rpms. For the exhaust, I'd run straight pipes with thin mufflers. I hollered over the noise. "We'll be just fine."

She stood back and crossed her arms. "Joseph?"

In the fourteen miles one way to school, I never—with God as my witness—broke the speed limit. Not once. Although every day, without fail, Allie propped her feet on the dash and we rode with the top down while she screamed at the clouds and sang CCR's "Fortunate Son" at the top of her lungs.

Then came the day the world changed.

# — 18 —

I crawled out from beneath the car, and Mom met me at the door. She'd been crying. "Let's go for a ride."

She didn't like riding in my car, so I knew something was wrong. We drove to the north end of the island. Slowly. Windows down. We parked up on a small rise looking out over the ocean.

Mom's hand was trembling. She was clutching a piece of paper. It was wrinkled. Tearstained. Too heavy for her heart to hold.

THE NEXT DAY, I found Allie on the beach. It was after sundown. Her hand was full of sharks' teeth. She was smiling. Breeze tugging at her hair. Bathed in a golden light. Bronze skin. Cutoff jeans and a white tank top. Her brunette hair streaked blond from a summer in the sun. In the difficult years ahead, I would hold on to that picture in my mind.

"Hey . . ."

She could tell from the look on my face. Tears welled.

I thumbed her hair out of her eyes. "I've got to go away for a while."

She dropped the sharks' teeth, scattering them in pieces on the ground.

I knew nothing I could say would make it hurt any less. "I'm going to California. Taking Bobby with me. Maybe cross into Canada. Try and outrun the war."

I held her as tight as I could, but I knew that no matter how tightly I held her, I could not stop the pain. Allie was cracking down the middle.

She sobbed on my shoulder.

Around midnight I walked her to her door and stood at the base of her steps. The screen door was open. She was holding my hand, looking up at me. Big blue eyes pleading. Her heart was breaking. "Come back to me?"

The pain in my heart was indescribable. I could barely breathe. "Yes."

"Tell me."

"I'll come back to you."

She pressed her forehead to my chest and spoke through sobs. "You promise?"

I stared out across the Gulf, took her hand in mine, and gave her the keys to the thing I valued most in this world. "I promise."

# — 19 —

Nine o'clock found me with my radio on my lap, staring at the ocean. While Suzy entertained us, Rosco and I studied the water. North of us, a bonfire lit the beach. Black shadows sat around it. Every few moments a candle-lit balloon, three feet tall, would rise off the beach, where the breeze would catch it and carry it west out across the Gulf toward Texas. I followed them through my binoculars, losing sight about five miles out.

After nearly thirty-six hours of sleep, Allie woke and appeared behind me. She put a hand on my shoulder. "Can I ask you a favor?"

I turned. Even her face looked rested.

She laid an official-looking piece of paper on the desk. The watermark showed in the light. "When we married, we took this policy out on Jake. Bought it through his company." She laid the check stubs on the table. "Been paying on it ever since."

I read the face page. It was a twenty-year term life insurance policy insuring Jake for $500,000. The weight of this squelched her voice to a whisper. She pointed. "There's a rider. Thirty dollars a month." She flipped to the last page and showed me the addendum to the policy. "It doubles the face amount if the cause of death is an accident." She spread the sheriff's certificate of death on the table and pointed at the word *accident*. She rubbed her face. "I called and got an appointment."

She was ready to be done with this.

"Let me clean up."

We drove to the national office of First General Life in Tallahassee where, to my surprise, we were taken to see the president, Dawson Baker. Evidently Jake's death and the nature of it had captured wider attention than we'd realized.

Dawson welcomed us into his office. "May I get you anything? Coffee? Water?"

He wore a white shirt. The carpet matched his red power tie. The royal blue drapes matched the thin stripe in his suit. Everything was wood, and the office was probably two thousand square feet or more. Pictures of his family covered much of the space on the desk behind him. Somebody had signed a wooden baseball bat that hung inside a display case on the wall. Behind his desk, in a small framed plaque, hung a shoulder patch for Army Special Forces. The accompanying beret sat on the shelf next to it. Followed by a framed Bronze Star, a Purple Heart, and a Distinguished Service Cross.

We sat, and Dawson held up a small stack of papers. "Jake's policy was paid and current. Most everyone in Florida knows what happened, so after you called, we fast-tracked cutting the check." He passed a piece of paper across the desk to Allie, who stared at it, her head turning sideways. Her bottom lip quivered just slightly. "But . . ." She spread her policy across his desk.

Dawson nodded and presented a stack of papers. Something in the expression of his face told me the rest of this was not going to go well.

"Jake canceled this policy three months after you purchased it. He transferred payment to this . . ." Another piece of paper. "The P&C on a Peterbilt."

Allie looked like she'd been shot. She spoke slowly. "P&C?"

He nodded. "Property and casualty insurance. That check you hold there is the accidental death and dismemberment rider to that policy."

I was getting confused. As was Allie. She scratched her head. "So—" She held up her policy. "What about this one?"

"Jake diverted payment to this." He held up the Peterbilt policy.

"So this is no good to me?"

He nodded. "Correct."

Allie was starting to get agitated. "Even though I've been paying on it for almost ten years?"

Dawson wasn't enjoying this any more than Allie. "To your credit, you have been paying, but not on that life insurance policy. You've been paying on this truck insurance policy."

"But—"

He looked at her check stubs. "See here, you even wrote the policy number for Jake's truck insurance on the check stub."

She compared the policy numbers. The number on her check stubs, and the one she'd written on the check, corresponded to the truck insurance. Not the life insurance. "But—" Allie rubbed her flushed face. The pieces of the puzzle were falling into place, and she couldn't make sense of the picture. She held up the life insurance policy. "Are you telling me this policy doesn't exist?"

Dawson took his time. "I'm telling you that you and Jake did initially purchase a life insurance policy, which he cancelled three months after purchase." He brought another sheet of paper from his file. "On this sheet of paper we have both your signature and his, with witnesses, showing the cancellation of that policy and the transfer of the payment to the policy that insured his truck. Your check stubs, the number you wrote on the checks, and Jake's truck insurance policy all agree with this."

She eyed the paper. "I don't remember signing that."

He held up the paper. "Is that your signature?"

"It looks like it, but I don't remember."

He then produced three certified mail receipts. "We sent three notices to your house, via certified mail, giving you both the option, over a ninety-day period, to reinstate the policy." He shook his head and spoke softly. "That never happened."

Allie had broken out in a sweat, and her left leg was bouncing. Her face was ghostlike. "So my husband had no life insurance policy with you?"

"Mrs. Gibson, I'm sorry. I realize this is a surprise, but you and Jake owned a policy with us that insured his vehicle." He was careful in how he answered. "Not his life."

Allie sat staring blankly at the wall. Finally she turned to him. "Well, if I've been paying the insurance on that truck, and that truck is now totaled, which I imagine is something you and I can agree on, shouldn't I get a check for the value of the truck?"

He nodded painfully. "You would if Jake had been driving the truck you'd insured."

Allie turned even paler. "What do you mean?"

Dawson pulled out several pictures depicting the burnt and mangled truck on the rocks. "This is not the truck you insured."

Allie slapped the pictures. "Of course it is. Jake was driving it."

"Yes, ma'am, Jake was driving it. But it's not a Peterbilt. It's a Mack. According to the VIN stamped on the frame and some of the other markings our investigators pulled from the wreckage"— Dawson pointed to individual pictures—"it was an older Mack truck not insured by your policy. Or by us, for that matter."

Allie's hands were shaking. She stood, stuffed half the papers back into her bag, and walked out. When we reached the truck, she walked to the grass, bent at the waist, and vomited. Then she vomited again. Her body tried to heave a third time, but the first two had emptied her, so she heaved dry.

The ninety-minute drive back to Cape San Blas was quiet. I drove to the cottage, thinking she would pull the covers over her head, but when she exited the truck she walked to the restaurant. Briskly. She unlocked the door and walked immediately to the bar, where she pulled out a dusty bottle of bourbon, poured a tumbler full, and turned it up. Followed by a second. Then a third. Finally she looked at me. "I don't ever remember signing that."

I kept quiet.

Another tumbler. "Never." She looked around. "I've lost it. For good." Without a word, she returned to the cottage and shut the door.

I stood at the base of the dunes scratching Rosco's head.

Something was bugging me about the whole life insurance thing. I believed Dawson was telling us the truth. I just wasn't sure he was telling us the whole truth.

I got a number from Allie's phone and dialed it.

He answered after the third ring. "Hello?"

"Bobby, it's me. Before you left, you asked me if there was anything you could do. I think there might be."

I told him what I needed, and he was quiet a minute. Finally he said, "Give me a few hours. Maybe a day."

"Thanks."

He stopped me. "Jo-Jo?"

I knew what he was about to ask, and he was right to ask it. "Yes."

"Let's say you're right. I mean, think about it . . . Are you sure you want to be?"

Politics had taught him well how to think two and three moves down the line. To ask what is the effect of this decision and the next. "No, I'm not. Honestly, I'd rather be wrong. But I have a feeling I'm not."

"I'll be in touch . . . You'd better give me your number."

I figured Allie would be asleep for several hours, so I returned to Tallahassee. I didn't know if Dawson Baker would be there or not. I imagined he kept a rather full schedule, but I only needed about sixty seconds. I rode the elevator to the sixth floor and spoke to the receptionist, who phoned his secretary. She came out to meet me. "I'm sorry, Mr. Brooks. Mr. Baker is tied up for the remainder of the day."

"Ma'am, if you could just tell him. I only need a minute. That's all."

She shook her head. "I'm sorry. I wish I could help. If you'd like to make an appointment for tomorrow or next week . . ."

"No, thank you."

With that, she returned to her office. While I stood there feeling rather foolish, the receptionist scribbled on a piece of paper, turned it upside down, and tapped it with a pencil. It read *Governor's Course. 2:30 tee time.*

I punched the button to the elevator and said, "Thank you."

The Governor's Course wasn't difficult to find. I found Dawson on the practice range. He saw me and leaned on his club. Staring at me through dark sunglasses. He was younger than me by maybe ten years. He did not look impressed that I'd found him. And while his voice had been kind inside his office, it was not now. "How can I help you?"

"Where'd you earn your Purple Heart?"

This took him by surprise. "Someplace we weren't supposed to be. You know something about them?"

"I've got a couple."

That got his attention. He took off his glasses. "Where?"

"Four tours. Most inside Laos. Or somewhere along the supply side of the Ho Chi Minh Trail."

He glanced at his watch. "I'm real sorry about your situation."

I stepped closer. "I realize you're in a bit of a pickle and there's only so much you can tell us, but . . . is there something you're not telling us?"

He used the blade of the iron in his hand to drag a ball out of the pile in front of him. He stood over it, swung backward slowly, and then struck the ball, which traveled about 175 yards in the air. When it landed, he culled another ball from the pile, stood back, and looked at me.

"Did Jake Gibson own a second life insurance policy that named someone other than Allie as beneficiary?"

He didn't respond.

"I'm not a legal expert, but I have a feeling that since Allie is Jake's legal wife, she can hire an attorney who can compel you to answer that question."

He took off his hat. "What do you gain from this?"

"Honestly, I will lose far more than I gain."

"Why then?"

I stared down the range, then back at him. "At one time I did a lot of things I'm not real proud of. Sometimes I think if I do some good, it will either erase or help me forget the bad."

"Has it?"

I shook my head. "No."

He stood over another golf ball, wiggling the head of his club. He chose his words carefully. "When you two left my office, you left some papers behind. I'll call my secretary and have them waiting for you."

I had a feeling my answer lay in those papers. I shook his hand. "Thank you."

I returned to the offices of First General, where the receptionist met me with a thin envelope. I tucked it under my arm and then sat in the front seat of my truck studying its contents. Four pieces of paper. The first three were certified mail receipts. The fourth was one legal-sized sheet of paper stating a change of address. It was dated a month after the purchase date of the policy. Jake had requested to change the mailing address of the policy from Allie's address on Cape San Blas to an address in North Carolina. None of this was making any sense until I looked again at the certified mail receipts. All three had been sent to North Carolina.

As I was driving back to Allie's, my phone rang. It was Bobby. "You own a smart phone?"

"No. Flip."

"Where are you?"

"Leaving Tallahassee."

"Buy a smart phone. Something with a screen and Internet access. Text me from that number when you get it."

"You find something?"

"Just text me."

Driving south on Highway 319, I stopped at a Verizon store and bought a no-contract phone with a screen that looked like a small tablet. When I asked the salesman if people actually kept these things in their pockets, he slid one out of his. He then educated me on how to send texts, surf the Internet, and use the maps program. He was launching into a dissertation on social media when I thanked him and paid my bill. An hour after having hung up with Bobby, I texted him. Thirty seconds later, my new phone chimed. Then it chimed again.

I opened Bobby's text. It read, *A little grainy but it's taken from 90 miles above the earth.* I clicked on the attachment and a video loaded. I pressed the play icon, and the video showed a dark road bordered by the ocean. That much I could see. Four seconds into the video a moving object appeared on the right of the screen, winding along the road toward the waterline where the road curved. The object was long, thin; headlights shone on the road in front, and as it stayed on the road, I could only assume it was Jake's semi. A half mile from the wall of rocks and the turn in the road, the semi veered into the other lane, the oncoming lane. As it did this, a second set of headlights appeared quickly on the driver's side of the truck. It moved in close, the truck door opened, and the driver hopped into what appeared to be an open-topped Jeep. The Jeep slowed, veered left down a dirt road, and disappeared from the picture about the time Jake's truck exploded on the rocks and a large white flash appeared on the screen.

I was having a tough time believing what I saw.

I returned to the crash site, following the same northerly path as both Jake's semi and the Jeep. A quarter mile from the crash site, a dirt road peeled off to the left, snaking through the woods and then making a complete U-turn, emptying south again onto the two-lane road that served the island.

While I sat on the side of the road shaking my head, my phone chimed a third time. Bobby again. *This is video taken from the surveillance cameras recording traffic onto and off the island. We have an "intelligence base" on the island. Have for years. Without it, these pics and video don't exist.*

I pressed play and two seconds' video footage from eye level showed Jake's semi, followed closely by a light-colored Jeep—top down—turning right, onto the island. From the rear, only the driver could be seen. No passenger. The video continued as the red taillights of both the Jeep and Jake's semi disappeared a mile down the road. Here the video had been spliced, as the timer on the bottom of the screen jumped forward several minutes. As the seconds ticked by at the bottom of the dark screen, a large flash was seen suddenly in the distance, turning much of the screen white. Again, the video had been spliced, as the timer jumped forward four minutes to a single set of headlights appearing in the distance, slowly growing larger and closer. The headlights were narrow, like a Jeep's. After a few seconds, the Jeep rolled to a stop at the flashing red light. Two people were now sitting in it. Given the reflection, I could not tell if they were man or woman. Just figures. The video continued as the Jeep turned left toward Port St. Joe, exposing its rear bumper where the license tag had been removed.

I sat on the side of the road, shaking my head.

# — 20 —

Allie was sitting in a chair staring out across the ocean when I returned. I didn't waste time. I pulled up a chair and sat next to her. "I need to show you something."

Surprise spread across her face when I pulled out my hour-old tablet phone. But not nearly as much surprise as what occurred when I pressed play. I turned the phone sideways, enlarging the picture. Jake's semi appeared in the video. Then the Jeep. Then the truck driver's jump to the Jeep. Then the separation of the two vehicles, followed by the explosion.

She was trying to make sense of it when I replayed it for her a second time. When it finished, I played her the surveillance video showing the entrance of Jake's semi and the Jeep—driven by one person—the flash, and then the return of the Jeep now showing two people.

She looked confused. "What? What is this?"

I leaned back against the chair. "I think it means that Jake Gibson faked his own death."

"What?" Her head was spinning. "Why?"

"I don't have the answer to that." I pulled out the envelope. "There's more." I spread the four sheets of paper across my lap. "This is a change-of-address form used by First General. It was filed by Jake a month after you two purchased the policy ten years ago. The new address is to a town in North Carolina. Oddly, it's about an hour from my cabin. It's near the interstate, so access for a semi like Jake's wouldn't be too difficult."

Allie was having trouble putting all this together.

"I think Jake purchased the life insurance policy with you and then transferred ownership to someone in North Carolina where, I would guess, he also reassigned the beneficiary—while still allowing you to pay on a policy you no longer owned. If you hire an attorney, I think you'll find this to be true. I also think you'll find he's lived at that address in North Carolina for quite some time."

She shuffled the sheets of paper. "Well, who lives in North Carolina?"

I didn't want to say what I was about to say. "I'm guessing Jake's first wife."

"What!" Her bottom lip was shaking and she was crying now, but it wasn't sadness. It was growing anger. "But why . . . ? What would . . . ?"

"I don't have answers for all of that. I could be wrong, but I'm guessing that Jake was married before he met you, and all the time you thought he was on the road, he was probably back home in North Carolina."

Her voice changed. "With his other wife?"

"Yes."

"But . . . that doesn't answer why. Why pretend all those years?"

"I can give you one million reasons."

She stared at the papers. "So here I am. The mourning widow. All torn up 'cause I think he's burnt to a crisp and my last words to him were so terrible. So hate-filled. And he's actually living with some floozie in another state."

I nodded. "With a million dollars."

"But . . . that would mean he planned this whole thing. That sadistic bast—"

I nodded. "A little more than ten years ago. And here's something else. How many times did Jake eat at the Blue Tornado before you two started dating?"

She shrugged. "Dozen. Maybe more."

"Did he stay at the motel?"

"Yes."

"Why would a guy that drives a semi for a living detour so far off the interstate when it's costing him time and money to do so?"

She shook her head. "Unless he was trying to find a woman who was tied to her eighty-hour-a-week job and hadn't left the island in years and never went anywhere on vacation. So she would never discover he was a lying sack of—"

"I think Jake was looking for someone like you when he found you."

"What, you mean, gullible?"

"Maybe *unsuspecting* and *trusting* are better words."

She sat back, shaking her head. "How do we find out?"

I held up the certified mail receipts.

# — 21 —

We drove up through Tallahassee, and because I loved driving back roads, we stayed on 319 up through Moultrie, then turned north on 33 up through Sylvester, finally dumping out onto I-75 at Cordele. Maybe Allie was trying to take her mind off what awaited. I'm not sure, but about the time our tires rolled off of Cape San Blas, she said, "It was good to see Bobby."

I nodded. "It was good to see him sober."

"You two ever talk?"

"You mean other than at Jake's fake funeral?"

She twirled her hair with one finger. "Yes."

"No. Not since we buried Mom."

"Long time."

"Yep."

She continued. "He looked older. Looked good in his suit and with those two handsome bodyguards."

"Maybe he's finally found his place on this earth."

She turned toward me. "I called him."

"He told me."

"He tell you I was actually looking for you?"

"Yes."

"He said he didn't know how to find you. Guess he found a way."

"Actually, he did not."

She looked surprised. "Then how'd you end up on the island?"

I told her. Starting with the snowstorm at my cabin. About Gabriella, Diego, and Catalina. About her brother, the trailer park, and how I saw the smoke.

"Bobby didn't call you?"

"No."

"And you turned toward home because you saw a spiral of smoke?"

I nodded.

"I guess Jake never counted on that."

"Tell me about him. Start at the beginning."

She backed up and described the last decade. How he was never really present. Married on paper only. They'd never had a vacation. He'd stay gone for literally months at a time. Calling every few days. Over the years, it dropped to once a week.

She said, "In ten years of marriage he was home maybe a total of a year. Maybe less. That truck only made money when it was rolling, so he was always on the road. And even when he was home, he wasn't home. I don't think we've slept in the same bed in three or four years. Maybe more. We 'played' married. That's about it."

"And the phone call the night he died?"

"I was mad. Said some horrible things. Things I never should've said." She paused. "But knowing what I think I know now, I should've said more."

South Georgia rolled along outside the window.

"After we hung up, he *tried*"—she made quotation marks in the air—"to make it home. Tired as he was. You know the rest." She bit part of a cuticle and spit it onto the floorboard. "He had probably been sleeping in his other bed with his other wife and was good and rested when he jumped into that Jeep."

"What had you planned to do with the life insurance money before you found out there isn't any?"

She laughed. "Pay off my debt. Reopen the restaurant. The cottages."

"You still love it?"

"It's what I know. I know how to take that place and make people happy. I love seeing the smiles and hearing the laughter. Always have. My dad was a lot of bad things, but one good thing was his belief that people would come from all over to sit on that beach and stare out across that water and eat good food. There's something peaceful there. And I think he was right." She looked at me. "I think at one time you believed that too."

"I did."

"Can I ask you something?"

"Sure."

"And you'll tell me the truth."

"Yes."

"You give me your word?"

"Yes."

"What happened to you?"

"Which part?"

She tapped her chest. "The part that included me."

"Well, about forty-five years ago, I went on vacation twelve thousand miles away—"

She interrupted me. "You told me you were going to California."

"I lied."

"Why?"

"Didn't want you to worry." I paused. "But either way it didn't matter, because when I came home two years later, you were dressed in white and marrying my brother."

She rubbed her palms together and closed her eyes for a long second. "Yes . . . I did that. But . . . you disappeared. Silent for two years. I needed someone to hold me."

I tried to make light of it. "Well . . . maybe you could've chosen someone other than my older brother."

She leaned closer. "I needed to hear from you. No letter. No nothing. Why?"

"That might be tough to explain."

"Try me."

"If I died, and chances were good that I would, then I didn't want to leave you standing over my grave holding a handful of tearstained letters. If I left you nothing to hold on to, you could cling to someone else. I was trying to make it easier for you if I didn't make it home."

"Would've been nice to know that then."

"Even when I did make it home, you wouldn't have wanted anything to do with me."

"What happened? Where'd you go? Where've you been?"

I laughed. Something I hadn't always been able to do. "That's a long story with little to interest you. And a lot that I'm not real proud of."

"Does it hurt to tell it?"

"Some."

She placed her hand on my arm. "Tell me." She propped her feet on the dash and laid her head back against the headrest. Air coming in through the open window was tugging at her hair. "Jo-Jo, I want to know about your life."

I switched hands on the wheel. "How far back am I going?"

"September 15th, 1972."

I squinted. "Second most painful day of my life."

"What was the most?"

"The day you married my brother."

"You're not going to let that go, are you?"

"Well, we should probably talk about it."

She twirled a finger through her hair and looked away. "We already covered that. Worst decision I've ever made. Although, in light of recent events, it may be second worst. If it makes you feel any better, I've had two really bad marriages with very little love and zero tenderness."

We were talking with the ease of two kids, forty-five years ago.

"I've been with two men—"

I raised my hand. "And I'm not one of them, mind you."

She smiled. "True. As I was saying, I've been with two men, neither of whom sent chills up my spine the way your hand in mine once did. Or your kiss on my lips." She paused. "You ever marry?"

"No."

"Ever been in love?"

"Yes. Twice."

"When?"

"Once when I was younger."

She smiled and twirled a finger through her hair again.

"Then later, after I'd been in-country for a couple of years."

"Where was she from?"

"Europe. She was a singer."

"What happened?"

"The war." I shrugged. "Didn't take."

Her eyes were glassy when she spoke. "When you came back . . . why didn't you come back here?" A tear broke loose. "You promised."

I slid my hand into hers. I drove several minutes. Trying to find an entry. "I was in a bad way . . . I'd seen a lot that wasn't good, and it clung to me. I was trying to shake it and couldn't. I wanted nothing more than to be with you. I just didn't want you to have to be with me."

She reached up and placed her index finger on my lips. "But what if I wanted to be with you?"

"The guy that came back wasn't the guy that went away. He was a powder keg, and even I didn't know when I'd go off. Even now I have flashbacks and I'm not in control. You just have to trust me on that one. When I came home, so much in me was 'off.' The part in me that *felt* had been blown up. Literally. I landed in California to Berkeley kids spitting through the fence at me. Throwing rotten fruit. And I could not understand that. I'd just spent twenty-four months trying to stop people from dying, and then these people I didn't even know cursed me as I walked off the plane. I looked around and wondered, *What is wrong with this world?*

"We had to spend a few days debriefing in this huge warehouse. The military wanted to know what I knew. Most guys went home in a day. Me, they were still talking to after two weeks. They wanted me to re-up. I said, 'No, thank you. I've done my time.' All I wanted, the only thing that kept me alive in that terrible place, was the thought of coming home to you. Of a life with you. Of walking that beach and letting you and those waves wash all the evil off of me. So they finally let me go. I looked out the window and those kids were still screaming at the fence. I asked my CO, 'Do I have to wear my uniform out of here?' He said, 'You can walk out that door however you want.' I threw my uniform in the trash. I threw all my medals in the trash. I threw everything having anything to do with the military in the trash and slipped out the back door in civilian clothes."

I glanced in the rearview as a new T-top Corvette approached and passed us in the left lane. Tanned couple. Laughing. The guy was driving with one hand. Holding the girl's hand with the other. Her long hair was flapping in the breeze. They were singing a song I couldn't hear. He accelerated and their red taillights disappeared in the distance. It was a good picture of us. Most everything we'd ever dreamed and never lived was silently passing us by.

"Given all I'd encountered, the military recommended a few weeks at a war treatment program. I had a feeling that was a good idea, so I spent a month there. Trying to put the pieces of my mind back into one skull. After a month I checked myself out and rode a bus to the Cape. Thumbed a ride to the restaurant, and when I got there, I found a party in full swing. I was so excited. I—" I paused. Looking at her. Her eyes were trained on me.

"I had bought a ring before I came home. Silver. A green stone. They said it was an emerald. Had it in my pocket. I walked up the steps. And there was my older brother, dressed in military uniform, a chest full of medals, holding your hand. His ring on your finger." I paused as the memory returned. "I knew if I stayed there, I'd kill him. But I'd seen a lot of that and I had enough control of my faculties to know that would not fix the hurt in me. So I threw the ring in the ocean, returned to California, re-upped, and did two more years in a country where my government denied my existence."

She was quiet awhile. Then she whispered, "Tell me about the war."

I sucked between my teeth. "I've spent the last four and a half decades trying not to think about the war. It's difficult."

"Any good memories?"

"When we first landed, the first time, I was stationed at a place called Camp California. Sort of a play on words for all the drafters. Anyway, we had these outhouse-things, tall metal buildings, built over a fifty-five-gallon drum. Given that many soldiers, the contents of the drums had to be burned twice a day. My first day in-country, they asked for volunteers for poop duty. We had another name for it, but you understand. I raised my hand. Every morning and evening, when we weren't on patrol, we'd pull those drums out, fill the remainder with diesel, light it, stir it, and then tend it while the fire burned the contents. Nasty work, but easy. During the rest of the day, I lay in my hammock on the beach and watched what happened on base. It would pay dividends later.

"One of the guys that tended the fire with me was Tex Lewis. Great big ol' guy. Our second month in, we got in this mess one night and he got hit. Bad. I laid his head across my lap. He asked me to pray the Lord's Prayer over him. So I did. I prayed and watched the light slowly fade from his eyes. Somewhere in that moment, that's where the anger came in. And I let it. I told myself that if I was to get home to you, if I was to make it out of that godforsaken place, then I had to forget what I loved and learn to be worse than the guys outside the wire. So I did.

"When I re-upped and they sent me back, I didn't take anything off anybody. I built myself a hooch on the beach of the South China Sea and hung a hammock between two palm trees. I'd lie there at night and listen to the bombs in the distance. They were always bringing in entertainment for the guys at the rear, and one night they brought in this lady singer. Beautiful. Sultry. Sang like a canary. And for some reason she picked me. It was the strangest experience. During the evenings, she'd hop on a helo and they'd take her to another base, where she'd entertain the troops. I'd hop on another helo and they'd drop us in a country we weren't supposed to be in, and we'd serve death for dinner and then fly out. And then she and I would meet at my hooch, I'd bathe in the ocean and wash off the blood, and then we'd walk hand in hand down the beach like two normal people. The crazy thing was how normal it felt, when it was anything but."

"Did you love her?"

"I don't know that I was capable of that. I liked having her around, and she took my mind off of you, but there was so much beneath the surface. She saw it, and I think it scared her. By my third year I was having some pretty bad dreams. I woke up one morning, and she was black and blue and lying unconscious on the floor. I had no memory of doing that. Later that week, she took a gig somewhere in Europe. For the next decade or so, whenever she'd put out a new record or song, I'd listen."

"How many men were in your unit?"

"Sixty-two."

"How many came home?"

"Including me?"

She nodded.

"Four."

She swallowed and stared through the windshield a long time. "Do you keep in touch?"

"One committed suicide. One died of cancer. I lost touch with the last when they put him in prison. Don't know if he's still alive or not."

She sucked in a deep breath and covered her mouth.

I continued, "The military would fly me home to deliver my men to their families. Sometimes it was just me and one casket. One time it was me and twelve caskets. I'd leave over there, fly thirty-six hours, deliver my friends, or their pieces, to their loved ones, fly thirty-six hours back alone, land, hop on a helo, and they'd drop me back in the jungle. Somewhere in that process, the place in my heart that felt things like love and desire died. It just quit feeling."

---

# — 22 —

We drove a long time in silence. She looked at me, at the road, back to me. She did this a lot. I wasn't sure what we were going to find when we got where we were going. The only thing I knew for sure was that we were going. Our drive took us through Cordele, onto I-75 North, and into Atlanta, where we stopped at Das BBQ for lunch. Hands down, best barbecue I've ever eaten. We split a slab of brisket, a rack of ribs, and five separate side dishes.

On I-26 I continued my story. "When the war ended they kept me around for a year, intelligence mostly, moving between countries, but by then I'd had my fill. They brought me home, more war treatment program, more interviews, more intelligence, and finally at age twenty-three they discharged me and I flew home and entered what I call my Peeping Tom Period. I returned to the island, just trying to see clearly. Just smell the ocean. By then, you and Bobby were living behind a white picket fence. He was gone mostly, drinking or shooting up, and when you weren't at the restaurant working, you would sit in your kitchen and watch *The Carol Burnett Show.* I'd stand outside your kitchen window at night and, because I had little to laugh about, I'd listen to you laugh. But then Bobby would come home and whatever hole in me your laughter had healed, his presence tore open, and ugly stuff poured out. So I forced myself to leave before I hurt him."

"You really did that?"

"Lots of times."

As this sank in, a look of shock spread across her face.

"With so much anger, and a lot of training in how to hurt other people, I started what I call my Fighting Period. I joined this underground bare knuckle thing. We moved from Mexico to South America. India. Some time back in Asia. Cash payouts, and they were big. We moved from destination to destination on private planes that sort of skipped the whole customs and immigration thing. Seeing an opportunity, I started running guns. Lots of guns. People came from all over to see the fights, which exposed me to a lot of not-very-reputable people who wanted stuff that I could get them. I got really good at it.

"So five years pass. Whenever I was home, I'd land in Miami and drive north, stopping on the Cape. I'd sit in the dunes and stare for days at your cottage with binoculars. My idiot brother was high on the next latest and greatest drug. I wanted to knock on your door, but I knew that as bad as your life was, it would be worse if I unleashed me on you. I guess I was just hoping that somehow I could get back to the me I used to be.

"Over the months, I watched your stomach get bigger and I was happy for you. But then came the delivery and I didn't know what happened, but I knew Bobby wasn't there and you had trouble and the baby didn't make it."

When I looked at Allie, tears were streaming off her face.

"So I stayed until you were stable and then paid for a funeral, and since you'd mortgaged the restaurant to pay for his rehab, I paid the hospital bills."

Her eyes widened. "That was you?"

"I needed to do one good thing. I rented a room at the motel on the island by the week, and kept an eye on you while Bobby was in rehab."

"I never knew you were there."

I shrugged. "The military spent a good bit of money training me not to be seen. Then I had this fight. Pretty good payday. Miami. Got cut up. Stitches. Hospital. Same old stuff. But then I walked by a room and saw your name on the clipboard. Poked my head in and saw you were beat up. Face bloody. Eyes swollen. I sat through the night. If my brother showed I was going to kill him. And it wasn't going to be fast. It'd be slow and he'd hurt and beg me to make it fast. Then early the next morning, I came out of the bathroom, and there was Bobby on his knees crying. Holding your hand. Begging forgiveness. I walked out. I knew I needed to get as far away from you two as possible.

"The years rolled by. Bobby was in and out of rehab. Your debt skyrocketed. He went to prison. He was running a lot of drugs and had run up a lot of debt on the restaurant that you didn't know about. Finally you divorced him and ran the restaurant alone. I found you one night walking the beach, booze in one hand, Smith & Wesson in the other. You were way bad drunk. A rip tide pulled you out, I found you on a kayak, nursed you sober, took you home."

"That was you?"

"I had made up my mind to come home. To finally talk with you rather than just spy on you. I was listed in a fight. Big payoff. The more I hurt him, the more I got paid. So I hurt the guy. I got arrested, and that started what I like to call my Prison Period."

"You went to prison?"

"Five years. And while I didn't like it, prison was where I saw what hatred does to guys. Which was good. Most of my life, I'd been a people watcher. Given my tendency not to trust others, I grew up that way. A personality trait that would help keep me alive in dangerous places. Prison forced me to sit back and evaluate what I'd learned from all the people watching. To not just sketch their faces, but read what the lines were telling me. When I got out, I started my Business and Womanizing Period—I was trying to replace your face with others, trying to forget you."

"How'd that work out?"

"Not very well. When I was released from prison, my parole officer got me a job at the zoo. Literally walking behind the elephants, picking up what they dropped, and they could drop a lot. Maybe I'd taken too many blows to the head or been near too many bombs when they exploded, but that got me to thinking. It's just poop. So I started a portable toilet company called the Poop Coop."

Allie burst out laughing. "You can't be serious."

"Totally. Our tagline was *You poop it, we scoop it.*"

Her laughter grew. I continued, "I learned that the poop business was a profitable one, so business grew. Eight states. I was on the road a good bit, learned to drive semis. We supported big outdoor venues, a hundred or more units at a time. We would deliver, set up, wash, pump, clean, whatever. It didn't bother me. It could never be as nasty as what I'd seen over there, so I started making money hand over fist. A cash cow. Years passed, I guess this was in my late thirties, and then a guy came along and offered me four times book. I said thank you very much, have a nice day, here's the key. I sold it, banked the money along with a decade's worth of residuals in which I made three times what he'd paid me for the company.

"So I turned forty. Alone. Found myself driving a Porsche 'cause that's what rich, lonely, compensating, unmarried men do. And, if I'm being honest, I thought it would impress you. I'd swoop in and knock you off your feet. I'd been living in Miami, and by the time I got my courage up, I was on my way to the island. Had the flowers in the passenger seat. Driving up the toll road. A guy cut me off, shot me the bird, and I went total spider monkey on him. I ran him down and beat him senseless. The news the next day said he was on life support, and it took him three months to wake up. That's when I had my first thought that maybe prison hadn't cured me, and I knew I couldn't bring that man home to you.

"So I climbed into a bottle, wrecked my Porsche, bought another one, wrecked it, and started my Boozing Period. One night, drunk out of my mind, I got my third Porsche up to about

160 and tried to kill myself. To make the bad man stop. I flipped the car ten or eleven times and walked away. By then I was having some pretty bad night terrors. Flashbacks. I'd wake up in strange places. One day I was coming down the elevator of a high-rise where a girl I was seeing lived. An Asian guy, slanted eyes, shorter than me, started speaking into his phone. When they sent me down into the tunnels, I had to go with no light, so I followed the sound of their voices. That guy started talking in the elevator and I was back in a dark tunnel. So . . . I came unhinged. When the elevator door opened, he lay in a puddle on the floor. Breathing, but barely. I climbed further into a bottle and stayed there for the better part of a decade.

"You, in the meantime, had poured yourself into the restaurant. You looked good, you were working out. Paying down debt. I would dress up like someone else, wig, glasses, hat, and come into the restaurant and order dinner. If I'm honest, I just wanted to smell you. You have this beautiful thing about you that when you start to sweat and then it mixes with your Chanel—" I blushed.

"Jo-Jo, are you blushing?"

I laughed. "You would walk by and I'd close my eyes and just breathe. And when I got my nerve up to take off the wig, I'd look at my hands, at the cuts, the scars, and then I'd look inside and see all the scars there, and I knew there wasn't enough water in that ocean to wash them clean. I kept quiet because I didn't want you to know who I'd become."

Her voice cracked. "Why?"

"Because if there was any part of you that still wished for me, I wanted you to wish for the guy that went away, not the guy that had come home. I was spending so much time around there that I rented an apartment. I knew your schedule. I knew when you went to dance lessons every week, and I knew if Seth the dance instructor put his hand on your butt one more time I was going to break it off."

She laughed out loud. "Yeah, he kind of creeped me out. A little too touchy." She rested her hand on my arm. Her touch was gentle. "You were watching over me?"

It was both a question and a statement.

"Then there were those group dance nights, when you'd get all gussied up and put on four times the normal amount of makeup, and I can honestly say I was both hoping you'd find one you liked and hoping you wouldn't. That maybe if you could just wait a little longer I could get my collective stuff together long enough to be a man you could love and who could love you back.

"Then you started bringing in live entertainment. Bands on the Beach. Most were good and I enjoyed them, but then you brought in that screamer guy and I never could understand what attracted you to him."

"I was trying to attract customers."

"I'm not sure he did that."

"In hindsight, neither am I."

"Anyway, I didn't like him from the first time I laid eyes on him. And given the fact that I'd been well trained to spy on people, I did. One night he slipped something in your drink. I wasn't sure until I saw you stagger around closing time. You two were all alone. He made his move and so did I. A few minutes later I carried you to your bed, and maybe the most difficult thing

I've ever done is not climb in there with you. But I knew me, and I knew I loved you. I also knew I needed something to make me laugh. Take my mind off you. So I bought a carnival."

"You bought a what?"

"A carnival. You know. Merry-go-round, Ferris wheel, bright lights, popcorn?"

She looked at me like I'd lost my mind.

# — 23 —

We took I-85 out of Atlanta until it intersected I-26, where we turned northwest. Jake's address, what I had come to believe was his primary place of residence, was north of Asheville—only a few miles off the interstate. If he actually drove a semi for a living, then it'd be a smart place to live, with easy access onto and off of several main roads. If he didn't drive a semi for a living, it'd be a good place to not be found. Either way, I felt it was strategic.

My cabin sat about an hour from Jake's address. Rather than drive north through Asheville, I exited at Tryon and ambled through the back roads of Rutherfordton, Union Mills, Marion, and Busick. They were prettier, and we could take our time, and with it getting dark I figured we'd just wait until tomorrow to spy on Jake. Winter was still hanging on and, unlike sunny Florida, there was snow on the ground here. Allie had not brought winter clothes. I doubted she owned many.

When we exited the interstate at Tryon, she said, "So did you really buy a carnival?"

"Sure. I quit drinking cold turkey and poured myself into making people laugh. I hadn't done a lot of that throughout my life, so I thought it sounded like a good idea. I built it up. It thrived. While everything in my personal life was a mess, every business I ever touched turned to gold. Even my mistakes made money. I had my own booth too, just for fun. I was really good at guessing people's weights. I was usually within two or three pounds. We really took off when I hired this group of four guys out of West Virginia with a motorcycle act inside a large cage that would make your head spin. Total absurdity, but it was fun, made people laugh. And just like the Poop Coop, it made money.

"The carnival was good for me. I was approaching fifty and thought maybe I'd laid my demons to rest. When I finally got my nerve up to come back, I walked into the restaurant, just me, no wig, and found you sitting at the bar talking to a guy with a cane and a friendly smile. Looked like he couldn't hurt a flea. You were smiling. He had grease on his hat. And I thought, *Finally a good guy, one without all the anger.* I thought maybe our chances were just gone. So I backed up, got a room at the motel, and watched you laugh for three days with Jake. I figured I'd better not get in your way. I returned to my carnival . . . but truth be told, I wasn't sleeping much at night. Bright lights and sudden noises weren't the best therapy for a guy who didn't like bright flashing lights and sudden noises.

"Then one night I was just minding my own business. Wasn't angry about anything. Wasn't really thinking about anything. I'd just gotten a kid some popcorn and helped a lady win a big stuffed animal, and this guy brought his kid in. One of my machines was broken. Took his money. He wanted a refund. He wasn't real kind in how he asked, but he was just some hardworking guy with his name on his shirt and had probably worked hard all week to take his kid to the carnival for a good time and there was my machine stealing his money, and so he got a little uppity with me. An hour later, I found myself waiting for him in the parking lot. Gun, knife, baseball bat. I wasn't going to just hurt him, I was going to erase his scent from the earth, in front of his son."

Allie didn't want to hear what happened next. "And?"

"His son laughed. Just about the moment I was gonna hurt him, the boy laughed, and it reminded me of you. Right there, I knew I needed to get away from everybody. I didn't trust me in the world in which I was living. As hard as I'd tried, I knew that the evil in me was still there, still bubbling beneath the surface. And I couldn't just kill myself and be done with it because I had this funny feeling that killing myself wouldn't kill it. It'd just jump from me to someone else. I'd seen it happen. Evil doesn't die with you. It just finds somebody else to latch onto. So I thought, *If I just go away, take it with me, it can't hurt anyone else.* So I shut down the carnival, locked the gate, moved into the mountains, and started my Monastery Period."

"You became a *monk?*"

I laughed. "No."

She exhaled. "Thank goodness."

I laughed. "You worried?"

She shook her head once. "There for a minute . . ."

---

"They let me live in a house alongside the mountain. I tended the garden. Pruned their grapes. They left me alone and I kept quiet. Somewhere in there I found Suzy True on the radio, and Rosco found me. One of the monks was a doctor. He helped me understand my blood sugar issues and got me set up on a monitor and taught me how to give myself shots in the stomach. Feeling healthier than I had in a long time, I built myself a cabin twenty or thirty miles away on a piece of property that shouldered Mount Mitchell. And there I have spent my days quietly, trying not to think about the life I left behind.

"Every six or eight months I'd drive down to check on you. You were mostly alone, and the restaurant looked old and needed a face-lift. I heard that Jake had convinced you to reverse mortgage the restaurant. Then he convinced you to let him give the money to an investor who promised big returns, although he failed to mention the high risk and lost it. Although, knowing what I know now, I have my questions about that money and whether or not it was really lost. At the time, I figured it was none of my business, and as bad as things were for you, you were still better off without me.

"So I returned to my cabin and turned sixty alone. I figured the best of my life had passed me by. Then came sixty-one. Sixty-two. Life was just clicking by, and I thought I'd die in some snowbank surrounded by bad memories. Then about a week ago, I heard this kid scream in the distance. And when I did, I heard you screaming from your bedroom, and in my mind I saw your mom on the floor and . . . the next thing I knew I was running through the snow."

As I had no food in my cabin, we stopped and bought groceries and dog food. Enough to last a day or two. Highway 221 passed under the Blue Ridge Parkway. Afternoon had given way to evening, and that beautiful purplish-blue light hung atop the mountains. The clouds had sunk down in the valleys. Stuffed like cotton balls in the cracks. Up here, on the ridgeline, the night air was cool and clear. I exited the paved road onto gravel and then dirt. We rolled slowly a few miles. When the road turned up, I shifted into four-wheel drive and began crawling toward the cabin. Allie watched the road with curiosity. When we leveled out onto the top of my mountain and rolled to a stop in front of my cabin, I finished my story. "Here we are."

With the temperature in the thirties and Allie wearing a T-shirt, I grabbed her a fleece jacket, a down vest, and a wool scarf and beanie. I lit a fire in the cabin, bathing the inside walls with a warm light that had become a comfort to me over the years. Allie kicked me out of my kitchen and made us some soup and cheese toast. Rosco stretched out on his bear rug, and we ate in front of the fire, peeling off the fleece and down as the inside temperature of the cabin grew cozier.

It was the most at home I'd felt anywhere in a long, long time.

# — 24 —

With Allie asleep, I tucked the blanket around her, but she never moved. Her sleep was peaceful and deep. At nine o'clock I tuned in Suzy, and I listened as the fire crackled and wind pulled on the evergreens outside.

In the early years of my calling Suzy, her producer would answer and then put me on hold like all the other guys. They'd make their way down the line and vet each of us, asking us what we wanted to talk about. What was "on our heart." I never really knew how to answer that. For a year or two I'd wait an hour. Sometimes two or three. Somewhere in the third year, Suzy was vetting the callers and she said, "What's on your heart, soldier?"

I responded honestly. "I'm not sure my heart can answer that."

She sounded surprised. "You don't know what your own heart feels?"

I spoke quickly. "You're assuming my heart can feel anything at all."

From then on, they patched me through.

I dialed the number. My caller ID registered. Suzy answered, and her voice walked three thousand miles through the line. "Jo-Jo! How you doing?"

Not wanting to disturb Allie, I walked outside and closed the door behind me. "Not real sure, Suzy."

She heard the uncertainty in my voice. "You okay?"

"Rough couple of days."

"You want to talk about it?"

"Not really."

She knew me well enough by now not to push it. She changed the subject. "What'd the doctor say?"

"Says I'm fine."

"Which means you haven't been to see him, have you?"

"I saw him."

"But . . . he wants to schedule a procedure and you're stalling."

"I feel fine."

"Except when you don't."

"It's getting better."

"You still eating antacids like chocolate chip cookies?"

"Not as much."

"How many a day?"

"I don't know—"

"Be honest."

"Fifteen. Twenty."

"Joseph, that's not normal. You need to see someone about that."

"Why is it when somebody wants to say something serious to me they always say my whole name?"

"Because we're trying to get your attention, but you're stubborn."

"I'll move it up on the priority list."

"Jo-Jo?"

"Yeah, Suzy."

"Tell me something you remember. Something good."

A memory flashed across my eyes. "I had a friend one time. He had my back. He plucked me out of more than one bad situation. Most mornings, we shared coffee. At a table overlooking the South China Sea. He'd light a cigarette and let it burn on the table between us, keeping the mosquitoes at bay. When we finished we'd leave our empty cups on the table and say, 'Till tomorrow.'"

"Why?"

"Because there was no guarantee of tomorrow. Only the hope of it."

Maybe it was the tone of my voice, but she let it go. "Can I play you something?"

"Sure."

"Anything in particular?"

"Grand Funk Railroad had a pretty good song back then."

"Good night, Joseph."

"Night, Suzy."

"And, Jo-Jo?"

"Yeah?"

"Until next time."

I hung up and smiled as she closed the show with "We're an American Band."

At midnight I found myself leaning against the couch, staring at Allie. For some reason she stirred and her eyes opened. My feet were stretched out toward the fire. She put her arm around me and hooked her heel over my shin. I'd seen vines do the same thing. After a moment she whispered, "I had a dream."

"Yeah? What about?"

"You."

I chuckled. "You sure it wasn't a nightmare?"

She smiled. "You were young. You'd been hurt." She looked up at me. "Wounded." She paused. "Were you?"

I nodded.

She slipped her hand inside my shirt, her palm flat across my chest. "Were you shot?"

"Yes."

"How many times?"

"I don't know really. We were all shot."

"Give me a number."

"A lot."

"That's not a number."

"I lost count."

"Do you have scars?"

I nodded.

"Will you show me?"

"Not sure that's a good idea."

"Show me."

I lifted my shirt. Left shoulder. "Bullet." Right rib cage. Longer scar. "Bayonet." Back. "Shrapnel." Scar along the left side of my neck. "Knife." Right hip. "Smaller bullet." I pulled my shirt back on. "There are others, but my pants are covering them up."

"Did you receive a Purple Heart?"

"Yes."

She touched the places on my body that I'd just shown her. "For all of these?"

"Yes."

"How many?"

"Don't really remember."

"How many?"

"For those of us who spent a lot of time over there, the whole medal thing became somebody else's concern. We just wanted to get home."

"So you got shot more times than awarded medals?"

"Sure. But so did everybody else in my unit. Medals are what people sitting at desks do back home. Trying not to die was what we did up front."

"Where're your medals now?"

"No idea."

"Really?"

"I don't think about them."

"Do you wish you had them?"

"What for?"

"To remember."

"I'd like to forget most of the moments they represent." I was quiet several minutes. "Maybe it's tough to understand, but all that happened over there, it's not like what you see in the movies. It's not like anything you've ever seen. It leaves its mark on a man."

She sank her shoulder beneath mine. Somehow, over the course of the afternoon and evening, any boundaries of personal space had been thrown out the window. If Jake had ever had a tether to Allie's heart, he didn't any longer. She liked being close to me, and I liked her being close. Which caused me some concern regarding tomorrow. I chewed a few antacids and admitted that wasn't my only concern.

"Why do you eat those?" she asked.

"Habit, I suppose."

"When did you start the habit?"

"Back when I was drinking."

"Why?"

"Stomach started bleeding."

"You had an ulcer?"

"Don't know."

"What do you mean you don't know?"

"Never really had it checked out."

She sat up and frowned.

I continued. "I quit drinking and started taking these. Bleeding quit. Problem solved."

She shook her head, leaned against me, and laid her hand flat across my chest again. "Life dealt you a bad hand."

I laughed. "Somebody did."

She reached into her shirt pocket and pulled out the index

card I'd laid on the bedside table the night I found her on the beach. I didn't know she'd kept it. Spilled coffee stained one corner. Water droplets another. The paper was wrinkled and some of the pencil had smeared. She held it between two hands. "You've improved."

"Practice does that."

I'd sketched her sleeping. Hair tucked behind her ear. Sheet and blanket draped across her legs and hips. One foot half covered. She pointed toward the drawing. "When I sleep, does my forehead scrunch like that?"

I nodded.

"No wonder I have so many wrinkles."

We slept in front of the fire. Warm. Close. Rosco sprawled out around us. The wind gently nudged the limbs, which brushed the sides of the cabin.

It was the best sleep I'd ever had.

# — 25 —

I woke before daylight and made coffee. Allie was wrapped up like a cocoon with one arm around Rosco. I poured myself a cup, stepped outside, and breathed in. A minute later, she slid her arms around my waist and pressed her chest to my back and held me. "Morning."

"Hey."

I turned and she wrapped her blanket around us, and we stood in the cold morning air. Two kids. I squinted one eye. "I think you're hugging me."

She strained on her tiptoes, kissed my cheek, and then brushed my face with her palm. Then she kissed the corner of my mouth. Then again, this time closer to the center.

She walked into the kitchen and poured herself a cup of coffee. I leaned against the counter. "You sure you want to do this? We don't have to go. I could go and do some poking ar—"

She sipped and didn't take her eyes off me. Her tone told me nobody was changing her mind. "We're going."

We drove down the mountain, taking 221 into Spruce Pine and then 19E through Burnsville. Three miles east of I-26 I pulled to the side of the road, read the map, and turned right on a dirt road. We drove a mile to a dead end and parked. I grabbed my binoculars out of the console, and we headed west through the trees and up a small ridge. On the ridgeline we turned south, then west again. Below us spread a meadow with a nice one-story ranch on the other side. Several horses walked in and out of the barn. Forty or fifty head of cattle dotted the hillside behind the house. A detached four-car garage lay perpendicular to the house. A late-model sports car of some sort, a Cadillac Escalade, a Ford F-250 diesel with aftermarket tires and bumpers, and a Mercedes SUV. Parallel to the garage sat a taller building with metal roof and open sides. Parked inside sat a mobile home—the expensive kind driven by rock stars or parked on the infields at NASCAR races. And parked along that sat a shiny new red and chrome Peterbilt. The trailer it was pulling had been painted with custom race car designs.

I passed Allie the binoculars. "That look familiar?"

She adjusted the eye relief and shook her head. "Never seen it." She handed me the binoculars. "But I'd like to know who's been paying the insurance."

While we sat hidden in our perch in the trees, a silver Jeep pulled into the drive. A girl, maybe sixteen, hopped out with a school backpack and walked inside, talking on a cell phone. At the rear of the house a woman, maybe early fifties, walked out wearing stretch pants and a workout shirt showing sweat down the back. She was sipping coffee and reading something on her phone. The only car that didn't fit was an older Honda SUV that must have belonged to the house help—a woman who exited the house about this time and refilled the first woman's coffee cup. A few minutes later the young girl, the driver of the Jeep, walked out and sat down with the woman. The two talked while looking out across the pasture at the horses and cows. The sun had come up over the ridgeline in front of them and shone yellow and clean on the grass below.

For an hour things around the house were relatively quiet. Then a Toyota Tacoma with large mud tires and a lift kit pulled into the drive and parked behind the Jeep. A good-looking kid jumped out and let himself inside. He wore athletic shorts and shoes, and he too was sweaty, as if he'd just come from a practice or workout of some sort. A minute later he joined the woman and girl on the back porch. At lunchtime all three left the house, each driving out in a different car. Over the next several hours, Allie napped while I studied the details below me.

The cars began returning at four. The woman first. She was nicely dressed, wore jewelry of some sort, and appeared to have a well-manicured body. Around five the boy and girl returned. The house helper lit the charcoal grill at five thirty and turned on the outdoor porch lights. At six a black Mercedes SUV with blacked-out windows pulled down the long drive and slowly approached the house. It wound around the used car lot in front of the house and paused long enough to remotely open a fifth garage door connected to the house. The door opened, the SUV entered, and the door closed.

At six thirty the house help came out and departed in the Honda. Soon a man appeared on the back porch, carrying a large plate of steaks. He laid the tray of steaks on the table next to the charcoal grill and stood sipping a glass of wine and staring out across the pasture, horses, cows, and meadow.

I handed the binoculars to Allie, who focused. Two seconds later the color drained out of her face and tears broke loose, cascading down her cheeks. She wiped her face on her shirtsleeve, bit her lip, and watched Jake stoke the fire and spread the steaks on the grill.

Five minutes later she handed the binoculars back to me. She spoke with clarity and control. "Jake has no cane . . . and no limp."

We sat there watching as he cooked steaks amid the world his lies had created. I spoke softly. "It's your call."

She stood. "Let's go."

We returned to the truck. I cranked the engine and we drove back down the dirt road to 19E, turned west a half mile, and then right. We ambled down a recently asphalted and nicely serpentined blacktop and finally came to Jake's mailbox, which ironically was a miniature Peterbilt. Allie calmly dialed 911. She was staring at her fingernails like a woman who'd just decided she needed a manicure when the dispatcher answered, "911. What's your emergency?"

"Yes, hi . . . you need to send several officers to . . ." Allie craned her neck and read the number off the box.

The dispatcher responded, "Is there a problem, ma'am?"

Allie tapped her front tooth with a nail. "No, but there's about to be."

The dispatcher was well trained and attempted to keep her on the phone. "What kind of trouble are you experiencing, ma'am?"

Allie smiled. "Well . . . I'm about to kill somebody . . ." And she hung up.

Small-town deputies are often starved for excitement, so I figured that would get their attention. They'd come running. I parked at the front door, and we got out.

I was surprised at Allie's demeanor. She was calm, cool, and totally collected. I thought about ringing the doorbell, but Allie walked right past me, gently pressed the door handle, and let herself in the front door. I followed, not wanting to miss what was about to happen. She wound her way through the foyer toward the sound of dinner being eaten in the kitchen. She turned right at the jumbotron screen and into the light of the kitchen, where Jake sat with his family eating dinner.

All four of them looked with curiosity at Allie, who stood in the center of their kitchen. The woman spoke first. "Can I help you?"

The only person who looked like he'd seen a ghost was Jake, who was as white as a sheet. He wiped his mouth with his napkin and attempted to scoot his chair backward, but I stepped in behind him and put my hand on his shoulder. "Sit tight, Houdini."

Allie pulled up a chair at the table. Both the kids to her right. The woman across from her. Jake on her left. She folded her hands on the table. Even her breathing was calm. Her right hand was spinning the wedding band on her left. An empty vase sat in the middle of the table. She slid it slightly off to the side giving her a clear view of the woman. She looked at the woman several seconds. "Do you know who I am?"

"No."

I had a feeling she did, but that would come soon enough. Allie looked to both the kids. "You two have any idea?"

They shook their heads. I actually believed them.

Allie never looked at Jake. She was watching the eyes of the other three. She said, "Jake, why don't you tell them?"

He was about to say something like "I don't—" but I patted his shoulder and encouraged him otherwise. He turned to the woman. "Kids, this is Allie."

When he stopped talking, I prompted him. "And she's . . . ?"

The pain I was creating in his neck convinced him to keep talking. "She's my . . . my other wife."

The children looked confused.

It was obvious that the woman was in on whatever Jake had cooked up, as she was not the least bit shaken by Jake's words. He was about to turn toward me to exert his authority, but I cranked down on his left ear, pinning it between the end of his steak knife and my thumb. He tried to sip his wine, but his hand was shaking so he set his glass down. "She's, um . . . she and I are married."

The boy looked at his mom. "Mom, what's he talking about?"

The woman wiped her mouth on her napkin. Cool as a cucumber. "Just nonsense. I don't know who these people are."

Allie reached across and slapped the woman as hard as she could across the face, knocking her out of her chair. The boy stood, but at my invitation quickly sat back down. The girl started crying. From the driveway I heard several car doors slam. Before the police walked in, Allie turned to Jake. While she had captured his attention with the stiletto finger jabbing him in his face, she grabbed the woman's steak knife and drove it down through Jake's right hand, pinning it to the table. That seemed to get everyone's attention. When the woman climbed back up to the table, Allie lifted the vase and broke it against the woman's jaw.

AN HOUR LATER, JAKE sat silently cuffed in an ambulance while medics tended to his hand. The look on his face suggested there were a million other places he'd rather be. His first wife, Sylvia—of twenty-four years—also sat cuffed and sitting not-so-quietly in a patrol car in the driveway. She was doing a pretty good job of exercising her first amendment right. Unfortunately, Allie also sat cuffed in yet a third vehicle. The sheriff listened to my story with a raised eyebrow. When I finished, he shook his head. "I appreciate your trouble, I really do, but you can't just go around breaking into people's houses and stabbing them in the hand."

I gave him the number at First General and told him Dawson Baker would confirm and document everything I said. As would local law enforcement. He still wasn't buying it. The sheriff added, "Not to mention that we have her on record as stating she intended to kill someone."

I dialed a number, and Bobby answered. I asked, "You got a minute?"

"For you? Yes."

I explained our predicament. Bobby said, "Put him on."

I tapped the sheriff on the shoulder. "Excuse me, Sheriff." I offered the phone. "This is Chairman of the Joint Chiefs, Senator Bobby Brooks. He'd like to speak with you."

The sheriff stuck the phone to his ear and spoke with no small disbelief. "Yeah, this is Sheriff T. Wayne Higginbotham. To whom do I have the pleasure of—"

The sheriff was quiet several seconds while the color drained out of his face. When he responded, he said, "Well, sir, I'd be negligent if I didn't at least hold her. I mean, at a minimum, we've got assault with a deadly weapon, and we do have her on record as having threatened to kill someone . . ." Slowly, disbelief gave way to something else. His eyes began to grow large and round and his tone of voice changed. Pretty soon he was nodding in agreement. "Uh-huh . . . uh, yes, sir . . . Well . . . yes, sir. Her threatening him in that manner did definitely get our attention." Another laugh. "Yes, sir, I imagine we set a few land speed records getting here." He paused. "No, sir, I hadn't thought of it that way." More seconds passed. More nodding. Followed by a chuckle. "Well . . . when you put it that way, no, sir, I don't in fact see how anyone could be arrested for assaulting someone who's already dead." At this point, he belly-laughed. "I understand . . . No problem, sir. No, I appreciate that, but I don't think it's necessary. If I need you, I'll contact your office. It's my honor and privilege . . . Yes, sir . . . I will, sir. You have a good night, sir. And you keep up the good—"

Bobby must have hung up. The sheriff closed the phone. "That's a new one." He lifted Allie gently from the back seat of his patrol car and unlocked the handcuffs, freeing her wrists. "How do you know him?"

Allie rubbed her wrists and opened her mouth, but I answered for her. "That's a longer story than this one."

He turned his attention to Allie and held the phone aloft. "Can I reach you at this number?"

Allie smiled. "Yes, sir."

He handed me the phone but spoke while looking at Jake. "If you've been married to him ten years, and he did what you're saying he did . . . I 'magine he deserved a lot more than just a steak knife through the hand." He walked off shaking his head and talking to himself. "You can't technically assault someone who's legally dead."

Before Allie climbed into my truck, she took a long look around. Taking in the enormity and prosperity of what had been Jake's life. If she had words, she didn't speak them. We drove slowly to the cabin. Jake's sand castle was about to come crumbling down and those kids were about to lose their mom and dad. Allie had already lost a husband. And for what? Just money. Stuff. It was pathetic, and so was Jake Gibson. Prison would teach him that soon enough.

Allie fell asleep in the truck. When we parked at the cabin, she said, "Think I'll get some sleep." I got her settled, but when I spread a second blanket across her legs and toes, she said, "All the times he was gone from me, he was here with this family . . . two kids who had no idea. And there I was back home, hurting, thinking what a lousy wife I am. I was never anything to him other than a payday. What kind of man does that? And why me?"

The next morning I woke her with a breakfast of eggs, toast, jelly, hot coffee. She didn't eat much, but she appreciated the gesture. Hovering over her coffee, she stared into the coals and said, "You think he'll go to jail?"

"Just as soon as they sew up the hole in his hand."

She looked out across the mountains. "I thought about driving it through his heart, but then I remembered he didn't have one." She leaned against the sofa and wiped her face with both hands. "I didn't see this coming. And I have no idea what to do now." She was quiet several minutes. "Does this mean I'm not married?"

"I think it means you never were. At least . . . not to Jake."

I poured her a hot cup of coffee and sat opposite her. Just being present without feeling the need to talk or try to fix everything. After breakfast she closed her eyes. "You mind if I rest awhile?"

ALLIE SLEPT THE BETTER part of three days. She'd wake, eat, drink something, sit by the fire, then climb back into bed. At night she slept deeply, fourteen hours at a stretch, her eyes rolling behind her eyelids. I recognized, maybe for the first time, how tired she was. Not just sleepy, but bone- and soul-tired. She'd been holding both ends together so long, trying to recover from betrayals and rejections. Treading water while tied to a cement block.

Rosco and I never ventured far from the cabin. When we did, we left the door open so she'd know we were close. On the third day she woke, rubbed her eyes, and found me looking at her. She said, "How long have I been sleeping?"

"Better part of three days."

"I could sleep a week."

"I have a request."

"Okay."

"Will you let me show you something? It's a bit of a drive."

"What is it?"

"It's better if I show you."

# — 26 —

I packed knowing I wouldn't be back for a while, and the three of us drove out of the mountains. When we reached Atlanta I turned west on I-20, then took Highway 431 north out of Dothan, Alabama toward Abbeville, where we turned west on Highway 10 and south at the flashing light in Clopton. Rosco had sprawled across the center console, slobbering on Allie's thigh and expressing his incessant need to be literally in the middle of everything all the time. The cup holder next to me held three of Gabby's crayons. I remembered watching her gently peel the paper back and sharpen each. Below my tachometer I'd taped a small picture she'd drawn of a stick-figure man next to a stick-figure dog. The picture tugged at me.

When the hard road turned to dirt, we drove a mile to a pecan grove and stopped at a red gate. Somebody had stolen the sign. I unlocked the gate, and we pulled through the pines down a dirt road and up onto a small rise to an open field. Standing in the center of the field was a large metal-roofed building with no walls and a fifty-foot ceiling at its apex. Maybe a square block in size. Buildings like this were originally constructed to house outdoor rodeo venues.

Allie's eyes had grown large as Oreo cookies. The roof protected most every kind of carnival ride known to man: merry-go-round, bumper cars, go-karts. Those rides too tall to fit inside the building surrounded it. She pointed at my carnival ghost town. "This is yours?"

"Kind of a neat place when it's all lit up at night. Provided you don't mind bright flashing lights."

"How long has it been here?"

"Twenty years or more."

"How long's it been like this?"

"What, you mean dilapidated?"

She laughed. "Yes."

"I locked the gate more than a decade ago and haven't been back since. I'm kind of surprised it's still here."

"Why'd you put it so far out here in the sticks?"

"I didn't initially build it to draw a crowd. I was just giving my hands something to do while my mind spun itself. One bolt led to another. Before long I had a merry-go-round. Then a shooting range. Baseball toss. Bowling lanes. A dunk tank. Whack-a-mole. Guessing people's weights. The power meter thing where you see how hard you can swing an ax like Paul Bunyan. Snow cones. Cotton candy. Popcorn. Candied apples. Photo booth. Pony rides. Horse shoe toss. I'd dress up like a clown and take pictures with people."

Allie laughed. "Did you really dress up like a clown?"

"I wanted an old-fashioned carnival. But what I learned was that when you turn on a light at night, people want to see what you're doing. Turn on ten or twenty thousand and they really get curious. Add carnival music and . . . Most nights I operated at capacity. We even had amateur rodeo night once a month."

I led her through the maze of rides toward the only enclosed section of the building, the restaurant. It was nothing fancy. Function over form in every way. Picnic tables with enough seating for about two hundred. A cafeteria-style buffet line. Behind the counter was the kitchen. I wound through the line and back into the industrial-sized, commercial-grade kitchen. A stainless-steel ghost town.

"We used to serve several hundred a night. Sometimes a thousand." I pointed as I talked. "Fryers. Griddles. Grills. Exhaust fans. Refrigerators. Freezers. Ice makers." Cobwebs had spread across the corners.

She surveyed the expanse of once-shiny machines. "How many people did you employ?"

"In our heyday about sixty, but that included folks making balloons, people in dunk tanks, pony walkers, folks parking cars . . ."

She walked through the kitchen, her fingers gently rolling through the dust along the tops of doors and handles. "We never had equipment this nice at the Tornado."

Rosco was sniffing behind a fryer, his tail rhythmically thumping the sides.

"I have a proposition for you."

She slid her hands into her jeans. "Okay."

"Let me help you. I'll stick around, we'll put the Tornado back the way she was when we were kids. Once it's up and running, if you want to run it, you can. If not, sell it and make a little money."

She raised an eyebrow. "You'd do that?"

"If you let me."

"Why?"

"Because you need a break." I waved my hands across the kitchen. "Some of it might need a little work to get it going again, but it's yours if you want it."

She pushed her hair out of her face and leaned against a griddle. "I appreciate the offer, but the Vacuum needs more than a kitchen to get her up and running."

"Like what?"

"Wood rot repair, to start with. Walls. Floors. The roof is zinc, but it needs a few sheets. The whole thing needs to be replumbed. Rewired. And, yes, it needs a kitchen."

"What happened to the last one?"

"Sold it to pay the property taxes." She crossed her arms again. "But all of that work does nothing to pay down the debt."

"How much do you owe?"

She shrugged. "I try not to think about it."

"Ballpark."

"400K plus."

"Any second mortgages? Unpaid taxes? Anything else?"

"Nope. That's pretty much it." She summed it up. "My father used the restaurant as collateral and accumulated debt my mother could never climb out of. I paid that off, made a little money, and then the whole Bobby thing happened. His rehab wasn't cheap.

Now I get sucker-punched by Jake. Truth is, I love everything about that place, but it does not love me."

"You want to make another go of it?"

She laughed. "Did you not hear anything I just said?"

"I have some money."

She chuckled. "How much?"

I shrugged. "I told you I was good at the poop business."

"I'm being serious."

"I've got more than enough to help you get back on your feet."

"And what if, after all your best intentions and all your hard work, the restaurant tanks and you lose it all?"

"What am I going to do with it?"

"I don't know. Travel?"

"I've done that."

She did not look convinced.

"Allie, I'm just offering you a chance. A fresh start. If you want it."

She pointed out toward all the rides. "What about all that stuff?"

"That's yours too, if you want it."

"Where will you be in all of this?"

"I'm pretty handy with a wrench."

"What about your cabin?"

"It's not going anywhere."

She let out a deep breath. "Jo-Jo, I'm pretty fragile right now. Starting with my dad, every man I've ever trusted has . . . not proven trustworthy. They've lied to me, stolen from me . . ."

"I have only lied to you once."

She nodded. "Once was enough." She spoke as much to herself as to me. "I'm not sure my heart can survive . . . another."

"And I won't steal from you."

When her eyes found mine, they were looking decades behind us. "You would do all this . . . even after . . . ?"

"After what?"

She looked away. "Everything that's happened."

I walked her to the merry-go-round, dusted off two horses frozen in full gallop, and we sat, she leaning her forehead against the brass pole, looking at me. I studied the quiet world around us, frozen in time, just waiting for someone to throw the switch and jump this place back to life again.

"You and me, we're a lot like this place," I said.

"What, old and decrepit?"

We laughed. "Maybe that too." We were growing comfortable around each other. I pointed. "I used to sit over there at night, close my eyes and just listen to the laughter. Watch the smiles on the kids' faces."

We climbed off the horses and walked between the booths and rides.

"This was never intended to be this way. It was designed for something else. Something better. But when I killed the power, it froze. Stuck here in time. And what was once alive and warm became dead and cold to the touch. Like me. Or at least parts of me." I shook my head. "So I locked the gate and drove away.

"Now I'm trying to figure out how *not* to go back to my cabin and end up like one of these horses." I looked at Allie. "A long time ago, when you and I knew laughter and love and we were full of hope and dreams, something pulled the plug on us. Ever since, we've been stuck in this cold, dusty, frozen place. Just waiting. But for what? I'm sixty-two. I live alone, don't hear as well as I used to, can't live without insulin, I have bad dreams, there's stuff in my life I can't begin to talk about. I'm not the man I'd hoped to be. But these last few days, I have enjoyed being with you. Seeing your strength and your frailty."

I grabbed her hand, and we sat on a picnic table staring at the crazy world I'd created and then abandoned. "I'm feeling something I haven't felt in a long time. There's a part of me that feels like I don't deserve it. That if you really knew me, if you could see the pictures I see with my eyes, you'd want nothing to do with me. But if that horse back there could talk, and I walked up and asked him, 'Mr. Horse, what can I do for you?' he'd say, 'Old man, hop on and let me take you for a ride.'" I paused and rubbed my hands together. "There are a thousand reasons not to, but I think we should throw the switch one last time and then listen for the laughter."

She slid her hand in mine and laid her head on my shoulder. "Life's not been easy, has it?"

I wrapped my arm around her shoulder. "No. It has not."

"Make me one promise."

"Okay."

"Be truthful with me. Even with the stuff that hurts."

"Sometimes I don't have words for the stuff I see, but with the words I do have, I won't ever lie to you."

She kissed my cheek. "That's good enough."

WE LOCKED THE GATE behind us and pointed the nose to Cape San Blas. Three hours due south. We had just pulled off Highway 231 onto I-10 east when my phone rang. It was my doctor's office, calling to tell me I'd missed my appointment.

I sent it to voicemail.

A few minutes later my phone rang again. I punched the mute button, again sending it to voicemail. But when it rang a third time, I checked the caller ID. It was a Mississippi area code. I flipped it open. "Hello?"

The accent was thick. "Mr. Jo-Jo?"

"Catalina?"

She was whispering. "Mr. Jo-Jo, I don't know who to call. We are in a bad way."

"What happened?"

"Men were waiting for us."

"Are you okay?"

"Yes."

"The kids?"

"Scared but good." She paused. "My brother . . ." I heard some-one groaning in the background. "He's not too good."

"Where are you?"

"Outside New Orleans."

"Do you have transportation?"

"No."

I made an illegal U-turn in the median. "Can you stay safe for a few hours?"

"I think so. We are hiding behind a rest area on the 10 interstate."

"Do you know the name of the closest town?"

She whispered something to someone next to her, then returned to me. "Gulfport."

"I'm about five hours from you. Sit tight. How many are you?"

"Me, the kids, my brother, and three other men. My cousins."

"Are you hungry?"

"Yes."

"Does your brother need a doctor?"

"He's in and out of consciousness. I don't know."

"Is he bleeding?"

"Not anymore. I stitched him up. But his ribs are badly bruised. He's having trouble taking a deep breath. And one eye is closed."

"Sit tight. I'll call you when I get close."

"Mr. Jo-Jo?"

"Yes."

"Thank you."

# — 27 —

At nine p.m. we crossed into Gulfport. Allie leaned over and touched my arm. "We should pick up some food. The kids'll be hungry."

We pulled into a small twenty-four-hour grocery store and bought groceries and some pain medicine along with some first-aid items, a pillow, a few blankets, and an inflatable pool raft long enough for a man to lie on. At the checkout counter, I said, "Chocolate. The kids like chocolate."

Finding the rest area wasn't difficult. We pulled in and parked, and before I could call Catalina on the phone, she had stepped out of the shadows and was bringing the kids to us. When they saw me, they ran and jumped into my arms. Gabriella was crying. Diego clung to my leg. I carried them both to the truck while Allie helped Catalina.

Manuel was a different story. They'd worked him over pretty

good. He was lying on the ground, and three men sat alongside him. One of them was my friend Javier. I knelt and held Manuel's hand. "Manuel?"

He opened his eye and tried to smile. "El Gato."

The four of us lifted him. He was a thick, muscled man and he was in a lot of pain. It took all of us to get him to the bed of my truck.

He patted my hand. "Gracias, señor."

The men climbed into the truck to sit with Manuel. "If you need anything, tap the window."

I drove back roads and avoided the interstate as much as possible. It took longer, but I figured a 45-mph wind would be gentler than a 75-mph wind. While we drove, the men in back blew up the raft, rolled Manuel onto it and covered him with a blanket. Up front, Catalina relayed the story. They'd made it to a trailer park near Hattiesburg, Mississippi. They'd only been there a few days when a truck arrived in the middle of the night and three men got out. They pulled Manuel out of the trailer and worked him over with baseball bats. Wanting to make an example.

We pulled into Cape San Blas well after midnight. Manuel had slept most of the way, which was good, but he'd stiffened up more, so moving him was not fun. We got him inside Allie's cottage and into bed. Most every square inch of his body was bruised and swollen.

Allie called a doctor, then she helped Catalina get Gabby and Diego cleaned up and tucked in alongside each other in the small second bedroom. They were asleep before she pulled the covers up.

When the doctor, a woman in her forties, arrived, she examined Manuel and started IV fluids that included a broad spectrum antibiotic and enough pain medicine to knock out a horse. Within minutes he was sleeping soundly. Breathing better. She left us with two prescriptions. One if the pain was bad. The other if the pain was real bad.

"I can only do so much here," she told us. "It's been over twelve hours since the beating. If he had any substantial internal bleeding, he'd be dead by now. I can't guarantee you that he's out of the woods, but he's strong and the bruise pattern suggests his ribs did what they were intended to do. The next twenty-four hours will tell you a lot."

DAYLIGHT BROUGHT THE SMELL of coffee and somebody cooking breakfast. I walked inside to find Catalina teaching Allie how to make tortillas. Evidently they'd already been to the store. Allie poured me a cup of coffee, and I sat as Catalina produced a breakfast fit for a king.

"She really knows her way around a kitchen," Allie said.

I crammed scrambled eggs into a tortilla and smothered it in Catalina's homemade salsa. I spoke around a smile. "Wait till you taste her fajitas."

We spent the day lying low and tending to Manuel, who slept peacefully. The doctor returned late in the afternoon and was not displeased with his condition. She also examined the three amigos—Javier, Peter, and Victor. Despite their silence, they had not escaped the bullets and the bat. She put ten stitches in

Peter's shoulder, where she'd extracted a piece of bullet shrapnel he'd not told us about. She also put seven stitches in the back of Victor's head, while confirming there was a good chance he had suffered a concussion.

Feeling helpless on the second day, I disappeared for a few hours and drove to Port St. Joe and the main branch of Florida First Bank. I sat down with the branch manager, explained what I wanted to do, and he got on the phone with the regional manager. When I returned, Allie asked, "Where you been?"

A strange emotion surfaced. I had been missed, and I liked it. "Trying to help."

She slid her hand in mine. She'd gotten more touchy-feely in the last few days, and I liked that too.

Manuel continued to improve. On the third day he sat up, and Catalina fed him some soup she'd made. Allie and I had introduced the kids to the addictive practice of looking for sharks' teeth, and they had already half filled a Mason jar.

The two of us took a tour of the restaurant, making a list of what needed doing. And a lot needed doing. Walking through the dining room, where a roof leak had left a puddle on the floor, Allie tucked her arm inside mine. "More than you bargained for?"

"She's in pretty bad shape."

The three amigos were used to working sunup to sundown, and they needed an activity. Their English was not as good as Catalina's, but they could communicate. They followed us, watching. Listening. At one point I discovered Victor looking at the electrical panel. "Can you do electrical work?" I asked.

He nodded matter-of-factly.

"What else can you do?"

He shrugged. "What you need done?"

Allie and I walked him through and around the restaurant. He asked, "You have tools?"

"No."

This did not seem to faze him. He spoke rapidly in Spanish to Javier and Peter. The three nodded. "Okay."

"Okay, what?" I asked.

He waved his hand across the restaurant. "We fix."

"The whole thing?"

He nodded. Again, matter-of-factly. Catalina pushed open the kitchen door of the restaurant then and found us standing in the dining room talking about roofs and plumbing and all things electrical. She explained, "All three have worked construction. Peter has built houses. Victor can wire most anything. Javier is good with wood and plumbing."

Allie tugged on my shirtsleeve. "We'd better check with the bank before we start work. What if we can't work out a deal?"

I turned to the men. "If I drive you to a store, a big one with lots of tools and lumber, do you know what you need in order to get started?"

They nodded and Peter spoke for them. "Sí, señor."

Allie and I drove them to the Home Depot outside of Tallahassee. Each of us grabbed a cart. You can learn a lot about a man by how he values his tools and why he buys the equipment he buys. You can also learn whether or not he knows how to use them. Three hours later we had filled eight carts, placed an order for several thousand board feet of pressure-treated wood, and spent almost eight thousand dollars. Allie looked like a ghost. The store manager was beaming. Knowing we'd never fit all this in my truck, I struck a deal with him on a high-wall, dual-axle trailer. I also set up an account that would allow the men to buy what they needed without my being present.

When we returned, Manuel was sitting at the kitchen table looking at the kids' beach pickings for the day, which included twenty-seven sharks' teeth. As the moon rose above us, Peter and Victor and Javier worked into the night, setting up a staging area for equipment in the open space below the restaurant, where guys working in the kitchen used to wash the fryers.

Allie pulled me aside. "You really think they can do what they've said they can do?"

I smiled. "I guess we're about to find out."

# — 28 —

The sound of demolition woke us the next morning. Hammers, reciprocating saws, sledgehammers—it didn't take them long to make a giant mess. Manuel leaned on me and we walked slowly to the restaurant. Knowing they needed a dry place to work, his three cousins started on the roof.

Over the course of the week, hiring the three of them proved to be one of the wiser choices I'd ever made. By Friday they had gutted every piece of rotten wood and repaired the roof with new sheets of zinc. They worked from daylight to sundown, only stopping a few minutes for lunch. And they played music from their stereo that made everyone want to smile and dance. Including me.

By the end of the week, against our petitions, Manuel was slowly swinging a hammer alongside them. Catalina and Allie made a hundred trips to the Dumpster, and I paid cash for a used three-quarter-ton long-bed Chevrolet that allowed the three amigos to get what they needed when they needed it. We were in full-blown construction mode.

THE FAMILY, AS I'D begun calling Catalina, Gabriella, Diego, Peter, Victor, Javier, and Manuel, fixed us dinner on the porch. The place was swept and clean, but walls were missing. Wiring exposed. Pipes disconnected. They spread out a feast unlike anything I'd seen. It gave a whole new meaning to the word *fajitas*. Some of the best food I'd ever had. And then Catalina fried sopapillas. I forced myself to stop at eight.

Two weeks in, the three mess-makers, as Catalina referred to them, had finished the kitchen renovation. They'd rewired, replumbed, and were ready for inspection, proving that they obviously knew more about commercial construction than I did. I called the city inspector, and he made us correct a few things and then gave his approval and told me what licenses I'd failed to apply for. He left me with some pretty clear instructions about how to function as my own general contractor. Turns out he grew up eating at the Blue Tornado and was eager to see her reopen. I made a mental note to buy dinner for him and his family when we reopened.

Manuel recovered enough to travel with me to Clopton to start bringing back pieces of kitchen equipment, using both trucks and the trailer. Allie worked tirelessly alongside us. The first day we loaded the kitchen appliances, cookware, benches, and tables. Over the next couple days as the others worked to retrofit the new kitchen, Manuel and I made two more trips. On the second trip, as we were packing up, he pointed to the carnival rides.

"What do you plan to do with all this?" he asked.

"No idea."

"You want to bring it to the island?"

"That's a little bit bigger project than just renovating a restaurant. Can you do that?"

He nodded. "But do you have a place to put it?"

"I don't, but Allie does."

Allie watched the transformation with wide eyes and old tears. We would walk the beach, and each day, with each fallen tear, more of the hardship of her life washed away.

Rosco had taken to island life just fine. He was always at my heels except come time to walk the beach. As Allie and I started walking through the dunes, he'd tear off through the sand and head north up the coastline. Well after dark, when it came time to go to bed, he'd reappear and hop up on Gabby's bed.

I'd return to my cottage alone and sit on the porch, listen to Suzy, where I'd stare out at the stars until after midnight. And sometimes sunup.

# — 29 —

By the beginning of April, the men had returned the Blue Tornado to her prior glory. Better even. Either repaired or replaced, every square inch of the restaurant had been touched by their fingers. Rather than paint, they'd put a high-gloss finish on much of the wood. It not only protected it, but gave every room a warm, golden glow. The inspector approved of their work and even applauded it—asking if he could recommend them elsewhere on the island.

We turned on all the breakers and every light came alive. The guys had installed a new LED spotlight above the actual Blue Tornado vacuum, still protected in its glass case. When she saw it, Allie cried.

A week later she began accepting deliveries from local fishermen vying to become her primary seafood supplier. In the meantime, she and Catalina worked in the kitchen, cooking up new and old recipes.

One day about lunchtime I followed my nose to the kitchen, where the two of them were in full-on food-production mode. Julia Child would have been proud. The kitchen was a sea of bright lights, loud Spanish flamenco music, stainless steel, and brilliant color. Fryers. Grills. Flank stank. Beans. Peppers. Handmade tortillas. Rice. Guacamole. Onions. Then there was the seafood. Shrimp. Prawns. White fish. Scallops. Blackened. Fried. I ate three plates.

To put me completely out of my misery, Catalina prepared sopapillas and covered them with honey and powdered sugar. I pushed back from the plate on the precipice of a sugar-carb crash. I needed a nap.

The two of them watched me literally scrape the last flake of doughnut off my plate and spin it in honey residue. Allie asked, "Good?"

I shook my head.

Catalina put her hands on her hips. "No?"

"Not even in the same ballpark."

She pointed. Angry. "Get out of my kitchen."

"*Good* is a greasy diner cheeseburger. Maybe a milk shake with whipped cream. A hot dog at a ball game. This . . ." I waved my hand across the table. "This is what God eats for dinner."

She smiled and used the apron to wipe the sweat and flour off her forehead. "Okay, you can stay."

She started clearing the table and I stood. "I got this. Dishes are my specialty. Ask Allie."

I rolled up my sleeves and pushed past the two women to reach the sink of sudsy water, but Catalina tried to bump me out of the way. "In Mexico, men do not work in the kitchen."

I smiled and took hold of the sprayer. "News flash. I am not Mexican." And then I soaked both of them with the sprayer.

DIEGO AND GABRIELLA WERE starting to find a rhythm of their own. Like two other kids I once knew, they were seldom far from the beach. We spent a lot of time searching the shoreline for sharks' teeth. For the first time in our short relationship, Catalina grew tight-lipped and tense. She had given me a few looks, something she wanted to say but didn't, and I wondered if I'd offended her. I asked Allie, "I do something?"

We watched the kids run up and down the shoreline chasing Rosco, splashing in and out of the waves. Catalina didn't take her eyes off them.

"Can they swim?" Allie asked me.

"I don't know."

"Well, if you were their father, and they were in the water and couldn't swim, would you be worried?"

Sometimes it's the little things.

"Catalina?" I hollered.

She spoke without turning. "Sí?"

Whenever she was lost in thought, she'd unknowingly answer in Spanish.

"Okay with you if I teach the kids to swim?"

She looked worried. "What about the sharks?"

In the short time we'd been at the Cape, we had nearly filled a quart-size Mason jar with sharks' teeth. I laughed. "You know the teeth that we find on the beach are very old."

"How do you know?"

"When the shark first loses a tooth, it's white in color. It only turns black after it's been in the water a long time."

She looked doubtful. "How long a time?"

"About ten thousand years."

Her eyes narrowed. "So the sharks are . . . ?"

"Dead. Some folks believe those teeth we find are a million years old."

Her face relaxed. "Dead sharks are better than live sharks."

"So can I teach them to swim?"

She took off her apron. "Only if you teach me too."

While Diego took to the water like a fish, swimming within minutes, Gabriella took some coaxing. Allie and I stood waist deep, ten yards apart. The cool thing about teaching somebody to swim in the ocean is that they can always put their feet down—provided you don't venture too far from shore. Gabby walked between Allie and me, moving her arms as if she were swimming, but we could not get her to launch her feet off the ground. She was making her way from Allie to me, swim-walking, when a wave rolled over her head. When the wave cleared, she screamed, and Rosco came running. He crashed into the waves and swam straight toward her. He circled her twice, let her pet his head, and, when he heard her giggling, returned to the beach. Apparently inspired by Rosco, Gabby picked her feet up and swam toward me, reaching me in a few strokes and then treading water without touching bottom. It was clear to me that the bond between the kids—especially Gabby—and the dog had grown close.

That night I realized just how close. The four honeymoon

cottages along the beach had become our homes. Allie lived in the first. Manuel, Javier, Peter, and Victor in the second. Catalina and the kids in the third. And I lived in the fourth. And while most would say that Rosco was my dog, I didn't command where he spent the night. He came and went as he wished. For the last several weeks he had been staying with the hands that rubbed his tummy the most and fed him scraps from every meal.

At night, before I went to sleep, I'd walk by Catalina's cottage and check on the kids. I'd find Rosco curled up between them, Gabby's arm draped across his stomach. His tail would slap the bed as he'd look up at me, making no effort whatsoever to get up. I would whisper, "Stay," and he'd lay his head back down.

PROGRESS ON THE TORNADO continued apace, and the kids and Catalina were happy as clams, but something seemed to be troubling Allie. I had a feeling I'd done something wrong, but I didn't know what. Some of the touchy-feely tenderness was missing. At night after work, dinner, and a walk on the beach, I'd walk Catalina and the kids to their cottage, then I'd meet Allie at her cottage. She called it our porch time. Or knee time. Where we sat close enough for our knees to touch. She'd drink wine, I'd drink tea or Sprite, and we'd prop our feet on the railing and listen to the ocean and watch the moon shimmer on the water.

The attire was casual. I'd show up in jeans or shorts or whatever I'd been working in that day, and she'd meet me after a shower, smelling great, wearing a nightgown or a pair of pajamas. Legs freshly shaven. And while I can be a bit slow on the uptake when it comes to all things feminine, I did notice that the gowns and pajamas were getting shorter. Looser. Revealing more. I began to grow a little nervous.

One morning at daylight, I woke to find Allie sitting next to my bed. She was staring at me, and her coffee cup was empty. Her lips were pursed and one eyebrow hung lower than the other. My mother used to give me that same look when I was in trouble. I sat up. "What'd I do?"

"Why didn't you tell me?"

"Tell you what?"

"About the dreams."

"What dreams?"

"Your dreams."

"I don't have dreams."

"I've been watching you sleep the last few nights, and, yes . . . you do."

"Why've you been doing that?"

"To give Catalina a rest. She's been sleeping on your front porch the last month or so."

"Those aren't dreams."

"What do you mean?"

"Dreams are made up. Mine are memories."

"Same difference."

"Not if you're me."

"Catalina told me about a dream you had in Manuel's trailer."

"Yeah . . ." I scratched my head. "I'm still sorry about that."

"What can we do about them?"

"I've been asking myself that question a long time."

"Catalina says that night at her place, Rosco hopped on the bed, started licking your face and whining. He woke you up. Stopped the dream. Or memory. And you went back to sleep. She said he did that a couple times throughout the night."

I nodded. "That's how we met."

She waited.

"I was up on the mountain and had dug out a hole beneath the trees. A place to sleep. Rosco found me. He'd wake me up during the nights. Stop the memories."

"Based on what I've seen the last couple of nights, you need something or someone next to you." She pointed at me, my clothes on the floor, and the fact that while I started out sleeping in clothes, I always ended up naked and in a wrestling match with my sheets.

"It helps."

"Is this why you haven't stayed with me?"

"I don't want you to be afraid of me."

She let out a breath. "I was starting to think I was tainted."

"Tainted?"

She shrugged. "Or you didn't find my lace pajamas attractive." She pushed the hair out of her face. "Like maybe I'm too old for you. Too wrinkly. Too saggy. And . . ." She glanced next door to Catalina's cottage.

I laughed, sat on the edge of the bed, and covered myself with the sheet. "Allie . . . the reason I sleep alone has nothing to do with you and everything to do with me. And while I think Catalina is beautiful, she doesn't hold my heart in her hands."

"So I'm not too old for you?"

"Um . . . no."

"And you still find me somewhat attractive?"

"Um . . . yes."

She smiled and raised an eyebrow. "You telling the truth?"

"Yes."

"How about you let me lift this sheet off you, and we'll see if you're telling the truth."

I slid my hand beneath hers. "Allie-girl, you were once the most beautiful girl I'd ever seen. But who you were then can't hold a candle to who you are now."

She blushed. "Been a long time since you called me that."

"You don't mind?"

"I don't mind." Another raised eyebrow. "Can I borrow your sheet? . . . My car just hit a water buffalo and . . ."

My shorts lay in one corner. My underwear had spilled off the bed. "Not right this minute."

She stood and walked to the door, allowing me a close-up view of those same enticing short, silky, lacy pajamas. "Your secret's safe with me. I had to cover you up twice last night."

I shook my head.

She glanced over her shoulder. "And you're blushing."

# — 30 —

That afternoon found me staring down at Mom's grave. Arms crossed. A wrinkle between my eyes. Mom had never remarried. Said the first time just hurt too much. After Bobby and I left, she lived alone, doing laundry at night and cleaning rental houses during the day. Then Bobby returned, but he melted down soon after. She and Allie shipped him off to rehab, where he spent the better part of five years off and on. Once he sobered up, they divorced and he ran for state legislature. He made a name for himself and eventually ran for US Senate and moved to Virginia, keeping a condo in West Palm Beach.

I, meanwhile, was trying to outrun my memories and bouncing between a dozen different places. Cape San Blas was not one of them. So Mom lived the last decade of her life in relative isolation. Allie would check on her from time to time, but Allie was a painful reminder. One day Mom had a stroke pumping gas. She was dead before she hit the ground.

Not knowing how to find me, Bobby delayed the funeral a few days. He used the FBI to track me down. I showed up and we buried her, but I never said a single word to Bobby nor he to me. He knew better than to open his mouth, because the second he did I was going to shut it.

Somewhere on planet Earth, if he was still alive, my dad would have been sixty then. I hadn't seen him since the broken-plate day. But that didn't mean time had softened my feelings. If I was good at one thing, it was hate. We lowered Mom's coffin, threw some dirt on top, and I climbed into a rental car to make my way home.

I leaned against Mom's headstone, peeled open a new roll of antacids, and popped four into my mouth. Strange how I'd grown to like the chalky, minty taste. Since leaving North Carolina, the pain in my chest had become more constant. Sharper.

The breeze pushed the leaves along the grass and tugged at the moss hanging in the scrub oaks above Rosco and me. I scratched behind his ear and he rolled onto his back, paws in the air. Rubbing his tummy, I spoke aloud to the cold, granite memory of my mother.

"Strange how one man's absence can leave such carnage in its wake." The dull pain in my chest had graduated toward knifing. And if I'm being honest, even shortness of breath. I massaged the muscle just below my collarbone, then my shoulder, but it didn't help. As if I needed another reminder, my phone rang. Caller ID registered my doctor's office, calling to reschedule my missed appointment. I pressed Decline and sent them to voicemail for a third time.

White cottony clouds drifted silently above. I spoke again, this time to Rosco, who didn't care what I said as long as I kept rubbing. "I can't remember any of my dreams coming true." He groaned in agreement and closed his eyes. "Now I open up and try to love, and find nothing but dead chunks of flesh and shrapnel where my heart used to be."

I ran my fingers through the carved letters of Mom's name. She'd been gone a long time. Trouble was, my heart had never really accepted that. Too many words had been left unsaid. "You and I alone know the truth. If you see a way around all this, I wish you'd let me know."

## — 31 —

Life had returned to Cape San Blas. Word spread. Locals appeared daily to witness the progress and ask when we were opening. Gabriella and Diego got in on the action and sold tea, bottled water, and sopapillas to the spectators. Media outlets from Pensacola to Orlando had heard the news about "the coming Tornado" and sent reporters and camera crews. In the space of two weeks Allie had been interviewed a dozen times. From managing what was needed, to running back and forth to pick up supplies, to "Here, hold this board," I pitched in where I could, making myself useful while trying not to get in the way. To some extent, I was the glue. I was also the checkbook, but I knew that going in.

Allie had secured her suppliers, and then hired and trained servers and dishwashers and line cooks and bartenders. She was in full restaurant-management mode and seemed happy. Controlling food costs, managing employee schedules, planning food presentation. Nothing got past her. With one eye on the completion schedule, we scheduled a "soft opening."

MANUEL, JAVIER, PETER, AND Victor had cleaned up their mess, arranged for the removal of the Dumpster, and washed and waxed the work truck before I realized they needed something else to do. They couldn't go back to the migrant world. Couldn't go back to Mexico. And they didn't have the paperwork to get hired in the legitimate world. The process to citizenship was too expensive.

That afternoon Allie and I pulled the four of them aside and walked across the street to the vacant property. When Allie's dad purchased the land some sixty years ago, the original deed included twenty acres across the road. At the time it was considered worthless; they couldn't have given it away. As the restaurant prospered, they used an acre or two for parking, but the rest remained wild and unusable.

I put my hand on Manuel's shoulder. "Can you put the carnival here?"

Manuel nodded confidently.

"It will mean disassembling most everything up there and bringing it down here. Including the metal building that covers most of it."

He nodded. Still confident.

"And when it's up and running, we're gonna need some guys to manage it. Maintain the rides. Pop the popcorn. Fix the go-karts."

Manuel shook my hand. His eyes were glassy. I've seldom seen gratitude like that.

I took them to the bank, opened joint checking accounts for each one, and made cash deposits in the form of a work bonus, bringing their opening balance to $7,500 each. Victor teared up and gave me a hug, then turned to Manuel and spoke in rapid-fire Spanish.

Manuel pointed him back to the teller and then explained to me. "He wants to send money to his wife and children in Mexico."

I didn't even know he was married. Peter held up one hand with five fingers extended.

"What?" I asked. "He has five kids?"

Peter shook his head. "No, me. I have five kids."

I looked at Javier.

He held up three fingers.

I walked away, realizing they had worked without complaint, grateful just to be working, never feeling sorry for themselves. I shook my head. "I need to learn to speak Spanish."

The following morning, I woke to the sound of a rented bull-dozer. Manuel and the three amigos were back at work.

I got out my phone and called my brother. He didn't answer, so I left him a voicemail. "Bobby, you said if I needed anything . . . Well, I need some help with a citizenship issue. I've got some folks down here that aren't here legally, but if we send them home, they'll die a painful and violent death, and probably their kids will too. The reason is long and complicated and has a lot to do with me. Just tell me what I need to do to start the process. I'll pay for it. Point me in the right direction and then cut through all the red tape I'm about to bump into. "

I STOOD ON THE porch of the restaurant, lured by the enticing smell of fresh coffee. The wafting aroma was akin to Morse code and Allie had tapped out the invitation. Without a word, it whispered, "Come be with me. I want you here with me." It was as innocent as a love note passed between two kids in grade school and as intentional as a tender hand slid beneath the sheets.

As a girl, Allie had always been beautiful. In our teens, my eyes opened as I'd watched straight lines develop into curves. In my time away, she'd become a woman, knowing hardship, accomplishment, and confidence. But now she was a woman in full bloom. A presence to be reckoned with. And neither high-school Allie nor curved Allie nor powerful Allie could hold a candle to Allie now.

When we walked the beach alone, her arm locked in mine, she continued to ask me questions about my life. I answered as best I could. Sometimes when I didn't have the words, we walked in the quiet, and she was okay with that.

Despite age and time and whiskey and fights and businesses and success and money and isolation, the touch and smell of Allie brought back images of my early life that I'd tried for years not to see.

One afternoon she wrapped her arms around my waist and pressed her chest to mine, her sandy toes on top of mine. "Is this difficult?" she asked.

"Which part?"

"The looking back part."

"It's a reminder."

"Of?"

"When I was over there and we had a break, a few days in the rear, dusk would fall and the only sound was the gentle roll of waves on seashell. I would sit up on the dunes beneath the palm trees with my head in my hands and try to remember what your face looked like. How your hair smelled. The taste of you. Then I would look at my hands and ask myself the simple and unanswerable question, 'How do I get back to good?'"

Sometimes it was hard for Allie to listen. Sometimes she would sob and cling to me. Often she would just stop me and kiss me. Trying to make up for all the years apart.

Then there were the nights. She'd told Catalina to give up her vigil on the porch and get some sleep, and then she crawled in bed with me. You might think it was sexual. It was not. Sure, I wanted it to be, but when I closed my eyes, sleep fell and my body remembered what my mind had forgotten.

Allie held me night after night, while I sweated and shook and screamed in my sleep. I woke sometimes, surprised to see her face and the fear she was trying to hide. I also saw that those nights convinced her that something I'd encountered had tormented me a long time. Night after night, she clung to me, pulled me to her, wrapped around me like a vine. I began to know sleep like I'd not known in a long, long time.

WITH THE SOFT OPENING less than two weeks away, Allie found me late one afternoon in the restaurant bathroom, painting one of the stalls.

She leaned against the wall, a sneaky smile on her face. "You got a minute?"

I rinsed my brush and met her outside. As we walked to my truck, she held out her hand. "Keys, please."

I hesitated. "I'm a little picky about who I let drive my truck."

"Give me the blasted keys, Joseph. You can't always be in charge."

I handed her the keys and she drove us the long way to Apalachicola. When we reached town, she wound her way around to a small, dilapidated house for which the only hope was some gasoline and a match. Behind the house stood a small and slightly leaning garage. She parked in front of the garage and said, "It's not in the best of shape, as I haven't really had the money to keep it up. I thought about taking out a loan to do the work, but I imagine you'd want to do that yourself." She rested her hand on the garage door handle. "I'm sorry it's not in better condition, but that's the thing about horses frozen in time . . ."

She lifted the door.

Inside, covered with a tan tarp, sat a car. Despite the fact that all four tires were flat and dry-rotted, I knew the body shape. I just couldn't believe that what sat beneath the tarp might actually be what I thought it was. "Is that . . . ?"

She smiled that sneaky smile again and began pulling back the tarp.

I stood there. Jaw hanging. My '67 Corvette. The one I'd given to Allie before I left. Now fifty years old. I didn't know what to say. She reached in her pocket and slid the very same keys into my hand that I'd given her on the day I left. She looked at the car, then at me. "If you could ask these 550 horses what they'd prefer, they'd say, 'Old man, turn on the juice and let us take you for a ride.'"

I stared at the keys. Nodding. The swell of emotion was more than I could hold back. She held my face in both her hands, leaned up on her toes, and kissed my cheek. Then my lips. Then again. If I thought I had loved her at one time, I had another thing coming. I looked down at her and wrapped my arms around her waist. "Allie-girl, you need to know something."

"What's that?"

"I have fallen for you. Totally."

She kissed me. Tenderly. "Good."

"Can you kiss me again?"

When she finished, she said, "You know, the whole kissing thing is great, but it gets better. Right? I mean, you do know that?"

I shook my head and opened the car door.

With four flat tires, we couldn't push it. So we wiped off the seats, put the top down, and sat in the front seat. She propped her feet on the dash and we sang "Fortunate Son" and "American Pie," and we held our imaginary glasses high toasting whiskey and rye.

A once-dead part of my heart came alive in that moment. It was pumping again. Feeling again. Listening to her sing, and watching her toe tap the dash, I felt my cold, gray heart turn warm and red.

That was both good and bad. Feeling something that good was a welcome emotion. But as I sat there singing with Allie, I felt the hair standing up on the back of my neck. A shadow over my shoulder.

If the good had returned, the bad wasn't far behind.

# — 32 —

With Allie's encouragement, I took a break from the restaurant and got my hands greasy, spending a week with the Corvette. Between Port St. Joe, Tallahassee, and Apalachicola, I got the parts I needed to get her running. From day one, I had a helper. Diego. He was curious and possessed an innate understanding of how mechanical things worked. He helped me pull the engine, where we soaked her in an acid bath and started over. New rings. Gaskets. Plugs. Wires. Cables. Hoses.

Allie said she used to drive it once a month to keep it running, but that ended years ago. A decade maybe. So anything that could rot, had. Diego and I drained all the fluids; replaced the bearings, U-joints, and brake pads; turned the rotors; and bought a new set of Goodyears. If I needed a wrench, pan, rag, anything, Diego hopped up and got it for me. I explained everything I was doing to him, and pretty soon I was letting him do a few things himself.

After a day of elbow grease and buffing, the exterior color returned. Some of the chrome had rusted and bubbled slightly around the edges, but I couldn't bring myself to replace it. The rag top was dingy and maybe on the verge of dry rot, but I looked at the canvas the same way I looked at the chrome. I just couldn't bring myself to throw out something because it was old and no longer shiny.

With the soft opening less than a week away, I let Diego install the battery, and then we sat in the seats. I pushed in the clutch and let him turn the ignition. Cut from her cage, she roared to life. I revved the engine and sat there listening to the sound of my youth. Diego's smile spread from ear to ear. I toweled the grease off my hands, pulled down my sunglasses, put the top down, and we eased out of the garage and cruised through town. On the outskirts I turned onto 30E, downshifted into second, revved it to 6,000 rpms, dropped the clutch, and burned rubber for an entire block.

I pulled up in front of the restaurant and sat there, engine idling. Allie came running out. She handed her apron to Diego. "Honey, tell your mom I'll be back later." She was a picture of the teenager I once knew. We put three hundred miles on the odometer before dark. With the sun falling west over the Gulf, we drove the coastline. Allie laid her head against the headrest, closed her eyes, and let the wind tug at her hair. I drove with my right hand and surfed the wind with my left. Dark found us parked facing the beach, moon above us, stars shining down, Allie leaning against me. Neither of us saying a word. Soaking in what had long since drained out.

After an hour of sitting in each other's quiet, she turned and looked up at me. "How long have we been back in each other's lives?"

"Couple of months."

She shook her head. "Four months. Seven days. Two hours."

I smiled. Not sure where this was going. "Okay."

She placed her hand on my chest. "And in all that time, why haven't you made a pass at me?"

That was a good question. The answer was not. I was about to say something when she said, "I mean, I've made like a hundred passes at you, which have done me little good, so I'm just wondering if you've lost your mojo."

"My mojo?"

She laughed. "Yes. Mojo."

I stammered, "I was thinking we'd get there when we got there. You just lost one husband and I thought . . ."

"You 'bout done?"

"Done with what?"

"Thinking."

"Well . . . I don't know."

She leaned into me and kissed me, pressing her face against mine. While the other kisses had been kind and gentle, this was more of a pass a passionate teenager might make. When she sat up and peeled away from me, I actually uttered the word, "Wow."

She sat up, perplexed. Staring from my lips to me. "This whole exchange is better when two people do it. It's called 'kissing.' It's when your lips speak what your heart feels. Or have you forgotten how?"

I laughed. "I might have. It's been a long time."

She kissed me again. When she'd finished smothering me, which I didn't mind at all, she wiped her smeared lipstick off with a finger, smiling. "Well, that's a start."

She sat back in her seat and threw her feet up on the dash. "You're going to give me a complex if you don't make a pass at me soon." She pushed her hair back. "I mean, we're not that old. First it was the pajamas, and you did nothing. Now I'm practically throwing myself at you, and . . ." She undid her top button. "I'm still a kid at heart."

I put my arm around her. "What you're getting, or not getting, from me has nothing to do with you."

"Why then?" She half smiled. "If you tell me you're married, I am going to shoot you in the face."

I laughed. "I'm not married. I promise."

"Good, 'cause I'd hate to have to turn your head into a canoe." We laughed. She leaned against me. "That's the first time I've been able to laugh about that whole thing. Ten years wasted from my life, and here I am laughing about it."

"That's good."

"But that still doesn't answer my question."

"I thought we were finished talking about that."

"Nope. And you haven't said, or more importantly done, anything that makes me think we're any closer to you wrapping your arms around me and making out with me."

"Are you this forward with all your car dates?"

"Just you."

I tried to explain. "There's a thing that happens when you

watch guys . . . get gone. And as their numbers add up, and the months pass and their faces flash with some regularity before you . . . you begin to feel guilty for . . . feeling. For desire. For hope. For laughter. For kissing a beautiful girl. Like somehow, to have any emotion that is good, or to be with anyone else, is like spitting on their memory. I know that sounds crazy, but the moment I start to let myself feel anything good, their faces pop up in my mind. And . . . any good emotion feels like a betrayal."

"A betrayal of who?"

"The guys who never had the chance." I rubbed my hands together. "Letting myself experience or desire pleasure is like a shot through the heart of their memory."

To her credit, Allie didn't listen and then try to fix me. She just listened. After a minute she slid her hand inside my shirt, placing her palm flat against my heart. "You need to know something." Her hand felt warm across my chest. "I've been holding my love a long time. Twice disastrously married doesn't change that. I've never given my heart to anyone the way I once gave it to you. Right now, it's full. I don't know that I can hold it in much longer." She spoke softly. "I don't want to make light of anything you just said, but if those red-blooded guys that you hold in your heart were here in this seat with us, I think they'd tell you it was okay. They'd cheer you on. They'd be fist-pumping and knuckle-bumping and whatever it is guys do."

I wrapped my arm tight around her. Smiling. "They'd be saying a lot more than that."

She smiled. "Then you should listen to them."

# — 33 —

The soft opening arrived. As did crowds of hungry people. We opened for lunch and had anticipated being open for dinner, but by three p.m. we'd sold out of everything but water. Two of the first customers were my cigar-smoking, Harley-driving local who'd never met a stranger and the building inspector. I sat them each in a booth overlooking the ocean and bought their lunch. For dessert my Harley friend ordered a plate of hush puppies and polished them off with a cigar on the porch.

The second day, Allie doubled her food order and we sold out by three thirty. This continued throughout the week, and by Friday night there was a two-and-a-half-hour wait at the door. She looked at me from the hostess stand, shaking her head. "Where did all these people come from?"

We survived the weekend. Allie had decided that we'd close Mondays to give the staff a break and allow the cleaning team time to scour the restaurant.

Monday afternoon found all of us relaxing. The family was playing on the beach while Allie and I sat on the porch. She was counting the receipts from the week, and I was rubbing her feet. I said, "Are you cooking the books, or balancing them?"

She shook her head. "No need to cook them. If my math is correct, we netted seventeen thousand dollars. That means I can start paying you back."

As the sun was just dropping over the edge of the Gulf, giving way to my favorite time of day, a courier drove up the drive with a package addressed to Allie. She signed for it and then sat on the porch overlooking the dunes and ocean. Her mind was spinning with a dozen things, not least of all the foot massage, so she totally ignored the sender and simply tore open the package.

I saw the return address, so I had a pretty good idea things were about to get interesting. I stood and walked down the steps to the edge of the dunes and the path that led to the beach. I could hear the kids laughing along the water's edge. She opened the envelope as I watched.

She pulled out the paid-in-full notarized receipt for her back taxes and other liens, along with a paid-in-full notarized receipt for the satisfaction of her mortgage, along with the stamped and recorded deed to the Blue Tornado.

She stared at the papers. Reading. Rereading. Turning them sideways. Once it sank in, she crumpled and turned into a puddle on the porch. A pretty good reaction.

After she composed herself, she looked my direction and held up the papers. "I thought we had agreed you were just going to pay the back taxes. Make interest payments." She made quotation marks with her fingers. "'Get me on my feet.'"

"Correct. I paid back taxes. And made"—I held up a finger—"one interest payment."

She shook the papers at me. "Along with all the principal."

"It was easier to write one check."

Calmly she placed the papers back in the envelope and laid them on the porch table. Then she started racing toward me. "Joseph Brooks!"

Allie chased me through the dunes and out onto the beach where the kids found her hysterical screaming and my laughing rather comical. Rosco ran in circles around us. We weaved down the beach, then back up. I was laughing so hard I was having a tough time putting one foot in front of another. Finally she caught me along the edge of the water. When she did, I picked her up and carried her into the waves, where we fell into waist-deep water. She stood, soaking wet, hair matted to her face. I pushed it back behind her ears. She cupped my face in her hands and kissed me square on the lips. Then again. "I can never pay this back . . . you know that, right?"

"It's a gift. You don't pay those back."

Her face took on a serious look. "Are you broke?"

"Why? You trying to decide if you still like me?"

"No, I didn't mean it like—"

"No. I'm not broke."

"I can't believe you did that." She studied me. Head tilted. "Why?"

"Sometimes . . . our debt is more than we can pay."

"But . . . ?"

"Long time ago, a friend gave me a gift I can never repay. The longer I live out the reality of that gift, the more I come to understand the enormity of what I owe and what is required to wipe the slate."

## — 34 —

Opening day was an explosion of people, color, lights, sound, and a good bit of chaos thrown in for good measure. When the restaurant opened at eleven a.m., a two-hour wait was lined up at the door. We'd set up a bar on the porch along with a walk-up window with a reduced menu for people who wanted just appetizers or something to eat with their drink on the porch.

Allie reminded me that the tension with any great restaurant is how to produce a product so good that folks are willing to stand in line to get it while not making the people feel rushed who, sitting in their seats, are enjoying the product. New technology allowed us to text people when their table was ready. That meant they weren't tied to the front steps and could make their way to the beach where the sea breeze, sunshine, and waves gently rolling across the shoreline added to the ambience.

Allie was in her element. And if anyone knew how to run

a restaurant—which included anticipating problems and fixing unanticipated problems—she was a pro. She never looked frazzled, made people feel welcome, and yet had a keen eye for presentation, food quality, timeliness, service, customer satisfaction. She could multitask on a level I couldn't comprehend. And somehow, in the midst of this exercise in controlled chaos, she found the wherewithal to actually sit down at tables with patrons and check in on so-and-so's momma or daddy or distant relative in Siam or Topeka.

I figured I was of the most help behind the scenes. Washing dishes. Mopping floors. Stocking the bar. Cleaning bathrooms. The less people interaction the better. I knew if I just kept my head down and focused on the systems or machines that helped us operate, I'd be fine. When the lights and the noise and the number of people grew too much, I'd stop and count forks or plates or sketch a face in a booth or some stranger sitting on a barstool. My stack of index cards was never far away.

WHILE THE CARNIVAL WAS still a work in progress, Manuel, Javier, Peter, and Victor had succeeded in reassembling the merry-go-round on the edge of the parking lot. Along with a few toss-and-throw games and the Paul Bunyan hammer swing. We'd strung lights and laid down hay for people to walk on. Gabby and Diego offered free lemonade and popcorn. The added distraction helped occupy those waiting.

We finished Saturday's shift about two o'clock Sunday morning. We'd been up close to twenty-four hours, and yet Allie was still smiling and darting around like the Energizer bunny. The entire staff had yet to go home, and yet we were scheduled to be back in the restaurant in seven hours to start prepping.

Even the kids were still awake. Gabby lay on the floor using Rosco as a pillow. It was a good picture. I propped my feet up and transposed it to paper. As I was finishing my sketch, Allie thanked the staff and then said with a sly smirk, "Make sure you tell your friends to come tomorrow. Should be an interesting evening."

I sensed that I had missed a memo.

I gave the card to Gabby and whispered, "Tell your friends what?"

She shook her head. "Not telling."

I turned to Allie, who grabbed my arm and said, "It's a surprise."

"I don't do well with surprises."

She nodded matter-of-factly. "I know."

SUNDAY MORNING I WOKE with a headache, which coffee did not alleviate. Maybe I was just dehydrated. I drank some water but nothing improved. That should have been my first sign. I made it to the restaurant, pitched in with everyone else, and by noon we were slammed. Word had spread from the night before, and a three-hour wait did little to deter diners.

By three o'clock I was elbow deep in suds trying to keep up with the dishes when Allie found me. "You okay?"

I squirted her with the spray nozzle. "Yep."

She was giddy. "Just checking."

Sundown came, and my feet were killing me. How did Allie keep this up?

I was pretty well soaked from the speed and fury of the dishwasher when she came to get me. She handed me a towel and instructed Peter and Victor to pick up where I left off. I wiped my hands and face. She smoothed my hair with her fingers, which did absolutely nothing, and then tied a handkerchief around my eyes. She led me by the hand through the kitchen and into the dining room, which seated over two hundred people. I knew the room was full, but somehow everyone was hushed and whispering as she led me in and then told me to stand still. Feeling fully exposed, I checked my zipper, bringing a laugh from somewhere in front of me. Then I heard a shuffling and somebody took my hand and said, "Hello, Joseph."

I knew that voice instantly. But this time, rather than hearing it over the radio, I was hearing it next to me. Her voice on my face. She wrapped her arm in mine and peeled the blindfold off my face. Speaking into a microphone, Suzy said, "Everybody give it up for Sergeant Joseph Brooks. A seven-time combat-wounded veteran and recipient of the Congressional Medal of Honor."

Over two hundred men, women, and children stood, whistled, and applauded. Their response was the welcome home I had wanted forty years ago. It was more than I could handle. Not just for me, but because I was seeing and hearing what so many others deserved.

FOR THE NEXT THREE evenings Suzy broadcast from the restaurant, drawing hundreds. At one point, Allie counted five hundred people outside. In between songs, Suzy would interview

me. Snippets. Five- and ten-minute stories. Boot camp difficul-
ties. Flying in-country. Conditions. Number of men in my unit.
The number of men who came home. She asked about my trips
flying home to deliver the bodies. Was it quiet on the plane? Life
in the tunnels. The medals I'd been awarded and for what. What
was it like to be sitting in Laos when the president declared that
the United States had no active service personnel inside Laos?
She skirted the edges on the number of kills and how many times
I had seen a buddy blown up. She steered the conversation to
the beach, my hooch, the singer girlfriend, a German shepherd
I befriended, anywhere she felt something tender. The second
night she asked me, "Ever steal anything?"

"All the time."

"Do tell."

"We would stay gone for weeks at a time. Sleeping on the
ground. Often wet. Ten trillion mosquitoes. When we would
get back to the rear, conditions were little better. I'd been there
about a year when we returned to find our camp in pretty bad
condition. We were just sleeping in holes in the ground. But next
door was a barracks reserved for officers when in-country. It was
quite large. Clean. Spacious. Would house our entire unit and
then some. But it was empty. So one night I, along with most of
my unit, disassembled the building, moved it to our side of the
fence, and reassembled it. I installed hot showers, decent bathrooms, bunks, offices. We called it Camp California.

"There was also a vehicle. A truck. Another camp needed it.
They were closer to our supply line, so we traded the vehicle for
booze and beer and steaks, you name it. Pretty soon, guys were

coming to Camp California for R&R. The fact that it sat within two hundred yards of the South China Sea didn't hurt. We held concerts on the weekends, but I think what the guys liked most were the hot showers."

"Ever get caught?"

"We'd been up and running about two weeks when I was ordered to receive a helo on the landing deck. It was raining buckets. A monsoon. The chopper landed, I saluted the colonel who stepped off, and then I escorted him to the only dry place around. I took him to his quarters in Camp California, a room we had reserved just for him, and as I'm standing there in muddy boots soaked to the bone, he asks me, 'Sergeant, you got anything to drink around here?'

"We weren't supposed to have hard liquor, but I responded, 'Sir, we have whatever you'd like.' He held his thumb and index finger about three inches apart and said, 'Scotch.' I retrieved it. Twenty years old. He sipped, studied me, and said, 'I hear tell you stole a building.' I responded, 'Yes, sir.' 'You admit it?' he asked, taking another sip. 'Yes, sir.' He sipped again. 'You realize I am obligated to have you arrested at that admission?' 'Yes, sir.' He spun his glass on the table. 'You mind telling me where you took it, and the military vehicle that went with it?' 'Sir, as for the building, it's currently keeping you dry. As for the vehicle, you are drinking it.' He nodded. 'Carry on, Sergeant. You need anything else, you let me know.'"

Suzy's producer said that night, during my stories, they had the most callers ever in the history of the show. Suzy scooted closer to me and leaned her head on my shoulder. I searched the crowd and spotted Allie leaning against the back wall. Hands in her pockets. She looked warm. Happy. Truth was, she was glowing.

Suzy looked up at me. "One more question before we break. A lot of guys I talk with wrote home every day. Did you?"

I shook my head. "No."

"Really? Can you tell us why?"

I rubbed my palms together. My eyes found Allie's. "When I left here, my heart was breaking down the middle. I had to leave the only girl I'd ever loved. Once I got there, I looked around and knew I might never go home. And if I didn't, I didn't want her standing over my grave holding tear-soaked pages of my heart. I'd seen a lot of guys go home in flag-draped boxes, and those letters never brought them out of the grave."

Allie crossed her arms.

"I wanted her to go on with her life. Not stay stuck to my memory."

Suzy's voice was soft when she spoke. "Did she . . . go on with her life?"

Allie smiled and thumbed away a tear. I didn't know how to answer. "I think maybe we all died a little over there. War has a way of killing you whether you die or not."

Suzy put her arm around me and spoke to her audience. "We'll be right back."

We sat in silence a long time. Suzy had tears in her eyes. Nobody approached me. Suzy didn't try to talk and make me feel better or pull me out of the moment.

After a commercial she asked, "Anything else?"

I was back there. Walking through those trees. Hearing that poisoned water slosh about in my canteen but knowing it was all I had and I didn't really care if it killed me. I wasn't sure I wanted to say what I was about to say. I glanced at Suzy, who saw my hesitation. "It's okay."

"End of my fourth tour. I was ready to come home. When you've been there awhile, you get selective about your friends. As in, you try not to make any, because friends die. But me and this other guy had become pals. He was . . . a good man. Anyway, I was someplace my government denied me being and things went real bad and nobody would come get me except this one guy who disobeyed a direct order, stole a helo, got shot down, and crash-landed not far from me. Couldn't walk. Only way to get him out was to drag him, so I did. For two days. Somewhere on the third day, he died. I couldn't leave him there because they were so brutal to the guys we left. So I made a sled and pulled him behind me while I walked out. I didn't know it at the time, but people who have died get heavier the longer they stay aboveground. I wanted to get him home to his family, but . . . after dragging him for eight days, I put him in the ground. It wasn't fair to him."

"Do you remember that man's name?"

"Yes."

"If you could say anything to him right now, what would you say?"

Without a pause I said, "I'd ask him to forgive me."

"For?"

"Not bringing him home."

A tear dripped off Suzy's cheek. The silence in the restaurant was deafening. Suzy leaned across the space between us and kissed me on the cheek.

Turning to the microphone, she said, "This is our last night here on Cape San Blas. To all of you listening, we'd like to dedicate this show to Sergeant Jo-Jo Brooks and to all of you brave men who served like him." Then in her signature fashion she signed off. "You are not forgotten."

When I walked out the front door, several hundred people were standing around a dozen or so bonfires holding a beer or coffee or child, listening to the interview on vehicle speakers. I stepped out on the porch and they applauded. It lasted several minutes. Several hundred people hugged me or shook my hand. Asked me for a picture. It made me feel uncomfortable.

Unworthy.

At midnight, Allie found me on the beach. I was crying. No, I was weeping. And had been. Snot and tears smeared across my face. My soul was spilling out my mouth. Allie put her arm around me and just held me. Finally she turned me toward her and squeezed me tightly. I cried an angry, bitter, broken cry forty-five years in the making.

She asked me, "What can I do? Tell me. Anything."

I stared out across the ocean. Then down at my feet. "I need someone to forgive me."

She cupped my face in her hands. "For?"

"For living."

# — 35 —

Suzy came by at lunch the following day to report that last night's listening audience was the largest in their history. She said her television production company wanted to film today's show at the restaurant, live, and she asked Allie and me if we were okay with that.

I shrugged. "Sure."

Allie, knowing the pain of last night, paused. "You sure?"

"I'm sure."

The two-hour show aired live at four o'clock. The corner of the restaurant had been turned into a TV set, complete with down-lighting and microphones and twenty people moving around like ants pulling cables. When the show started, Suzy, ever the force to be reckoned with, took me back through many of the questions of the previous nights, replaying the audio for the television audience. Then she asked expounding questions. We talked for almost thirty minutes before she broke for commercial. When we returned, she continued with her line of questioning. I answered as best I could.

Sixty minutes into the show, one of her producers came to her during commercial and showed her several slips of paper. Suzy grew instantaneously angry and verbally reamed the producer a new orifice. Fifteen minutes later, again during commercial, the producer returned with more paper. This time the producer was white as a ghost.

As was Suzy.

When we returned to the show for the final segment, Suzy sat ashen, staring at the papers on her lap. When the red light flashed green and she gathered herself, her face was hollow. She turned to the camera. "Years ago, I started this gig trying to find the truth about my dad. I could not, but I soon discovered that a lot of other people were also seeking truth. So that's what this program became. A search for the truth. About the guys that went. Those that didn't come home. And . . ." She turned to me. "Those that never went."

If there was any air in the room when she started talking, it was sucked out the moment she said the words *never went*. She held the papers in her lap. "I have here documents, signed by witnesses, showing that during the years in which you say you were in Vietnam, you were actually in California. They say your favorite drug was LSD, though you were no stranger to heroin, and that you always had a vivid imagination and loved to spin a story. I have a signed lease agreement with your name on it. Pay stubs from a bar where you worked. Further, I have your birth certificate showing you were never drafted—as you were only sixteen when you claimed to enter the service. And furthermore . . ." Her voice was growing in volume and tone. "I have confirmation from rather high-up military sources that you do not possess a military record or identification number and that you never served in the United States military. The evidence is irrefutable." Suzy choked back a sob.

I could hear my heartbeat throbbing in my ear. She leaned toward me. The pain and anger in her eyes were pulsating through the veins in her head. She was shouting now.

"So tell me, Joseph Brooks, what makes it so easy to lie to us? To me!" She was spitting when she spoke. "How long did it take to become so convincing? What'd you do, park yourself at the VA and listen to other men's stories, stealing them as your own?"

Two tables back, a bearded guy about my age, wearing black leathers and motorcycle boots, stood up, holding a beer bottle. He pointed. "You lying, Jo-Jo?"

I just looked at him.

He gestured with his beer. "I drove up from Miami." He shook his head and walked toward the stage. I knew what he intended and I didn't stop him. He swung the bottle, breaking it across my forehead. Beer and blood ran down my face.

A woman, probably a widow, walked around behind him and dumped her plate of food on top of my head. Another guy squeezed an entire bottle of ketchup across my face and chest.

Allie was the last one. She stood shaking her head, tears pouring down. "You said you'd never lie!" She slapped me across the face. Then again. She poured an entire pitcher of beer over me, then swung the pitcher down on my head. At this point, people were throwing anything they could get their hands on.

I stood, walked out of the restaurant, down the steps, and out into the crowd, where people spat on me and threw more food at me. One skinny kid walked up and punched me square in the mouth. I stopped at my truck, where Gabriella and Victor stood holding Rosco by the collar. Gabby didn't understand what was going on, but she was crying.

Rosco stood, wagging his tail. I held out my hand like a stop sign and said, "Stay." He sat on his butt. I climbed into my truck, backed up, and drove out as men threw beer and soda across my windshield.

Sometimes the truth catches up with you, and when it does, life just hurts.

# — 36 —

I tossed both my flip phone and my smart phone out the window as I drove north. In a couple days I reached my cabin. I gathered a few things from inside, then doused the rest with ten gallons of diesel fuel and lit it. I backed out of the drive as the flames grew forty feet in the air.

I drove to the same diner in Spruce Pine where Catalina and the kids and I had eaten. My waitress friend had managed to lose a few of her pregnancy pounds and seemed more comfortable in her jeans. She smiled when she saw me. "You need a table?"

I shook my head. "Wanted to bring you something."

"Really?"

I laid the keys to the F-150 inside her hand. "Take care of that boy. A good momma is hard to find."

"But I can't—" She eyed the keys, then the truck, and started crying.

Her boss appeared over her shoulder, a spatula in one hand. "What's the problem here, bud?" He put his hand on my shoulder with some force and not-so-good intention, so I sent him to the concrete. He lay there trying to breathe.

I turned to go, but the waitress clutched my arm. "Please . . . but why?"

I kissed her forehead, shoved my hands in my pockets, and walked ten miles to the storage unit in Micaville, where I cranked the Jeep.

I drove west. Tennessee. Arkansas. Missouri. Kansas. At Iowa I turned north and drove to Minnesota and into Canada, where I spent a few weeks. When I returned to the US, I came in through North Dakota. Drove through Montana, Wyoming, Colorado. From Colorado I meandered through Arizona and New Mexico, eventually into Mexico and the Baja Peninsula. From the sun and heat of Mexico I returned north up through Nevada, Oregon, and Washington, finally making my way back into Canada, up through British Columbia, and into Alaska. I didn't watch the news. Didn't read the papers. Didn't listen to the radio. I sat in my Jeep and stared out through the windshield. And drove.

Eight months into my trip to nowhere, I found myself in Seattle in the rain. I had not shaved or cut my hair since I left. Despite my news avoidance, I picked up on the fact that my charade had made Suzy famous. Both her radio and TV spots sat in their respective number one spots across all time zones and markets. Her discovery had launched her into the stratosphere, and I had been labeled the greatest soldier of fraud in the history of modern media.

A month later I found myself in northern California. Sonoma. Sitting in an outdoor coffee shop, watching the city square, when a giddy couple, just kids in their late twenties, sat down and started talking about their winery. Every morning they showed up. A week passed. The picture of the two of them was tender. I came back each day just to watch them hold hands and listen to their laughter. Their love for each other oozed out of their pores like garlic. Not gooey like two people who need to get a room, but simple and pure affection. Tender love. Two kids enjoying the adventure of this life and wanting to live it with each other. They were young enough to be my kids, and maybe that was part of their appeal too.

One day the guy turned to me and said, "Pardon the intrusion, but I'm just curious. You've been here all week. You always order two cups of coffee, then drink one and pour out the other. There's got to be a story there. And what's with the lit cigarette you don't smoke?"

We started talking.

I learned that they had some big problems. Not with each other, but with the life they lived. From what I could piece together, Tim and Becca had partnered with a majority investor, and while these kids knew wine, the investor had the money and called all the shots. The Becca Winery was teetering on the verge of losing it all.

Sitting at the café, I applied for a job.

Tim looked at me and said, "How old are you?"

I had to think about it. "Almost sixty-three."

Becca looked uncertain. "Can you handle it?" She palmed her sweaty forehead. "It's difficult work."

"If I can't, you can fire me and don't have to pay me a penny."

Over the weeks, they taught me to tend the vines. They knew more about wine, how to make it, and what makes it really good, than I'd ever know. They had lived a decade in Italy, France, and Spain and poured their life's savings and everything they could borrow into this venture. I also learned about their partner. The money guy. And how his profit-making decisions were often at odds with their award-winning, wine-making intentions. Tim educated me on cabernets and chardonnays and tried to help me understand what my palette was trying to tell me. He was a good kid, but I sensed a growing heaviness in him I couldn't place.

Oddly enough, they didn't own a TV, so they spent their evenings wrapped around each other like two vines, listening to a transistor radio on the porch. What would they listen to? Suzy True. They never missed a show.

The only window into the outside world that I had came through Suzy. I still didn't watch the news. Didn't read the papers. Didn't own a phone or a TV. But one thing became painfully obvious. My interaction with Suzy had shattered something inside her. Whatever she believed about me, and the pain my betrayal had caused, had cracked open the only remaining reservoir of hope she had. Her tone of voice changed. Where she once was intimate and would crawl through the airwaves, she now seemed distant and indifferent. Callers praised her for her extreme weight loss and asked her how she did it. She danced around them, talking about "deciding she needed to do something," but the truth was, I had broken her heart and she'd lost the taste for food.

Harvest came, and it was a good one. Tim and Becca made me a manager, and for the next several months I tried to help them climb out of the hole their partner had dug. But one day I came into the barn and found Becca crying. Tim holding her. They had come to say good-bye. They were going to lose everything.

I started asking questions. Didn't take me long to learn that when they'd signed their agreement with their partner, they had inserted a buy-back option. Meaning if things went badly and the assets had to be sold, either party could end the partnership for a predetermined sum. I don't know how they arrived at the sum, but it was pennies on the dollar compared to what had been invested, and if I didn't know any better I'd say the partner had scripted the agreement this way so that he could own his own winery for a fraction of what it would cost otherwise. He knew they had poured everything in, and he knew he controlled both the purse strings and the decisions.

As I listened to them relate the decisions he'd made, all I could think was nobody with any business sense whatsoever would do what he'd done. My conclusion: he had purposefully sunk the winery. Or devalued it to the point that it was almost worthless. He had also crafted the agreement in such a way that he had veto power over any other partners they wanted to bring in, so even if they found the money he could deny them. Very clever. Becca and Tim didn't have two nickels to rub together, and no bank in their right mind would lend them money, and their partner knew this.

They had dreamed of a winery. Of building something together. Their partner had never dreamed at all. The more I heard, the angrier I grew.

The sun was going down, and Tim opened one final cabernet. A long silence passed as they stared out across the vines they had pampered, sung to, and nurtured. Everything they loved had come crashing down.

I swirled my wine, watching the dregs drain down the inside of the glass. "Just curious, how much do you owe? What's the buy-out clause?"

They told me.

"How long do you have?"

"Twenty-four hours."

I said, "I have a proposition for you."

I had not cut my hair in a year. Had not shaved. Had not bought new clothes. Wore flip-flops. Overalls. Admittedly, I did not look impressive.

"Oh, really?" They chuckled.

"How about if I loan you the money?"

They looked at me like I'd lost my mind.

"I'll transfer the money today, now. Tomorrow you can enjoy the sweet satisfaction of walking into your partner's office and laying the check on his desk. After you two unwind all his bad decisions and turn this thing around, you can pay me back."

Becca didn't quite know what to make of me. Tim looked incredulous.

"Are you on the level?" he asked. He'd been burnt by one partner. He'd vowed not to let it happen again. "And what do you want in return?"

I sipped my wine. "I loved a girl one time. Still do. We were a couple of dreamers just like you two. But something got in the way. Never got straightened out." I pointed out across the vine-yard. "I want to see your dream come true." A tear broke loose and stained my face. "If you'll let me, I'd like to help."

To say their partner was surprised would be an understate-ment. He was furious. He'd played chess and lost. Tim said he threw quite the conniption when Tim laid that cashier's check on his desk. Paid in full.

Becca and Tim became sole owners and offered to name their first child after me. I laughed. "No need. But you want to do some-thing for me?"

They nodded.

"Two things."

Tim said, "Name 'em."

"First, nobody knows my name. Not ever. Look up 'silent partner' in a dictionary and you'll find me. When you tell your story of this place and what happened, you just refer to me as the old man. That's all. Besides, the mystique will create publicity, and publicity boosts sales."

Tim raised his glass. "Done."

Becca leaned in. "And the second?"

I stared out across the vines. "Love each other. Even when it's hard."

With our harvest, Becca and Tim set out bottling this year's production. And in a rather slick marketing move, given that the name of their winery was simply a girl's first name, they began naming all their subsequent wines with other girls' names. A rather romantic notion. For reasons I can't explain, a sommelier of serious reputation tasted Sonoma's latest boutique label, the Allie, and gave it 97 points.

Things took off from there.

The media and the tourists arrived in busloads. People were dying to know what happened, but Tim kept his word and I worked under the radar. Given my haggard appearance, nobody gave me a second look. I let my overalls get dirtier, stopped wearing deodorant, and pretty much everybody left me alone. As for Becca and Tim, they started making money hand over fist. The more they refused to reveal the mystery around the reclusive, ascetic owner who kept to himself and preferred seclusion over recognition, the more the label grew.

Everything I touched turned to gold. Except people.

MEANWHILE, IN FLORIDA, A wine distributor who had picked up our label was making his rounds of the Florida restaurants. He sat down with Allie and presented the Becca label and last year's award-winning Allie. "What a coincidence," he said with a laugh.

Allie studied the brochure, which showcased Tim and Becca and told their story. The up-close picture showed the two of them with their vineyard rolling out behind them. Grapes about to explode. Along the edge of the picture, some distance away, stood the gardener. Tending the vines. His overalls were dirty and tattered. Hair long. Beard longer. Flip-flops on dirty feet. He was turned slightly away from the camera so his face was obscured, but something trailed out of his left front pocket. A small clear plastic tube. The kind used to detect blood sugar levels in diabetics. Allie stared at the picture, the name of the wine, the gardener, and the angle of his broad shoulders.

Three hours later, she boarded a plane.

# — 37 —

I was standing in the vineyard alongside Tim and Becca, cutting grapes and laying them carefully in large bins. Despite their success and the fact that the White House, some famous French restaurants, and multi-Michelin-star restaurants across the US were now serving their wine, they couldn't resist the chance to get their hands dirty. It was late in the afternoon, the sun was going down, we were laughing. They were asking questions about my life, and I, as usual, was tight-lipped. They knew I'd traveled, had owned some businesses, but they knew almost nothing about my history. Including my real name.

A figure appeared atop the hill. The sun shone behind the visitor's back, so all we could tell was that she was female. The wind blew her hair sideways. She shaded her eyes, studied us, and then began walking toward us.

Tim said, "Looks like another lost tourist."

I watched her walk. The rhythm. The presence. "She's not lost."

Allie closed the distance until she stood less than an arm's length away. She brushed my long hair out of my face. Gingerly. Tears streaming down. "Been looking for you everywhere. Bobby too."

I nodded. Tim and Becca were listening with rapt attention.

"I've called your phone number ten thousand times."

I said nothing because I didn't know what to say.

Tim cleared his throat, and I turned toward them. "Becca and Tim, I'd like you to meet Allie."

Tim hopped down off the back of the flatbed and toweled off his hands. "This is Allie? Like . . . *the* Allie?"

I nodded. To her surprise, Tim hugged Allie and said the two of them had long wanted to meet her.

I asked, "How'd you find me?"

Allie held up the brochure and pointed at my picture in the background, then she slipped her hand into mine. "I need to ask you something, and I need an honest answer. Okay?"

I nodded. "I've only lied to you once in my life."

"When?"

"When I told you I was going to California to outrun the war."

"Did you really go?"

"Yes."

"What about Suzy's evidence? The fact that you have no record?"

"For me to tell you the secret of my life means I have to destroy someone else's. And while part of me might wish that . . . I can't do it."

Allie's eyes narrowed. "Bobby."

I didn't respond.

She shook her head. "But Suzy said you have no military record, and they have all kinds of stuff showing you were in California."

I shrugged. "That wasn't me."

"How can you say that? They have your signature."

"Doesn't matter."

Allie pounded my chest. "It matters to me. You matter to me."

"How're Gabby and Diego?" I asked. "And Rosco?"

She shook her head. "Thick as thieves." She paused. "For once and forever, I need you to tell me why you won't tell the truth."

"It won't change the past."

She clasped my face in her hands. "I'm not talking about changing our past, Joseph. I'm talking about changing our future."

I searched for the words. "I told you I had an ulcer once."

She nodded. "Yes."

"It was anger. Anger eating a hole in me."

Allie clung to me. "Can you prove any of what you're telling us?"

"Yes."

"Will you?"

"No."

"Why?"

"For me to do what you're asking is to go back to what I know, which is killing, and I won't do that. Not anymore. Whatever life I would gain is not worth what it will cost."

"But—"

"Allie—" I brushed her hair out of her face. "Anger, rage . . . they're as real as you and me. They don't have bodies like us, but they live . . . live in us. Take up residence in our soul. If I do what you're asking, I let them out where they spill out across the world and spread to other people. But if I don't . . . then they die with me. I take them to the grave. It's the only way to win a war I've been almost fifty-four years fighting."

"But what about me!" She clutched my shirt and pulled herself to me. "What about me?"

Becca wrapped an arm around me, and the four of us walked to the house, where we sat on the porch and Allie listened to me tell the story of the last year and then some. I guess I don't need to tell you that she cried through much of it.

When I finished, she relayed the story of life on Cape San Blas. Manuel, Javier, Peter, and Victor had transferred most of the carnival and set it up across the street. Business was so good that they'd had to hire some friends from the trailer park. Bobby's people had come through, and she'd been able to help them and their families navigate the path to citizenship. Catalina was almost single-handedly running the restaurant. The kids were in school. Rosco seemed happy enough, but often in the afternoons he'd stand on the porch and stare in the direction he last saw my truck. The Blue Tornado had prospered, the critical reviews were astounding, and my Corvette was lonely and waiting for my return.

"And you?" I asked.

She slipped her hand in mine. "I walk the beaches at night. Still holding my love."

While we were watching the sun fall, Tim returned from the kitchen with the radio. "You two better listen to this."

The distraught voice belonged to Suzy's producer. "We'll keep you posted throughout the night and tomorrow, but I've known Suzy a long time, through all the ups and downs. This started with a desire to find her father. That never happened. Then the Joseph Brooks debacle of last year." A pause. "I don't know if Suzy will ever return to the microphone. She's alive, but . . . I just don't know. I think we may have lost the one voice who made us believe."

Tim turned off the radio and explained that Suzy had been found unresponsive at her Los Angeles home. An empty bottle of pills next to her. They'd gotten her to the hospital in time.

I sat quietly a long time. Eventually Allie asked me, "What're you thinking?"

"I'm thinking how a forty-year-old war can still kill people." I turned to her. "You in a hurry to get back?"

She spread her fingers inside mine. "I'm not letting you out of my sight." She kissed me. "Ever."

# — 38 —

We drove to the City of Angels and found the hospital. I was pretty sure they'd never let me see her, but I had to try. I made it to the sixth floor, where her production company had placed two broad-chested security guards to prevent the media from making her attempted suicide any more of a circus than it already was. They put their hand on my chest and shook their heads. "Not a chance."

"I have something she's going to want to hear."

"Sorry, pal."

The producer overheard the commotion and walked into the hall. When she saw me, she pointed a finger. "What're you doing here?" Then she spotted Allie, and her composure changed. Less steel wall. More wooden fence.

"I have something to tell her."

She did not look impressed. "Right." She turned to go. "Haven't you done enough damage?"

"It's about her dad."

"Really?" She raised an eyebrow. "You have information about her father?"

"I know what happened."

"How would you know?"

"I was with him."

"And you can prove this?"

"I can."

She studied me. "Why now?"

"It's painful."

"To you or to her?"

"Both."

She looked at Allie. "You believe him?"

"I do."

She shrugged. "You might duck when you walk in. She'll probably unload at your head."

I walked in, Allie close behind. Suzy lay there, staring out the window, a thousand miles away. I sat next to her bed, risking being slapped or punched, and slid my hand into hers. I whispered, "I need to tell you a story."

She slowly turned her head toward me. "I'm not sure I can handle any more of your stories." When she saw Allie, she looked confused. "You too?"

Allie nodded. "Just listen to him."

A security guard stood over me. One hand on my shoulder. "You want us to remove him, Ms. Suzy?"

She studied my eyes, then shook her head. "Thanks, George."

George went out, shutting the door behind him.

———

I sat back, took a deep breath, and started in. "When I first landed in-country—"

Suzy interrupted me. "Before you go any further, can you prove any of this?"

"Yes."

"Beyond any shadow of doubt?"

I nodded.

She laid her head back and stared at the ceiling. "Because if not, George is going to break both your legs."

"When I returned for my second tour, years three and four, they continued sending us into Laos. Well into Laos. I'd take teams of ten to twelve men in at a given time. We were trying to disrupt their supply lines. They'd fly in low, drop us twenty miles behind the lines, and we'd make our way out after we'd done what we came to do. A good chopper pilot was tough to come by. The good ones didn't last long, because to be good meant they had to get into and out of places that nobody would want to get into or out of. They had to care more about someone else than themselves.

"We had this young guy, fresh out of West Point, green behind the ears, kept a picture of his girl on the instrument panel. To begin with, he was not a good pilot. He was afraid. Green. Trying not to get shot. We were all afraid of what his fear might cost us, because it wouldn't let him get us where we needed. I tried to get him removed, but everybody was sick of the war and they were sick of hearing complaints, so mine landed on deaf ears. We were stuck with him.

"On our fourth mission he landed some five miles from where

we were supposed to be. To make matters worse, we were sur-rounded by some very angry people. By then I could fly that bird well enough to get us home. My team was looking at me, and I knew that they knew that I knew I needed to do something so this dumb sucker didn't get us all killed. So I reached up and put both my hands around his throat and started squeezing. I'd done it to the enemy. What was one more? He turned blue and his eyes began popping out of his head. He was seconds from checking out, and I was just a few more seconds from dumping his body in a rice paddy and flying home, when he pointed to the dash. To the picture. His daughter. Just a few months old. I looked at that picture and something in me remembered."

I pulled Suzy's baby picture out of the envelope in my pocket and set it in her hand.

"Something in me remembered that I had, at one time, loved somebody too. I let go, he choked, vomited, cussed, and flew us home, threatening some sort of court martial. When we landed, I dragged him out on the beach and had a conversation about who and what he wanted to be when he grew up. He told me, through tears, that he wanted to be your dad. That you and your mom were all that mattered. That he was just trying to get home. Somewhere on that beach, I saw a scared guy who still loved. Who reminded me of the kid I used to be. And in that moment, I'd have given everything to be just like him. So I made a decision I was going to get him home.

"Every morning we shared a cup of coffee. Told stories of home. If I wasn't there, he'd buy me a cup and set it in my place in hopes I'd make it home to drink it with him. We talked about his girl, about Allie, about fast cars, and he said he wanted to make it home to drive my Corvette. If he was flying I'd buy two cups, drink one, and keep the other full and hot until he could enjoy it with me. We did this for a year. We thought we had it beat. We were starting to let ourselves think about home and the possibility that we might make it back. He had gotten really good. Best I ever knew.

"I had taken a team in. The team had done their job, but things had gone badly. The team had been split. In the confusion they'd rendezvoused at Bravo and left me at Alpha. I'd been cut, shot. Half blown up. Lost some blood. Things were not looking too good. I patched myself up, crawled into a hole, and kept quiet. The bad guys were monitoring the radio.

"After two days I ran out of water, so I drank out of a stream. Upstream was a dead buffalo that I wouldn't find until the next day. By then the dysentery had already set in. I became dehydrated. I'd try to walk and my whole body cramped up. I'd been alone a week when I called it in.

"They said they were glad to hear from me; they needed me fifteen miles south. I told them I needed some antibiotics and what they could do with their fifteen miles. They reiterated their order to hump it south. I reiterated my previous statements and told them if I made it out, I'd hunt every one of them down. I'd kill them, their wives, their children, their dog. Even their dreams.

"A minute later, the pilot's voice echoed on the line. He said two words: 'I'm coming.' Two hours later he landed, dragged me into the chopper, started an IV of antibiotics, and we lifted off.

---

We thought we were in the clear, but an hour and a half from Camp California a rocket cut our rudder. Sent us spinning in a circle. Somehow he landed. I climbed out of the wreckage, pulled him out, and the two of us disappeared into nowhere with a whole bunch of bad somebodies chasing us. By the end of the third day, I was carrying him on my back.

"The first bullet caught me in the stomach. The second passed through him and was headed into me when this stopped it." I set a book in her hand. "When I told you the story of the man's body I'd carried for eight days . . . that was your dad."

Tears were pouring off her chin. I set his watch and dog tag in her hands, and turned the brass Zippo in my hand.

"Against a direct order, and in a stolen helicopter, your father came to get me when no one else would. He was the best of them. The best of them all. He gave me what I didn't deserve and took what I did."

We sat in the quiet several minutes. Her eyes were closed as she let her fingers trace the leather cover and letters of his dog tag.

"It's a gift I can never . . ." I trailed off. Moments passed. "For a long time, I couldn't understand what would make a man do that. To drop into hell and give himself for another." I was crying now. "Lying there in that mud, his warm red life trickling out beneath my fingers and the light in his eyes fading, he started laughing. He said, 'Joseph?'

"I was trying to keep pressure on the hole. Keep him talking. 'Yeah?'

"He smiled. 'I want to let you in on a secret. It's time you knew.'

"I was too busy to look at him. I said, 'Yeah, what's that?'

"He tapped my chest. 'Evil won't kill evil.' He tried to take a deep breath and couldn't. 'Not ever.'

"I couldn't stop it. His life was seeping out between my fingers.

"He pulled my forehead to his and whispered, 'Only one thing does that.'

"I was crying. Crying hard.

"He smiled and placed his hand flat across my heart. He closed his eyes and spoke through a whisper. 'And it's the only thing we really need.' Then he was gone."

When I could muster the words, I said, "Suzy, I've wanted to tell you that *I'm sorry* for your whole life."

We sat for an hour. Neither of us talking.

THE MOON ROSE OUTSIDE the window. She blew her nose. "So . . . everything you said in your interviews with me was true?"

"Yes."

She choked back a sob. "Joseph, I am so—"

I placed a finger across her lips. "You don't owe me anything."

"Forgive me?"

I shook my head. "No."

"Please."

"I'll tell you the same thing your father told me when I asked him that same ridiculous question."

"Which was?"

"There's nothing to forgive."

Suzy sat up and hugged me for a long, long time. Tears fell. Tears that had been stuffed inside me an even longer time. I don't know where they all came from, but I cried a lot. I didn't know my heart could hold that much.

She studied me. "There's more to your story, isn't there?"

"Yes."

"But you can't tell me, can you?"

I turned the index card in my hand. A picture of her tear-stained face—of a soul coming clean. "No."

"Can't or won't?"

"Won't."

She looked at Allie. "Does she know?"

"No."

"Will you ever tell us?"

I gently laid the index card in her hand and shook my head.


WE SPENT THE AFTERNOON laughing. I told her a hundred stories about her dad, his sense of humor. I described his laughter, his affinity for cigars and good Scotch, and his love of all things related to her mom. How he talked about her. How he wanted to move to the mountains of Carolina and build a cabin and sit by the fire and hold her hand. Teach her to ski. Walk her down the aisle.

By evening Suzy's producer had ordered pizza, pulled up a chair, and sent the security guards home. Suzy was sitting up, eating. She'd turned the corner. The voice that made us all believe, believed again.

At midnight I turned to leave. She tugged on my arm. "I need a favor."

"Anything."

She told me and I said, "You sure?"

"Positive."

I kissed her forehead. "I'll be there."

# — 39 —

*They go from strength to strength;*
*each one appears before God in Zion.*

—PSALM 84:7

Suzy had spent the last month getting healthy and spreading the word. She'd returned to the air, told the story of her dad and me. The national networks caught on, tracked me down, and covered the story. At first they were cynical. Doubters and haters. Then they did their own homework, and while they could not put their hands on my military record, two of the folks in Suzy's office confirmed through an unnamed back-channel source (which smelled a lot like a leak from Bobby or his people) that I had one and that I had served four tours and been decorated at least eight times—including the Congressional Medal.

It had been an emotional couple of weeks.

When she broke the news that she was returning to Cape San Blas for another interview with me, RVs started appearing from all corners of the country. Gangs of gray-bearded bikers clad in black leather and straddling shiny chrome stormed onto the island with eardrum-bursting pipes. Veterans from all corners of the country filled every motel, hotel, and RV park for miles. Media trucks filled the parking lot. Police 24/7. Security. Directing traffic. We brought in tents from everywhere. Manuel's carnival was lit up like a runway and filled with color and sound and laughter.

Given the reach of Suzy's voice, the place was packed. Standing room only. She and I sat on barstools. She'd lost a lot of weight. Looked healthier. Lights shining down, six cameras, several monitors, and one prompter, and Rosco sitting next to me, licking my hand. He'd been happy to see me, although not so happy that he quit sleeping with Gabby.

Allie sat at a table in the front row, Gabby on one side and Diego on the other. Gabby had grown. Looked more like her mom. More beautiful. Diego was more muscled. Chin sharper. Both more tanned. In my absence they'd filled three Mason jars with sharks' teeth. Catalina stood at the kitchen door, smiling at me. I think I'd gained five pounds since being back, and she was to blame for most of it. Although the doughnut shop had helped. Becca and Tim had flown in, bringing wine for everyone.

When the light flashed green, Suzy turned to speak to me, but the emotion was too great. She started crying, shoulders shaking. I just held her. Me, holding the child of the man who came to get me when no one else would. She, holding the man her father went to save. Each holding the missing piece of the other. My arms have seldom felt so full. A photographer captured the moment, and it became the cover of several magazines and about a hundred websites.

What normally would have sent us to commercial brought the audience to their feet. The producer just let it go. For five minutes or more, Suzy shook with emotion. Shedding a lifetime of tears. When she finally composed herself, I gave her my handkerchief. She wiped her eyes and face and then spoke to the cameras. "Well . . . we'll be right back." It was a good moment. It broke the tension. The audience laughed.

When we returned from commercial, Suzy smiled. "Let's try this again."

"I don't know. I kind of liked the last segment." The audience liked that too.

She glanced at the papers in her hand. "A few weeks ago, you found me in the hospital and told me a story. Many have heard it. The larger networks have reported on it, including an hour-long documentary that aired two days ago. In case anyone watching this has been living under a rock the last few weeks, you mind telling it again?"

So I did. I walked back into the memory and told of my friendship with Suzy's dad. Of our life in-country. Of two cups of coffee. Of promises made. Then I told how he flew into a country he was ordered to stay out of, landed in a hot area, and picked me up, and how we flew a blissful thirty minutes until rockets blew off the back half of his helicopter. I told how we'd made a run for it. I talked of those three days, of the bullet that took his life and the book that stopped it from taking mine. I talked about the next eight days and how I would have given anything to hear his voice one more time. Of how I buried him beneath a tree with no marker. And, finally, of how I'd kept it a secret because I didn't feel worthy of the gift he'd given me.

When I finished, Suzy sat shaking her head. The people were quiet at first, and then the guy who had busted the beer bottle across my face stood and clapped. I felt uneasy. Allie picked up on it, appeared alongside me, and wrapped an arm around me. Without that support I think I'd have fallen over. When they finished clapping I cleared my throat. "If that was for me, it was too much. If it was for Suzy's father, it wasn't enough."

The next several minutes hurt my ears and soothed the painful places in me.

Suzy glanced at her papers. "You told me in the hospital that there was more to your story."

"That's right."

"But you also said you'd never tell me the rest of it."

"It's not mine to tell."

"You still holding true to that?"

I nodded.

"Before we sign off . . . Few people know this, but you have a rather famous brother who was also a war hero. Many times decorated. Senator Bobby Brooks. Heroism must run in the family." The people applauded. "Over the years, has he been a comfort to you as you two have talked about what you experienced?"

I glanced at my feet. Then back at her. "We've never talked about the war."

"Never?"

"Not once."

She was incredulous. "Why?"

"Some things are just too painful."

THE SHOW CLOSED, AND I walked through the kitchen and out the back door to get some air and sip some soda water. The hair involuntarily stood up on the back of my neck. I turned and saw Catalina off to one side. Frozen in a defensive posture and holding a large kitchen knife. The knife was shaking and terror riddled her face.

A few feet away, a man I did not know was holding a knife to Gabby's throat.

Juan Pedro's lieutenants had found us. Next to Gabby, Javier lay on the ground. Unconscious. Rosco lay next to him, completely still. A puddle of dark blood beneath him.

The man was speaking in hushed Spanish to Catalina. I couldn't understand his words, but his tone of voice told me that if either of us made a move he was going to finish Gabby. I also gathered that he was telling her to get into the turbocharged Dodge at the foot of the steps. I told her not to move, but he pressed harder against Gabby's neck and Catalina obeyed. She dropped the knife, walked around him and down the steps. She stood next to the car, where two more men waited inside. While Gabby cried and blood started trickling down her neck, the man holding her kept his eyes on me and backed down the steps. Slowly. Smiling. A cigarette dangling from his lips. At the base of the steps he stopped and was turning toward the car when I heard a piercing scream.

The man holding Gabby lost his grip and crumpled into a pile at the bottom of the steps. In the same second, Catalina launched toward Gabby, lifted her off the steps, and ran. The engine in the Dodge roared to life, and a hand extended out of the door to try and pull the downed man into the car.

I got there first and slammed the door shut, to the great discomfort of the owner of the hand. The blacked-out Dodge flung gravel through the parking lot as I raced toward the Corvette. The top was down, so I jumped in, cranked the engine, slammed the gear into first, and was about to let off the clutch when Diego appeared at my left shoulder, offering me Juan Pedro's bloody knife.

A half mile later, I'd pegged the accelerator at 160 mph. Both the Dodge and I were soon approaching the turn at the Rocks. Neither of us could make the turn at this speed. But if he made it through, he'd be gone. There was no way I could catch him. I had one chance—when he slowed just before the turn. I sat on his rear bumper, pushing him, wanting him to carry as much speed as possible into the turn. I knew the road would be slippery from a thin layer of windswept sand spread across the road.

He approached the turn at 120 mph. The Dodge got squirrelly, but he corrected, and that's when I figured out how good a driver he really was. He let off the accelerator, allowed the car to be absorbed by the soft sand on the side of the road, which stopped the spin he had begun, and let his momentum carry him through the sand and into the corner. If he didn't touch the accelerator, he'd emerge out the other side and disappear as the supercharger pushed the car over two hundred.

Halfway through the turn, I knew it was now or never. I swerved into the left lane, which would bring me into a perpendicular course with the Dodge when it corrected. The Dodge rounded the turn, began to straighten, and I T-boned him at over a hundred miles per hour.

Allie heard the crash at the restaurant. But unlike Jake's, there wasn't enough gas to cause an explosion. Just the sound of twisting metal.

The Dodge collided with the rocks and began flipping. As did the Corvette. I don't know how many times we rolled, but my roll bar saved me. When we came to a stop, we were both lying upside down on the beach on the other side of the rocks. The waves were rolling in beneath us. When the first one swamped me, I knew if I didn't get out I'd drown.

I unbuckled my harness, stumbled from the car, and stood weak-kneed on the beach, trying to shake out the dizziness and force my eyes to focus. There's a problem with spending your whole life trying to get back to good. Sometimes on the way back, you bump into the bad. And bad doesn't care. Bad is just bad. It likes it that way. And the bad is always hell-bent on you never getting back to good.

But in the last several years I had been trying. Making strides. Keeping to myself. A danger to no one. That ended on the beach when two strong, muscled figures crawled out of the Dodge and headed toward me. I didn't want to hurt them and I didn't want them to hurt me, but reason holds no place with people like that.

They didn't give me much choice. And thanks to the United States military, I'd always been good at fighting on a beach.

Twenty minutes later the police arrived. When they saw two bodies on the beach and Juan Pedro's bloody knife in my hand, they arrested me.

# — 40 —

The details would come out in court. Three illegal aliens, lieutenants of Juan Pedro, had attempted to kidnap Gabby and Catalina and return them to Mexico. When Diego and I prevented that, they fled. The prosecuting attorney neither admitted nor denied this. He focused on what happened the moment they drove out of the parking lot of the Blue Tornado. He was really good at his job and convinced the court and the jury that my castle doctrine defense ended at the boundary of the parking lot and what occurred thereafter, that is, my pursuit and the ensuing fight on the beach, constituted premeditated murder.

To an extent, he was right. Although I never verbalized that.

My attorney contended that I had a moral obligation to pursue. That my pursuit was a defense of those I loved no matter where it took place. Complicating matters was the fact that I'd just come off the airwaves where much of the radio-listening public had heard me talk about my military career. About how I was good at killing. The prosecution replayed carefully chosen snippets of Suzy's program to establish my "frame of mind," which gave rise to such a brutal outcome.

Contrary to my attorney's wishes and multiple objections, everything I'd said and done in the hour prior to the "encounter"—which included much of the admitted history of my life—was used against me to establish my mindset in the moments leading up to "the killing." The prosecuting attorney used pictures of the mangled bodies of Dummy #1 and Dummy #2 lying on the beach as evidence. I had not been merciful, and the pictures showed what he described as "excessive force." Dummy #3, who'd never walk again, sat in the witness chair and talked about my brutality. About the loss of his dearly departed friends. And how when he saw the error of his ways and tried to make his escape and climb into the car, I'd prevented him, breaking several bones.

Though I did not like him and wanted to rip his head off his shoulders, the prosecuting attorney did an excellent job of showing how three hungry, homeless, penniless, hardworking, and possibly misguided and not very intelligent men from Mexico, trying to put food on the table for their families, had attempted, and he emphasized "attempted" every chance he got, to steal some food from a large kitchen at a restaurant on the island of Cape San Blas. Not wise in their attempt, they got caught, and in their fear they made one bad decision to hold a young girl at knifepoint while they backed into their car and got away. Javier and Rosco had simply been casualties of their retreat. Their singular crime had been threatening Gabby, and other than a scratch on her neck, they'd intentionally harmed no one.

That was it. No mention was ever made of Juan Pedro or his organization or the fact that they were hired killers. Through much backroom wrangling and judge's quarters conversation between the attorneys, Catalina's history with Juan Pedro was not allowed to be admitted as evidence. Neither was the fact that they'd stolen the Dodge in South Texas two days prior.

Midway through the trial, my attorney read the writing on the wall and, in an attempt to help me, encouraged me to change my plea to guilty. I told him to put me on the stand. That I would speak in my defense.

He advised against that.

The state's attorney was salivating at the mouth when I took the stand. Given the cameras and the media frenzy, this was his ticket to the big time and he knew it. During his questioning, he asked, "Did you enjoy killing these men?"

"No, sir."

"You don't deny killing them?"

"Never have."

"Did you enjoy chasing them down after they had tried to leave peacefully?"

For a brief second I thought about jumping out of the witness stand and ripping his esophagus out of his throat, but then I looked at Allie and thought better of it. "I was defending myself and those I love."

"Be truthful, Mr. Brooks. You were angry and in a rage that they killed your dog."

He had a point there.

"That dog's name is Rosco, and he saved my life."

He liked the fact that he'd ruffled my feathers. "So you thought you'd make them pay."

"Sir, my intention was to stop them from threatening Catalina and Gabby. If they didn't want to die, they should've stayed in the car on the beach."

"And drowned?"

"It would have saved us all a lot of trouble."

"Do their lives not matter?"

"No, they don't." I looked at him, then at the jury, then I pointed at Catalina and Gabby. "Their lives matter."

THE TRIAL LASTED A week. When my attorney asked me if I needed anything, I said, "Yes, a stack of index cards."

The by-the-book judge never showed his hand. Judge Werther was judicially blind and just, never letting either side get away with much, and I must say I could not bring myself to dislike him. Under different circumstances I think we'd have gotten along. He was just a guy like me. Following orders. Given the national nature of the case, he allowed the media in the courtroom. Every channel had a live camera feed. The streets outside were jammed with trucks and telescoping antennas.

When the jury recessed, my attorney said, "You need to prepare yourself for the worst."

I poked him in the chest. "You need to make sure they understand that they killed my dog."

I could read the writing on the wall. They returned several hours later having found me guilty of manslaughter. Allie and

Catalina were inconsolable. Catalina stood and screamed at the judge and jury, forcing the bailiff to remove her. I was rather proud of her gumption. Sentencing was scheduled for a month later. Given my meritorious service record, the judge agreed to allow my attorney to bring character witnesses to the stand to speak on my behalf and petition the court for leniency. The possibilities for the length of my sentence ranged from several years to two consecutive life sentences.

They would not give me antacids in prison. As a result, my perceived discomfort grew steadily and the pain became constant. It would sometimes take my breath away. I said nothing, because if they gave me life, I didn't want to have a heart that worked.

Allie came to see me every day. I spent most of my time trying to console her. Manuel, Javier, Peter, and Victor came to see me. They sat across from me. Quiet. Not knowing what to say. I asked how the carnival was going, and they nodded. I asked how their families were settling into life in the States, and they nodded. I asked how the process to citizenship was progressing, and they held up their driver's licenses. They told me that Dummy #3, the man with the cut Achilles tendon, had been deported. "Sent home."

The governor went on the air and declared how all people, regardless of nationality, deserved the same civil treatment. That Florida was not the Wild West and that we were and are a nation of laws. That people did not need to feel afraid to live in our great state. He also did not want my case to get lost in the bowels of judicial wrangling. He let Judge Werther know he wanted justice served. And he let the people of the state of Florida know that he was monitoring the situation and would use the powers of his office to make sure we stayed on track. The people deserved a swift, public, and just outcome.

With a week to go, my brother came to see me. During the trial he'd kept his distance. His presence in the courtroom could have been misinterpreted and used by the other side. I knew that.

He sat down. Jeans and flip-flops. "How you doing?"

I tapped my heart with my pencil. "I miss Rosco."

He nodded.

I asked, "You got any feel for what the judge might do?"

He shook his head. "He's been on the bench a long time. Doesn't owe anybody any favors. Not real swayed by politicians. He's known for maximum sentences, and he hands them down with liberality."

"Great."

Bobby's lip trembled when he asked, "Can I do anything for you?"

"Take care of my family."

"Name it."

"Remove any red tape. Get them through the process. Give them a life here. I've got money. Whatever you need."

"And Allie?"

I paused. "Be a friend. She's gonna need one. I'm giving her all I've got so she won't need to work, but she'll want to. To give her hands something to do. She'll go crazy otherwise."

He stood to leave. Despite orders from the warden not to make physical contact with me in any way, he hugged me. Through tears he said, "Joseph, I'm sorry."

I handed him a card. A simple picture. A window, covered in bars. "Me too."

# — 41 —

The courtroom was packed. Standing room only. Judge Werther allowed my attorney to begin calling character witnesses. And so he did. Throughout the morning, he called Manuel, Javier, Peter, and Victor. Their presence seemed to make a positive impression on the judge, but he was tough to read. Then he called Catalina. With the judge's permission, she called Gabby and Diego and let them describe their relationship with me. His demeanor changed slightly when they spoke. He thanked them for their courage and he asked Gabby if her neck had healed. She showed him her throat. Standing before the bench, she said, "But this isn't what hurts."

The judge responded, "What does?"

"I miss Rosco."

Judge Werther nodded. "You mean your dog?"

"He slept with me. When that man put that knife to my throat, Rosco jumped on him."

The judge looked at me, then back at Gabby. "How was it that Rosco slept with you?"

Gabby pointed at me. "Uncle Joe told him to."

I'd never heard her call me that. I liked it.

The judge looked at me. "I thought Rosco kept you from having flashback dreams."

"He did."

"And yet you made him sleep with her."

I shrugged. "I knew he'd protect her."

The judge spoke almost to himself. "Which he did."

He motioned for Catalina and Gabby to step down. To my surprise, my attorney next called the waitress from the diner, to whom I'd given the truck. She wore a dress. Carried her son in her arms. She told what I'd done, and the judge thanked her for traveling to testify. Next to take the stand were Becca and Tim.

After lunch my attorney called Allie, and she gave her account of me. Of us. She took her time and told the story. The judge must have been a great poker player. He was stoic and had the expression of a piece of granite.

Lastly my attorney called my brother. Bobby had asked to be a character witness. The cameras in the courtroom clicked off a thousand pictures as he made his way to the stand. He was dressed in jeans, running shoes, sleeves rolled up. He swore on the Bible and stated that the words he was about to speak would be the truth.

# — 42 —

Bobby chewed on his lip and chose his words carefully. His posture wasn't political. The senator wasn't on the stand. My brother was. "Your Honor, there's a piece of this story that no one—including my brother—is telling you." He looked at me.

The judge responded, "Enlighten us, please, Senator Brooks."

Whatever story Bobby had come to tell, he'd come to peace with it. He adjusted in his seat, crossed his legs, and folded his hands. And while his eyes were focused on me, he was staring forty-five years into the past.

"In September of 1972, my number was called." He reached into his front shirt pocket and pulled out a yellowed and wrinkled document. "My draft notice."

It'd been a long time since I'd seen that sheet of paper. He turned it in his hands.

"When my mother opened the mail, her heart sank. I was . . ."

He weighed his head side to side. "Different then. Certainly not the man the voting public thinks me today. I liked books. Liked baseball. And pretty soon, I would like drugs."

The judge leaned back and showed surprise for the first time. The people in the audience who didn't know where this was going laughed. I did not.

Bobby continued. "Thanks to an experience in my past that scarred me, I was afraid. Of a lot. But mostly of other people. When it came to defending those who needed defending, I was paralyzed. It wasn't that I didn't want to, I just wasn't very good at it."

I spoke loudly enough for him to hear me. "You don't need to do this."

The judge turned to me. "Mr. Brooks, you have something to add?"

I stood. "Sir, I was just telling my brother that he doesn't need to tell this story."

Judge Werther pointed his gavel at Bobby. "He's requested, of his own volition, to do so. So please sit."

I did as instructed.

Bobby held up the draft notice. "My mother took this to Jo-Jo. My younger brother, Joseph. It was one week past his seventeenth birthday. Although I'm two years older, he was always the stronger one. He and my mother went for a ride in the car he had built. And on that car ride she asked him to take my place."

The sound of air sucking in rose up from the audience.

"And he did." Pin-drop silence roared. "My brother said good-bye to the love of his life. He told her he was taking me to California, maybe Canada, where we could outrun the war. Then he walked into the recruiting office and went in my place . . . with my name."

Behind me Allie began whispering, "No, no, no, no . . ."

Bobby spoke louder. "Ashamed of myself for letting him go, and trying to outrun the voices in my head, I told everyone I wasn't going to California. That I was enlisting. They gave me a send-off party, and I boarded a bus that took me straight to California, where I took Joseph's driver's license and rented an apartment and got a job and ingested every drug I could beg, borrow, or steal. But no matter how many I took, I couldn't drown the voices or medicate the pain."

Someone cussed Bobby from the audience. Judge Werther pounded his gavel and spoke to everyone. "I have instructed the bailiff to remove anyone causing a disturbance. And if that is all of you, then I will sit in my courtroom alone." He turned to Bobby. "Continue, please, Senator."

Bobby spoke to the man who cussed him. "You're right. I'm that and more. It gets worse."

My heart sank as Bobby committed political suicide in front of the whole world.

Allie's whimpering had become incessant. She was shaking her head and whispering no again and again.

"So after my two-year 'tour' of every drug hostel along the coast of California, I returned home. I convinced his girl that I had in fact gone to war, by telling her it was horrible and I couldn't talk about it, which was convenient because I wouldn't have known what to say anyway. Six weeks earlier, rather conveniently for me, my brother had come home after having honorably served two tours. He landed to mobs of people spitting on him. Given that he was covered up in medals, he was shining like the sun. He walked into an airport hangar and threw away everything having to do with the military—including his medals.

"After a week with the military brass trying to get inside his head and figure out what he knew that they needed to know, he spent a couple months at a war treatment program trying to get his head right. To figure out what to say when he got home. To explain who he'd become. During his program, his commanding officer—who was understandably proud of all that he'd accomplished—dug those medals out of the trash and sent them home where, upon my arrival, I opened the envelope addressed to me. I could not have timed that any better. And since I was already neck deep in the lie, I opened the envelope, admired my reflection in the silver and gold, and pinned them on my chest—"

The cussing had stopped. People sat in silent disbelief. Behind me, Allie made a dash for the trash can in the corner, hit her knees, and vomited. The sound of pain exiting a human body. It was raw, primal, and unadulterated. Cameras began to flash, people to talk.

Judge Werther pounded his gavel. "I will have order in this courtroom." He stood. "We're going to take a fifteen-minute recess."

The judge then asked the bailiff to get Allie a wet towel, which he did. But she was inconsolable. I pointed at her and asked the judge, "Sir, may I?"

He nodded and disappeared into his private quarters, taking my brother with him.

I knelt next to Allie, who threw her arms around me and sobbed, "I'm sorry . . . I'm sorry . . ."

I just held her. Wasn't much else I could do. Forty-five years ago, her soul had ruptured. Split down the middle. Somehow she'd stitched it back together. But here in this courtroom, listening to my brother, the stitching had been ripped open and the pain she'd long held inside was being released in front of me. In front of all of us.

The bailiff announced the return of the judge, and we all stood. He took his seat and told Bobby to continue.

Bobby looked at Allie. Then at me. "What I have told you is not the worst. Joseph exited the war treatment program, hopeful of what he'd find at home. He drove through the night, parked at the Blue Tornado, followed the crowd to the beach, and found me wearing a chestful of his medals and saying 'I do' to Allie.

"He turned around and went back to the only thing he knew. War. Where he spent two more years. During which time he would be awarded this." Bobby reached into his pocket, then opened his hand to reveal the Congressional Medal of Honor. The audience gasped. Even the judge's eyes grew large. The network guys sitting behind live camera feeds could not believe what they were hearing.

Bobby continued. "Back home, my life spiraled downward. After rehab and therapy and nearly bankrupting Allie in the process, I cleaned up my act and ran for state senate, convincing all of you that I was a man of my word. In truth, I got elected on the sympathy vote. I based my campaign, and every one since then, on a very good lie. The lie that I'd lived the life my brother lived.

It wasn't difficult. I simply asked the US military for a copy of my records. And since they were in my name, I got them. Somehow no one in the media ever studied my 'military record' in any detail. Had they done so, they'd have quickly pieced together that I could not possibly have been drying out in Arizona and at the same time leading special operations in Laos. Or Cambodia. Or wherever he was at the time. Once elected, I learned I was good at politics because I could lie with the best of them. So I traveled up the political ladder and ran for the US Senate. I've been re-elected five times, primarily because I was really good at spinning that same lie and who's not going to vote for a war hero and Medal of Honor winner? I'd made myself the poster boy for the Stars and Stripes. Wasn't long before I found myself appointed to committees whose sole purpose was to control much of what happened in the military. Those appointments came with top-secret clearance." Bobby took a deep breath. "A draft-dodging coward with security clearance . . ." He glanced at me. "Ironic, don't you think?"

The silence in the courtroom was deafening.

He continued. "Even the set of military records the government gave me upon my request were incomplete in several areas. Given Joseph's activities, much of which our government could not acknowledge, much of the file was highly classified; sections were black-lined or pages were simply missing. But with my classified security clearance, I dug around and patched back together the missing pages of my younger brother's military service record. Only then did I uncover the true nature and extent of his service, where he was and what he did. Luckily for me, he'd served so well, so secretly, and with such distinction that his entire life was classified. Still is."

He turned to Suzy, who sat in the audience with her jaw on the floor. "That's the reason you couldn't find it. Not to mention the fact that you were looking under the wrong name. But even if you'd had the right name, they'd have never given it to you."

Suzy was shaking her head. Tears streaming down.

"When I read the reports of what he'd done"—Bobby glanced in his lap where he held my file—"I felt both shame and extreme pride. I had done the unthinkable. Joseph had taken my place. Even my name. He said yes when I said no. I knew I could never pay for what I did to him, but . . . for reasons I've never understood, Joseph has never unmasked me." He looked at me and just shook his head. "For forty-plus years, he's never told the story I would have told a thousand times over. And for forty-plus years, I've been standing on his shoulders, taking credit for his steps."

Allie, sitting directly behind me, was muffling violent sobs. Suzy sat speechless. Nobody knew what to say or do.

Bobby turned to the judge. "The Latin word *meritare* means 'to serve like a soldier.' From it we get the word *unmerited*. My brother went to war when he wasn't technically old enough to go. Barely seventeen. He went without complaint. While there, we taught him how to defend those who could not defend themselves. He did that then. He's done it his whole life. He's doing it here, today." Bobby looked at the judge. "That gift to all of us was then and is now unmerited." Bobby was calm. Not the least bit anxious. And when he looked at me, for the first time since we were kids I saw my brother in his eyes.

Even the judge was speechless. Bobby paused, then looked back up at him. "A long time ago, my brother gave me what I did not deserve, and, ever since, has taken from me what I did deserve. He may be on trial, but he's not the criminal. If I could step out of this chair and take his chains, I would. I'd serve his sentence—whatever it may be. I ask this court for mercy."

# — 43 —

My heart was pounding in my ears. The pain in my chest had grown unbearable. I slumped over, causing my attorney to ask me if I was all right. I couldn't respond. Allie stood behind me and put her hand on my back. The cameras turned toward me. Whatever had long held back the pain in my chest was finally losing its grip.

I tried to stand, but I couldn't move most of the left side of my body. My heart sounded like Niagara in my ears and it felt like someone had shoved a spear through the center of my chest and out my back. I was having trouble breathing. Whatever I was doing got everyone's attention because all hell broke loose in that courtroom. Their faces suggested everyone was screaming, but I couldn't hear them. The world I was living in had gone quiet.

Somehow I ended up on the floor where the fluorescent ceiling lights seemed brighter. Somebody had ripped off my shirt, and somebody else hovered over me, holding two paddles. They screamed something, and I was pretty sure I didn't want them to do what they were about to do, but they slammed the paddles onto my chest and I remember seeing a flash of white light.

And where most people will tell you that in a time like that they saw some great light, I did not. My world went black. Not a sliver of light anywhere.

Since I was nine years old, while I had tried to force my mind to forget, my body had kept a debt ledger, a record of wrongs committed against it. When those things were spoken out loud, brought out into the open, they were torn from their cages, doors ripped off the hinges. What had so long been imprisoned in me now left my body in much the same way the pain had left Allie's. Involuntarily and with great speed.

The only way I know to describe what I felt is to say that my chest exploded.

And it felt good.

# — 44 —

My mother held the draft notice in her hand. Her hand was shaking. Tears were dripping off her chin. She was leaning on the hood of my Corvette, staring out across the water. I turned her toward the beach, and we started walking. For a mile, neither of us said a word.

Finally she spoke. "Bobby never met a stranger. He trusts everybody. It's one of the reasons I love him, but he won't last a week over there."

She was right. He wouldn't.

She crossed her arms. "And you'll be getting a notice in a few months." We kept walking. An endless shoreline. No hope in sight.

Mom had worked two, sometimes three jobs since Dad left. She'd clothed us, fed us, nursed cuts and bruises, put up with us. A single mom raising two boys, she'd given us everything she could. She had denied herself any small pleasure to see that we had shoes like the other guys, so they wouldn't make fun of us. To make sure Bobby had glasses that allowed him to read the chalkboard. To keep a roof over our heads. When times were tight she shopped at the Salvation Army and then wrapped the clothes in K-Mart bags so we wouldn't know. Mom had not known a life of luxury or ease, but she'd worked hard to make sure we had not known a world as harsh as the one she was living in. Walking down the beach, she held the piece of paper that was going to take everything she had in this world.

"I've got a little money saved up." She pushed her hair out of her face. "I want you to take your brother and go to California. Maybe Canada. You can come back when it's over." She straightened. "There's no shame in that."

I eyed the paper. "Does Bobby know?" I asked.

She stared out across the ocean. Shaking her head. "I couldn't . . ."

Mom stared at the paper, holding it in both hands. Then with anger bubbling, she tore it in two. Then again. Then she just stood there with the four pieces of her heart crumpled in one fist. "I will not live to see both my sons buried. I will not die a childless woman." She pointed at the Corvette, her resolve growing. "I want you to leave tonight."

"Mom?"

She knew what I was going to say before I said it. It's why she had brought me out there. Her lip trembled and she shook her head.

Dark clouds had blown in from the east. The air was thick with electricity. Lightning flashed in the distance. The wind turned and blew in from the south. We saw the sheets of rain rolling toward us. The earth bloomed and smelled of that pungent freshness that rises up out of the dirt just before the rain. I stretched out my hand, uncurled her fingers, and picked the four tattered pieces off her palm.

"Everyone's always saying how we look like twins," I said.

She tried to sound strong. "No."

I looked at my mom. "Don't tell him until I'm gone."

She knew I was right. She could keep one son or lose both. She whispered a second time, "No," but there was no resolve in it. It was as if she were talking to God more than me.

She crumpled into a pile on the sand just as the rain came down in sheets. The heavens opened and rocked the earth. A dozen times, maybe more, lightning flashed. At one point the hair on my neck stood up, and the thunderclap cracked above us.

Mom clenched her fists and tried to hold back the sobs, but soon the wave of emotions crashed over her. She rose up on her knees and screamed at the storm. "They're all I've got! All I've got!"

The thunder cracked. Lightning hit the dune next to us.

She turned and spoke into the flash. "What have I left to give?"

Another flash. Another thunderclap. Mom's voice was broken. As was she. She fell on me, wrapped her arms around my neck, and sobbed. I held my mom and I held those pieces of paper. And right then and there I buried the truth in me.

And the weight of it all crushed me.

Having spent its venom, the angry storm softened and blanketed us in large drops. As the rain washed the anger and tears, my mom stood. Drenched head to toe. She leaned into me and pressed her forehead to mine. When she spoke, she wasn't speaking to me. "Watch over my boy . . . all the days of his life . . . and let him live to see the rain." She closed her eyes. "Send down the rain."

FOR FIFTY-THREE YEARS I'D lived in a storm. Lightning. Thunderclap. High wind. But when my brother told the truth about us in that courtroom, the lies I'd buried came unearthed, and my chest exploded, and for the first time since that afternoon on the beach with my mom, I felt the rain on my face. I tasted the drops. And they tasted like tears.

On the floor of that courtroom, something in me came alive, but it wasn't my heart. At least not the one they were attempting to shock back to life. It was lower down. More toward the center of my gut. While chaos ensued in the courtroom, I lay on the carpet staring into a dark world. Then, without invitation, memories flooded like films across my eyelids. With the truth released, my body remembered the storm that my mind had forgotten. The memories were out of sequence and held no rhyme or reason. They just surfaced. The only common thread was that they were moments charged with emotion, and yet I'd not cried in any of them. I'd felt nothing.

That night on the beach with my mom, I'd closed my heart. And yet here I was now, more dead than alive, and I felt everything. I could smell people's sweat. Excrement. Dried blood. Fresh bread baking. Salt in the ocean. Hush puppies in the fryer. The way the earth smells before and after the rain. My mother's hair.

My father's aftershave. Engine oil. Burning rubber. The cabin of an airplane. The smell of death. And Allie.

I remembered the smell of Allie.

When I was a kid, I remember feeling with great emotion. My eyes would see and my heart would feel. The line between the two was taut, and when one pulled, the response was immediate and constant. I drank life through a fire hose. Then life dinged me, restricted the flow, and pretty soon the raging river was a dribbling trickle. Then some giant hand clamped down on the spigot nozzle and the trickle was reduced to nothing at all. Not a drop. Did it dry up on its own, or had my life just dammed it up? Either way, the flow of water was gone. Ever since, I'd lived my life through a dusty, calloused piece of lifeless meat.

That's a pain-filled way to live.

But lying on my back, with all those frantic people fussing over me, I watched the video of my life. And after all the hell and horror and evil and terror I'd known, something cracked through. As I stood there on the dry riverbed that was me, a trickle returned. And the more I watched, the more the flow increased. It swirled around my toes. Then my ankles. Wrapped around my knees. Waist deep, the current tugged at me.

It was both one second and one lifetime. The water around me was clear. I cupped my hand and brought it to my lips. It was sweet, clean, and cold. My body may have been in that courtroom, but my heart was standing in an ocean. I jumped in and dunked my head under the flow. I held my breath and pushed through the water, pulling with long, strong strokes. When I surfaced and sucked in a lungful of air, all the dirty, bloody places I'd carried around for so long had begun to wash off. What was once crusty became soft. What was dirty became clean. I took another breath and returned beneath the surface, kicking deeper. Where the water was cooler. I did that a long time. I don't really know how long. All I really know is that the water washed over me. It rose up from below. It fell from above.

The storm of my life was over. The rain had come.

# — 45 —

My eyes opened to a world of white. Everything was white. Including the woman at the foot of my bed. I asked, "Are you an angel?"

She laughed the most beautiful laugh. It echoed off the walls and fell across me like a soft blanket.

I thought to myself, *If she's laughing, then I can't be in hell, 'cause I highly doubt there's laughter in hell. I mean, what would people in hell have to laugh about?*

My chest wasn't hurting, so I asked, "Is this heaven?" Before she could answer, I said, "If you know all I've done, you'll never let me in."

She laughed again. That's when I was pretty sure I wasn't in hell. I tried looking around, but the world I'd awakened into was so brilliant and bright I couldn't look into it. I tried blinking my eyes into focus, but it didn't help. I'd awakened looking into the sun. Over my left shoulder, the sound of rapid footsteps echoed on a hard floor.

A face appeared over me. Then closer. Then I felt her cheek and lips pressed to mine. Then I smelled her. Allie was holding me.

Heaven had let me in.

My eyes slowly focused as medical personnel peppered me with questions and poked me and prodded me, and all I wanted to do was talk with Allie. There were six people in whatever room I was in and each was doing about ten different things. I held out my hand. "Hold it. Everybody stop."

Oddly enough, they did. About this time a man walked in. Gray hair. White coat. Stethoscope hanging around his neck. I said, "Other than me, who's in charge here?"

The man raised his hand. "That'd be me."

"Where am I?"

He answered, "Regional Memorial."

"What's that?"

"A hospital."

"Who are you?"

"I'm one of your doctors."

"One?"

"You have about eight."

"How'd I get here?"

He seemed to be enjoying this game, so he gave me short, staccato answers, hoping I'd keep playing along. "An ambulance."

"When?"

He glanced at my chart. "Sixteen days ago."

The word *sixteen* sank in. "What have I been doing?"

"Sleeping."

"What'd you people do to me?"

"You've been in a coma."

"Why didn't you wake me up?"

He laughed. "We've been trying."

"What happened?"

He spoke slowly. "Takotsubo cardiomyopathy."

I frowned. "In English, please."

"It's also called 'broken heart syndrome.' It occurs almost exclusively in women, so that makes your case that much more interesting. You're a bit of an anomaly."

I leaned my head back. "That's one way of putting it."

I was still pretty foggy, and the pieces of the puzzle weren't falling into place as quickly and neatly as I'd hoped. Allie was holding my hand with both of hers. She asked, "What's the last thing you remember?"

I pushed back the fog. "Bobby in the courtroom."

"As he was finishing, you had a heart attack. Or something like it. You died on the floor of the courtroom. These people brought you back."

The knowledge and weight of the world I had been living in returned. Along with my manslaughter conviction and impending sentencing. I turned to Allie. "What's my sentence?"

She shook her head. "We don't know yet; Judge Werther hasn't delivered one. Now that you're awake . . ."

I searched the room. "Where's Bobby?"

The doctor moved about two feet to the left. Bobby sat in a chair. Unshaven. A pillow next to him.

I lifted my head. "Hey, brother."

He nodded. Smiled. I could tell he was tired. "Hey."

The memory of his televised confession returned. "You okay?"

Another nod. "I'm good."

"I imagine you're sorta popular."

He half smiled. "In an odd sort of way."

"Folks want your head on a platter?"

"And they're the kind ones."

"You still got a job?"

"For the moment. I've been called to testify before a committee. Most think I should step down and let the governor appoint a replacement."

I waved my hand across the room and all the people staring down at me and all the machines. "You do all this?"

Allie answered. "Yes. He did."

I looked at the doctor. "So what now?"

He shrugged. "While you were sleeping, we ran a camera up your leg and into your heart. I was anticipating putting in several stents. After looking around, I did not. I can't explain it, but your heart is quite strong. Given the amount of time you were out in the courtroom, we didn't know how much brain damage you might have sustained. Based on the last five minutes, I'd say none." He patted my shoulder. "Welcome back." He then lifted a small sealed plastic bag from his shirt pocket and set it on the bedside table next to me. "We also found this in your stomach."

I stared at the mangled bullet.

"But I have a feeling you knew that was in there."

"I did."

Allie leaned closer and looked from the bullet to me.

The doctor laughed. "You're lucky they used copper. Lead would have eaten through you a long time ago."

Allie held up the bag. Staring closely. "When you were carrying Suzy's dad?"

A flash of searing heat appeared and disappeared in the side of my stomach. "Yes."

The doctor continued. "We happened upon it by mistake while trying to revive you. It showed up in the pictures." He crossed his arms. "Why didn't you ever do anything about it?"

I opened the bag and spilled the smooth bullet into my palm. The years inside my stomach had worn off the rough edges. "Didn't feel worthy."

# — 46 —

A week later they walked me into the courtroom. I shuffled, dragging my ankle chains. Walking like someone had tied my shoelaces together. Somehow the number of people in the courtroom had doubled. More cameras. More lights. More whispering. More eyes looking at me.

The bailiff walked in and raised his booming voice above the fray. "All rise. The Court of the Second Judicial Circuit, Criminal Division, is now in session. The Right Honorable Judge Jay Werther presiding."

The judge walked in and took his seat, and everyone else did likewise. He was quiet a few seconds. Digital cameras clicked and sounded, suggesting the Internet would soon be filling with pictures and video of the proceedings. He looked at me. "How're you feeling?"

"Better, sir. Although I'm real sorry for what I did to your carpet."

Everyone laughed.

I continued, "Looks like somebody washed out the stain, though."

This time the judge laughed. Along with everyone else.

He tapped his lip with a pencil. "Can I ask you a question?"

"Yes, sir."

He pointed the pencil at Bobby. "Do you hate your brother?"

I shook my head. "No."

"How is that?"

"What good would it do? Won't change anything."

Judge Werther nodded once.

"Sir, I've had the experience of being in a country where people were trying to kill me. Every day. That simplifies life a good bit. In matters of the heart, we have only two options. Hate them or love them. That's it. That's all we got. There's no middle."

He seemed surprised by this. The judge paused. Tapped the end of his pencil on his desk. "I'm curious."

"About?"

"The one part of your story that's not been told."

"Sir?"

"The part only you can tell."

"You talking about the conversation with my mom?"

He nodded.

"Sir, I can tell you, but the only other witness is dead. How do you know I'm telling the truth?"

"I don't."

I scratched my head. "And you're okay with that?"

"This is no longer a trial." He pointed at the cameras. "You've been out of commission for a few weeks, so let me spell it out for you. Joseph Brooks, you've captivated a nation. I'm told that several million people are currently watching these proceedings. There are more than a thousand men in black leather straddling enormous, eardrum-splitting motorcycles outside this courthouse right now. Schools across the country have canceled classes and are projecting these proceedings on giant screens in auditoriums. A record of living history."

He looked at Suzy. "I'm told that Suzy True's show has seen ratings increases unheard of in the modern radio era. I've had personal phone calls from the governor, the other Florida senator, the Speaker of the House of the United States Congress, and the Chief of Staff of the President of the United States. Each has called to make sure that justice is served. So let's just say for the sake of argument, and because that lady over there with hummingbird wings for fingers is recording everything you say, that I'd like to hear you tell me. I have a feeling you can remember."

"Bobby was working at the Blue Tornado, a restaurant back home. I was turning a wrench underneath my Corvette. The mailman walked up to our box, slid in the mail, and kept walking. Mom had been sitting on the porch. Wind tugging at her dress. One of the two she owned. She stood and made herself walk the forty-two feet to the box. She lowered the lid and I guess the notice was lying on top, because she sucked in a breath and covered her mouth with her hand. Clutching the mail to her chest, she walked back to the house, stumbling every few feet. She walked inside and shut the door. I crawled out from beneath the car and walked up onto the porch. I watched through the glass as Mom opened the letter, let out a noise that sounded like somebody had just shot her in the chest, and then dropped to her knees in the front hall. For about two minutes, she didn't breathe. She just knelt there. I pushed open the door, and when she looked up at me, she was cracking down the middle. She said, 'Let's go for a ride.' She stood up and leaned on me all the way to the garage. We drove north up the island where she sat with that notice spread flat across her lap. We parked and stood next to the dunes and I watched my mom come apart at the seams."

I paused, looking back. Stuck in the memory.

He pressed me quietly. "And?"

"She tore that piece of paper into four pieces and told me to take Bobby to California. Or Canada. To come back when it was over."

"When you and your mother made this plan, did the two of you ever think to give your brother a vote?"

"No, sir."

"Why not?"

"Because he'd have gone."

"You really believe that?"

"Without a doubt."

The judge let that sink in. "Continue."

"I'd seen what had happened to my mom when my dad cut out on us. It left a hole in her heart, and in ours. I knew if we both left, what life remained in my mom would drain out the hole and she'd die alone in that house. Especially if one of us didn't come home. To my mom, that draft notice was an obituary."

Behind me, Bobby blew his nose.

"I was savvier than Bobby," I continued. "Thought maybe I had a better chance of staying alive. The only thing to do was take the notice, along with his driver's license, and raise my right hand."

The judge tapped a pencil on his desk and leaned back. "I'm curious."

"Sir?"

"Where were you when Nixon canceled the draft in January '73?"

"Somewhere in Laos."

He dug through some papers on his desk and held up a single sheet. "This is your birth certificate." He handed it to the bailiff, who handed it to me.

"Is the date of birth correct?" the judge asked.

"Yes, sir." I handed it back to the bailiff.

"You realize, based on your date of birth, you never would have been drafted."

"Yes, sir."

Behind me, Bobby was crying.

"My fourth tour, near the end, I had a couple of really bad days and I was in pretty bad shape. In the four years prior, I'd gotten pretty good at getting myself out of tough situations, but on this particular day, I couldn't. I needed someone to come get me. The folks who put me there said they weren't coming. Too dangerous. Plus, they'd have to admit that they'd inserted me into a country where I wasn't supposed to be. That meant I was helpless." I looked at the judge. "Do you understand?"

He nodded once. "I do."

"Then a buddy, a guy with a wife and a daughter he loved, who had everything to live for and everything to lose, acted against direct orders. He stole a bird, crash-landed into hell, and lifted me out. I've had a lifetime to think about that. What would cause a man to do that?" I shook my head. "This may not make much sense to all of you, but as I was standing in that place, covered up in heat, bugs, bullets, and bayonets, I knew that the ground I was standing on and everything around me was flat-out evil. But when I heard those rotors whipping through the air, I knew that whatever was in that bird could not be evil.

"I'd seen what evil could do. Evil never gave itself for anyone. It takes what it doesn't own. Holds your head under the water. Rips your head off your neck and dangles it from the city wall. Evil dominates. Controls. Eradicates. Evil is a sniveling punk, and if you let it inside you then you spew hatred, which is just another name for the poison we drink hoping it'll hurt someone else."

I glanced around the courtroom at Allie, Catalina, Gabby, Suzy, and finally at the cameras.

"But not love. Love rushes in where others won't. Where the bullets are flying. It stands between. Pours out. Empties itself. It scours the wasteland, returns the pieces that were lost, and it never counts the cost."

Despite a packed house, the room was silent. After a minute, I continued, "Love walks into hell, where I sit in chains, where the verdict is guilty, grabs you by the heart, and says to the warden, 'Me for him.'" I turned and glanced at my brother. "Sir, we live in an angry, evil world. Where stuff doesn't always make sense. Where hope seems like something we did when we were kids and the love we cling to slips through our fingers like cold water, but"—I tapped my chest—"nothing that happens here today changes the fact that love heals the shattered places." I shook my head once. "It's the only thing that can—" The faces in the courtroom held steady on mine. "It's the only thing worth fighting for," I finished, then turned to Bobby. I'd like to think my eyes smiled. "So, no, sir, I don't hate my brother."

The judge nodded. Sat back. His chair squeaking. Another long pause. After a moment he sucked through his teeth and scratched his chin. "You present this court with a real problem, Mr. Brooks."

"How so, Your Honor?"

He held up the scorecard that the jury had returned along with the verdict. It was the formal listing of my crimes, along with mandatory sentencing guidelines as outlined by the State. He waved the paper. "In Roman times this was called 'the handwriting of requirements that was against us.' Here today, the State of Florida requires that I sentence you to a term of punishment based on your crime as dictated by the law."

"I understand."

He pointed to the twelve empty jury chairs in the jury box. "They found you guilty of manslaughter. They did not agree with either you or your attorney's argument that you had a moral obligation to defend that woman and her daughter"—he pointed to Catalina and Gabby, who were sitting one row behind Allie— "beyond the geographical boundaries of your home and place of work."

I nodded. "Yes, sir, they did."

He waved that piece of paper. "This brings with it a minimum requirement of eight years. And a maximum of two life terms to be served sequentially."

I did not like where this was going, but I nodded. "That's what my attorney tells me."

The judge sat back in his chair. For several minutes he tapped his pencil on his desktop. Then he said, "Mr. Brooks, please stand."

I did. My chains rattled.

The judge stood. "Mr. Brooks, I am sentencing you to life."

Allie gasped behind me. As did most of the courtroom. Two dozen cameras clicked hundreds of photos. Mutiny bubbled just beneath the surface. The bailiff and four well-armed police officers stepped forward.

Judge Werther pounded his gavel, and the courtroom slowly quieted. Staring out across the room of reporters and cameras, he focused on me. "The conditions of your sentence are as follows." He placed the gavel quietly on the desktop and folded his hands in front of him. If I'm not mistaken, his eyes had become glassy. "Go live your life. The one you never got to live."

"Sir, I don't follow you."

"I have considered the manifest weight of the evidence, and I am reversing the jury's decision. In legal terms it's called *sua sponte*. Meaning after forty-plus years on this bench, I am making a decision of my own, which I believe serves justice better than the decision of the twelve who sat there. I am throwing this verdict back at the state's attorney and telling him that he has to retry you. That I don't really care what the jury said. I think they got it wrong. And based on my conversation with the state's attorney, he does too. Given what has happened here, and been revealed, he knows it will be political suicide to retry you, and so he has no intention of ever doing that." Judge Werther shook his head once. "Mr. Brooks . . . you're free to go."

I once owned a carnival. On Friday nights, when we were operating over capacity, I called it controlled chaos. But it was nothing compared to what that courtroom became when he pounded his gavel one last time and said, "Bailiff, remove Mr. Brooks's chains."

# — 47 —

Bobby was called before Congress to testify. I asked to tag along. He didn't think it'd do any good, but I went anyway. Walking in amid shouts for his blood, he said, "You sure you want to be here? This could get nasty."

"I've seen nasty, and it doesn't really scare me. I wouldn't miss this."

Most of my brother's critics used the hearings as a chance to peacock. They drilled him with questions and he answered. Honestly. Not the least bit flustered. I sat in the chair next to him. His attorneys thanked me for my presence and my service, but reiterated that I was not compelled to testify. But given the public nature of my life over the last few weeks, they wondered if I had anything to add. They said this as if they were doing me a favor.

I told the story of the three events in our younger lives. My dad's absence. The tae kwon do debacle. And Mr. Billy. Of their effect on Bobby and me. Then I tried to paint a picture of Bobby in those early years. One of the senators strutted and told me those stories had no bearing on my brother's cowardice. He opined for about twenty minutes.

When he finished, I said, "Sir, you see this medal hanging around my neck?" It was dangling against the base of the microphone.

He didn't respond.

"The governing body that you now represent awarded it to me upon returning from war. With all due respect, I've earned the right to speak in this chamber, and if I want to tell you about my childhood, then"—I smiled—"you're going to hear about my childhood."

He huffed and tried to say something senatorial, but I cut him off.

"None of us are the men we'd hope to be. Not you. Not my brother. And certainly not me. We're all guilty. Despite what you may think about him, my brother has spent his life trying to get back to good. Paying penance. Here in this place. With all of you. How many of you can say the same?

"We've lost a lot of lives to something that's been over a long time. Something that up until now nobody's really wanted to talk about. You want to give it one more life? What good would it do?" I scanned all those angry faces. "As a kid I said 'yes, sir,' you sent me away, and I fought for you. Then I came home a broken man and fought a different war. Been fighting it a long time. Now I'm sitting here fighting again. Getting spit on by you. All of you value the knight who storms the castle, kills the bad man, and saves the girl. But you need to ask yourself, how does the knight live on the other side of the rescue? When he's sitting in his castle with armor that's rusty, a sword that's grown unwieldy, and a horse that's gray and old? There are a lot of us. I'm just the one talking at the moment." I sat back. "So no, Senator, I will not hand you my brother's head on a platter."

To their credit, they did alter my military records to permanently reflect my name, rather than Bobby's.

# — 48 —

At the invitation of the Vietnamese government, Suzy, Allie, and a host of other people traveled to Vietnam. Much had changed, and when the memories flooded back, they hurt. I couldn't have made it without Allie. She held me up. She shielded me from the cameras, asked a lot of questions, and then cried through most of my answers. It was good for both of us.

The hike in took several hours, but I led Suzy to her father's remains. One reporter asked me, "How can you remember the way?"

I turned to him. "How can I forget?"

A beautiful tree had grown above him. When they unearthed him, she sat for a long time next to the hole, talking to him. When I had buried him, I'd taken one dog tag and left the other. She sat there, turning the second dog tag in her hand.

Suzy wanted to bring her father home. She asked me to help

pick up the pieces and place him in a box. I reached into that black dirt and for the second time carried my friend. And in those moments, I wept like a child and told him I was sorry and asked him to forgive me. When we had all of him that we could find, we closed the box.

Suzy had brought a marker. Stamped in aluminum. It looked like a giant dog tag. The two of us nailed it to the tree above the hole.

Upon her return she buried her father in Arlington. Full military honors. And nobody spit on him.

ALLIE AND I RETURNED to the beach where we had long ago fallen in love. We married. Honeymooned along the beach. Allie was right. She'd been holding her love a long time, and when she gave it to me, well . . .

I bought a '72 Corvette. Fitting, I thought. I took it apart, put it back together better, and we drove it most nights. We rode the merry-go-round at the carnival. The flying chairs. We laughed. We visited Rosco's grave, where I ate a doughnut and then gave myself some insulin and told him that I missed him. We filled another Mason jar with sharks' teeth. We danced along the beach with Gabby and Diego. We did all the things that for years I'd felt guilty doing.

Sometimes I stand on the beach and cry for no reason. No reason at all. Allie found me one afternoon and asked me why. I said, "The place where the tears come from is full again." After not being able to cry for most of my life, I cry now at the drop of a hat.

And, to be honest, I like it.

# — 49 —

Voter opinion turned against Bobby. Smelling blood, the networks continued their feeding frenzy. The backlash was constant and severe. He was labeled a traitor. Public death threats multiplied. The airwaves were filled with large personalities, all of whom were standing on an angry soapbox. Many wanted to talk to me.

To turn me against my brother.

Given the growing storm, Bobby resigned. A live press conference. We watched it with sadness.

Later that afternoon I told Allie I needed to go for a ride. As we walked to the Corvette, Catalina hollered at me across the parking lot. "Joe? You'd better take a look at this."

Around the back of the restaurant, she handed me a flashlight and pointed to the crawl space. We knelt and crawled along the base of the dune until I came upon a smiling Gabby and Diego.

Next to them was a dog. It looked like a Rhodesian ridgeback and had evidently given birth to about eight puppies.

Catalina whispered, "That Rosco, he got around."

Gabby lifted a reddish-brown furball with big paws and floppy ears. Its eyes had barely opened.

"Do we know whose dog it is?" I asked.

"No idea," Catalina said.

Allie patted my back. "Congratulations, Papa."

I pointed at the squirming mess of fur. Each pup the spitting image of Rosco. "What am I going to do with all of those?"

Gabby now had a puppy in each hand. She said, "Can we keep them, Mama?"

Catalina raised an eyebrow at me. "See what you have done?"

I smiled. "Good old Rosco."


I CRANKED THE CORVETTE, and Allie and I drove the coastline southeast. I drove with tears in my eyes. Every few seconds, Allie would reach up and thumb one away. But not all the tears were sad.

Bobby wasn't hard to find.

During my brother's drunken years, which often coincided with mine, he kept a cabin in a little place called Yankeetown. It's a fishing village on the west coast of Florida, about two hours southeast of Cape San Blas. His cabin sat isolated on a point, and faced west. He'd crawl through the door, climb inside a bottle, and disappear until he couldn't remember why he started drinking in the first place. After a week or two he'd surface, buy some groceries, and return to the security and confines of his sunsets.

A tidal creek flowed just north of his property, spitting distance from the cabin door. Fifty yards across, the water moved with a fast current. During the painful periods of my life, I'd stand on the opposite bank and check on him through binoculars. Watching his movements. Originally, my intent was to hurt him, drown him, rip his head off, dump his body in the river, and post his head on a stake. I kept my distance and watched him through magnified lenses. The water between us was a barrier. If I lost my mind and jumped in, he'd see me coming and have a chance to get away.

Over the years I watched him fluctuate between puffy-faced and overweight to gaunt and bone-skinny. One thing became clear. If I knew torment within, Bobby lived it on the outside. And while his might have been self-inflicted, it was torment nonetheless.

# — EPILOGUE —

*As they pass through the Valley of Baca,*
*they make it a spring;*
*the rain also covers it with pools.*

—PSALM 84:6

I turned onto the coquina road and wound nearly a mile through palm trees, palmettos, and scrub oaks. Plants whose roots held fast through the last hurricane. We parked a half mile back of his cabin and slipped through the trees, moving slowly. The breeze blew from the north across our faces. We saw Bobby sitting on his dock. Legs dangling over the water. An unopened bottle of tequila next to him.

We stepped onto the dock and he didn't turn. The afternoon sun was falling. The light was golden red and soft, and layered the air with an amber glow. Allie sat down on one side of him and I sat on the other. None of us spoke for several minutes.

Finally he pointed north across the tidal creek to the patch of palm trees where I'd built a hide so many years ago. "I used to sit here and wonder why you didn't just put me out of my misery."

I stared at the trees. "Me too."

He turned the unopened tequila bottle in his hand. "Why didn't you?"

I watched the sun drop off the edge of the earth and bleed crimson into the Gulf. "Wasn't what we needed."

"What was?"

"Not that."

The outgoing tide ripped beneath our feet. He spoke without looking at me. "You ever wonder what life would have been like had I gone?"

"Not much anymore."

"But did you used to?"

"Sure."

"Ever come to anything?"

I laughed. "It's tough for me to see past what it all became."

"After you left, I used to sit up nights and listen to Mom cry herself to sleep. I'd get on the floor and press my ear to the air vent. She prayed one thing over and over."

I knew the prayer. Last time I'd heard it Mom was coming undone on the beach the night before I left. I pulled the brass Zippo out of my pocket. Dull from the decades. I held it up to reveal the worn engraving. My fingertips traced the grooves like Braille. STRENGTH TO STRENGTH. I flipped it over. SEND DOWN THE RAIN. I handed it to him. My tether to hope. "Had it done over there . . ."

"Why?"

"To help me remember."

"Remember what?"

"Mom's voice."

He turned it in his hand, flicked it lit, then slammed it shut on his thigh and passed it back. "You don't even smoke."

"Fire can be a comfort when you're lonely."

Bobby paused and waved his hand across me, him, and the world Mom had born us into. "You think this was what she was talking about?"

I surveyed the world. "Yeah."

He unscrewed the tequila top. I heard a somber finality in his tone of voice. "All my life, I've always wanted to be you. To make hard decisions no matter the cost." He shook his head and lifted the bottle to his lips. He held it there. Lips trembling.

I eyed the bottle. "How long's it been?"

His reply was slow in coming. Liquid courage hung two inches from his lips. "Long time."

I knew if he crawled in there he'd never swim out. I reached into my backpack, pulled out a gallon of chocolate milk and a package of Oreos, and set them on the boards between us. Minutes passed as he stared between the two worlds.

He studied the gallon jug. "When'd you start on chocolate?"

"When I tired of regular."

"When was that?"

I laughed. "'Bout the time you stole my girlfriend."

He nodded. Shot a glance at Allie. Then me. "Yes, I did that, too." He glanced at the roll of antacids in my hand. "I thought the doc said your heart was strong as a twenty-year-old's."

"It is."

"Why then?"

"I like the taste."

He eyed the Oreos. "How long we been eating these things?"

"Since we been brothers."

"They're probably the cause of your diabetes."

"No." I flung one out across the water. "That was floating on top of the water I drank when I was in-country."

"Agent Orange?"

"Yep."

He swallowed, but it was difficult to get down. Tears dripped off his cheek and landed on his jeans. "We missed a lot."

I stared out across the water. "We were born into a world at war."

"Why you think God did it this way?"

"I don't think this was His original intention."

"What was?"

I shook my head. "Not this."

He turned to me. A question on the tip of his tongue. "Why?"

"Why what?"

"Why didn't you ever tell my secret? Undress me before the world?"

I swigged the chocolate milk, licked the soft middle of a cookie, and then crushed the remaining wafer in my hand. I opened my palm and let the pieces spill onto the surface of the water. Then I checked my blood sugar and gave myself three units of insulin.

"Something happened when Suzy's dad came to get me. Something in the way I see. Evil became a person. As real as you and me. And when I came home, you were not that person."

He set the tequila bottle on his lap. Stared at it several minutes. Then, without saying a word, he turned it upside down and emptied it into the river. He pulled the draft notice from his shirt pocket. Yellowed. Tearstained. Ripped down the middle and taped together like a cross. He rolled it like a scroll and slid it inside the bottle, then screwed the cap back on.

He offered it to me.

I shook my head. "You do it."

Bobby stood, took two steps, and heaved that bottle as far as he could out across the tidal current. It spun through the air, reflecting light like a diamond, splash-landed, disappeared, bobbed to the surface, and began its long trip to the other side of the world.

Bobby sat, his shoulder brushing mine. I offered him the milk jug and he took it, swigging long. When he finished, the chocolate milk dripped off his chin. He whispered, "Good call on chocolate." He turned to me and tried to speak again, but his voice cracked. Behind us, rain clouds had blown in. The breeze pushed across our shoulders, turning the air cooler. He looked up at the clouds. Then back at me. Squinting. "Brother?"

I loved it when he called me that. Always have. "Yeah."

"Thank . . . you." The words were separated by pain and they were long and hard in coming. The empty tequila bottle bobbed in the distance. Glass reflecting sunlight. A diamond floating on the surface of the world. "For giving me what I needed." He swallowed and dug his hand into the package. "And not what I deserved."

I put my arm around my brother's shoulder.

---

We sat there a long time. Brothers. It'd been a long, long time. I sketched while he licked and flung Oreos. We finished off the milk and cookies. He started laughing.

I said, "What's so funny?"

The air had turned ripe and pungent. The last warning before the rain.

"I've just been fired." He raised a finger. "By the American people, no less. Literally got run out of town. Can't really get hired anywhere, by anyone . . . to do anything." He sucked through his teeth. "I have no idea what I'm going to do now."

"You ever thought about a career in the carnival?"

Allie laughed as all three of us watched the bottle disappear out where the ocean touched the sky.

He raised both eyebrows. "No. Never given it much thought."

"You've never really lived until you've guessed people's weights or torn tickets at the tilt-a-whirl."

"You hiring?"

"Matter of fact, yes."

"You hire guys like me?"

"No . . . No, we don't. We hire illegal aliens mostly, but . . ." I started laughing. "Thanks to you, most of them are legal now."

He chuckled. "I should fit right in."

We hadn't laughed this much since we were kids. It felt good.

I finished my sketch. "You got any dinner plans?"

He pointed at the water in front of him. "I hadn't gotten past the edge of this dock. Much less dinner."

"We've got this weird little Mexican-seafood-fusion restaurant on the island that's attached to a carnival. The food is off the chain, and the chef they've got is winning awards and being written up in magazines, and they've got these little fried doughnuts that I just can't get enough of. And when I finish eating, I walk across the street and pop popcorn, scoop ice cream, and then turn on the cotton candy machine and hand it out free to all the kids and then just stand back and watch them smile. And then I hop on the flying chairs and ride till I get so dizzy I can't stand up, and then I pick out a valiant steed on the merry-go-round and ride till the music gets stuck in my head, and then, when I'm done, I walk out on the beach and let the water wash over my feet and look for sharks' teeth and wonder how my life turned out the way it did."

"And then?"

"Then I wake up tomorrow and do it all over again. Although—" I paused. "Now I've got to add nursing puppies into the mix."

"Puppies?"

"It's a long story, but let's just say Rosco was never one to stay home very long."

I handed him the index card. It was a good likeness. The breeze had blown his hair across his forehead, and somehow I'd manage to capture that kid I once knew on the beach when we were boys. The one whose eyes smiled.

"So you two inviting me for dinner?"

"Something like that."

Bobby licked the middle of an Oreo. "I'd like that."

Allie wrapped her arm around my waist, placed her other hand over my heart, and leaned against me. Melting into me. Out in front of us, the ocean was a sheet of glass and the clouds were rolling toward us. Pushing the rain. We could see it coming.

*USA TODAY* bestseller *Long Way Gone* tells the heartwarming story of a prodigal son and his long journey toward redemption.

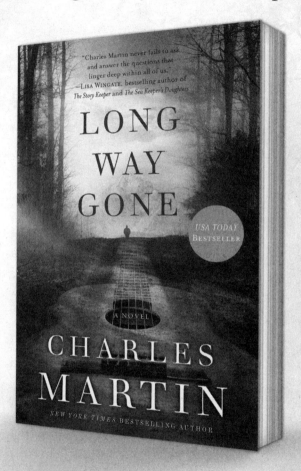

"Charles Martin never fails to ask and answer the questions that linger deep within all of us. In this beautifully told story of a prodigal coming home, readers will find the broken and mended pieces of their own hearts."

—LISA WINGATE, national bestselling author of *Before We Were Yours*

# — DISCUSSION QUESTIONS —

1. At the opening of the story, Allie is faced with two significant losses—that of her husband and the Blue Tornado. In what ways does she cope with her grief? How have you coped with similar losses? Can you relate to Allie's hardships? Her ways of coping?

2. Why does Joseph retreat to the cabin? Is he seeking something or avoiding something? Or both?

3. How might we compare and contrast Joseph's life situation with Allie's? In what ways are they similar? In what ways are they different?

4. Rosco may be Joseph's dog, but he is still an important part of the story. What role does he play? Suzy is another supporting character who plays a significant role. How does her character contribute to the story as a whole?

5. Joseph appears at the accident as if by grace. Does Allie react to his reappearance as you would expect? Does Joseph? Have

you had an unexpected reunion with past friends or significant others? If so, did you feel as if it happened for a reason, as Joseph and Allie do?

6. Much attention is given to the upbringing of Allie and Joseph, and the influence of family—fathers, mothers, and siblings. What did you notice about how these family relationships have affected the lives of each character? Can you relate? How have family relationships and memories affected you?

7. Joseph has seemingly given up on life, but something within prompts him to help Catalina, Diego, and Gabriella. What do you think that something is?

8. Catalina, Diego, and Gabriella are like castaways. They have been abandoned, and they are seeking a kind of shelter—a shelter Joseph is able to provide. Do they provide Joseph with something as well? What might that be?

9. Abandonment can be literal or emotional. Many characters in *Send Down the Rain* have been abandoned in some way. How so? What led to their abandonment?

10. A major revelation comes to Allie and Joseph regarding Jake. Were you surprised? Did you find this twist believable?

11. With their original homes lost, the characters seek a place to call home. Have you found yourself seeking a "home" at different times in your life? What makes a place feel like home?

12. The novel has a very strong sense of place, from the Carolina mountains to the Florida shores. How are these settings meaningful to the story? Likewise, much of the story takes place on the road, between places. Is the road symbolic?

13. Are the hopes of Joseph and Allie fulfilled? How so? Do you believe new beginnings are possible? If so, what makes them possible? If not, what makes them impossible? Are they partially possible, but only to an extent?

# — ABOUT THE AUTHOR —

Photo by Kerry Lammi, www.soulwornimages.com

Charles Martin is the *New York Times* bestselling author of twelve novels. He and his wife, Christy, live in Jacksonville, Florida. Learn more at charlesmartinbooks.com.

Facebook: Author.Charles.Martin
Twitter: @storiedcareer